# FADE TO BLACK

*By Tony Gibbs*


*The Harbormaster Series*

Shot in the Dark
Fade to Black


*FICTION*

Dead Run
Running Fix
Shadow Queen
Landfall
Capitol Offense


*NONFICTION*

Practical Sailing
Advanced Sailing
The Coastal Cruiser
Cruising in a Nutshell

# TONY GIBBS

# FADE TO BLACK

**THE MYSTERIOUS PRESS**

Published by Warner Books

A Time Warner Company

Mysterious Press books are published by Warner Books, Inc.,
1271 Avenue of the Americas, New York, NY 10020.

A Time Warner Company

The Mysterious Press name and logo are registered trademarks of Warner Books, Inc.

Printed in the United States of America

First printing: July 1997

10 9 8 7 6 5 4 3 2 1

Library of Congress Cataloging-in-Publication Data
Gibbs, Tony.
    Fade to black / Tony Gibbs.
        p.   cm.
    ISBN 0-89296-602-5
    I. Title.
    PS3557.I155F3   1997
    813'.54—dc21
                                                        97-701
                                                        CIP

*For all the family—Bill and Michelle, Jessie and Megan, Eric and Lisa, and especially Elaine*

The window was dark, but the miniature spotlights that illuminated the paintings along the walls also silhouetted the new lettering on the glass, and Jock paused to read it again:

## THE FEVEREL COLLECTION
## OF
## FINE ART

He still didn't like COLLECTION much, but he knew it was a hot word: everything was a collection these days, from condoms to real estate listings. Even if it didn't make much sense, it sounded classy—and in Santa Barbara, sounding classy was often an end in itself. Besides, the city already had a dozen places that called themselves art galleries, and if you were going to stay alive in this cutthroat business, you had to scramble for even the tiniest marketing ploy that would set you apart from the others.

Maybe, Jock reflected, it would read better without the OF. He couldn't quite visualize the change, but he'd have Wilbur scrape the letters off in the morning and see how it looked.

I

*Speaking of Wilbur, where the hell is he?* In the back room, no doubt. More than likely screwing up his own supposedly finished work. Wilbur Andreas might be employed as the gallery's night watchman, but he was a painter first—and a painter who simply couldn't pull the string on his paintings. Jock remembered with a surge of retrospective fury the time he'd just about sold Wilbur's epic parade scene, the 48" by 72" *Summer Solstice: State Street*, to a visiting Hollywood type, only to find Wilbur had sneaked in and changed the whole foreground, painting over the curbside figures the prospective purchaser had liked so much. A five-grand sale (two thousand of it Jock's commission) down the drain with a couple dozen brushstrokes.

Lately, though, Wilbur was different. There was something about him—something Jock couldn't define but made him obscurely uneasy. Like when Wilbur was supposed to be watching the shop, he now flatly refused to sit at the gallery desk, even though it was discreetly half-hidden behind an antique Chinese screen. "I can't stand it, being . . . *exposed* like that. Makes me feel like I'm for sale, too," he said.

But it was the way he said it—gritting on the words, as if they were sand between his teeth—that raised Jock's hackles. And Wilbur's round, Frans Hals face, its usual scarlet a pale mauve from barely suppressed emotion. Jock shivered at the recollection.

Wilbur was too much. He not only gave Jock the willies, he scared the customers. He would have to go. It was a decision that had been creeping through the tangled underbrush of Jock's brain, and now, fully revealed, it seemed inevitable. *I just have to tell Wilbur our arrangement is over. Tell him now.*

Propelled by his thought, Jock reached for the door handle. Pressed it without result. *Now, what the hell:* the tastefully lettered sign—Wilbur's work—read WE'RE OPEN TO SERVE YOU—PLEASE COME IN. But the door was locked. Grateful anger for this latest irresponsibility warmed Jock's soul. He fumbled his alligator keycase from his too-tight pants pocket and flipped it open.

The key turned and the bolt slid back, but still the door wouldn't open. Jock selected a second key and inserted it in the upper lock, thinking, *Well, he can't say he double-locked it by accident.* But the thought wasn't as comforting as he'd expected it to be.

"Wilbur?" he called. Thought he heard a noise from the storeroom in back. Like a groan. "Wilbur! That you?"

Jock stood frozen, his mind racing in neutral. Robbery? It was, alas, ridiculous: nothing to steal—but would a gangbanger up from Oxnard know that? The gallery looked prosperous, even wealthy. It was supposed to. But gangbangers would go for one of the convenience stores on Haley or Milpas. For sure they wouldn't knock off an art gallery around the corner from City Hall and three blocks from Police Headquarters.

The sound again. Definitely from the back, but hard to define. Not so much pain or fear as unbearable weariness. Sudden apprehension melted Jock's fear. He stepped through the curtain, ready for anything but what he saw.

Beyond the curtain, thick beige carpet gave way to scarred flooring. The stark room, lit by a single bare bulb, seemed even smaller than it was. Roughly carpentered racks, filled with unframed canvases and prints, lined its two longer walls. In the narrow space between facing racks Wilbur Andreas lay on his side, curled in a tight ball. His head rested in an unspeakable pool, and as Jock stood frozen, watching, he snorted thickly.

"Wilbur. Oh, Jesus," Jock heard a voice say. His own voice, cracking. He stepped forward, dropping halfway to his knees before he remembered his new slacks. He squatted instead, balancing unsteadily as he lifted Wilbur's head. His forehead was wet, his face a purplish gray. He was breathing slowly. His eyes opened, at first unfocused, then recognizing Jock.

"Lost my nerve," he said, with a ghastly smile.

"Feeling better?" Jock asked, half an hour later. His initial concern had soured to exasperation, and he could hear it in his tone.

"Worse, actually," Wilbur replied. He was slumped in the desk chair, which Jock had dragged from the gallery to the storeroom— the last thing he wanted was Wilbur visible from the street in his present condition. "Guess I'll live, though."

"Well, that *was* why you stuck your finger down your throat: suddenly deciding you wanted to live." To Jock the very idea of suicide was incomprehensible. No matter how bad things seemed, there was always a way out. All you had to do was find it. A considerable number of his clients were heavily into self-dramatization, however; this was not the first suicide attempt Jock had seen. Still, Wilbur was hardly the person he'd have expected it from—or was that what he'd been edging up to these past weeks?

"Not exactly wanting to live," Wilbur said at last. "Scared to die, that's all."

"Oh, for God's sake," Jock exploded. "What on earth would make you feel like—" He pulled himself up short as the dreadful possibility occurred to him. "Is it AIDS? Is that it?"

Now it was Wilbur's turn to be annoyed. "No, it is not AIDS. It's . . ." He groped, shrugged helplessly as the words eluded him.

Not fully convinced, Jock tried another tack. "You polished off half a bottle of my Wild Turkey—you know that's for the customers, damn it—and all of a sudden you decided to kill yourself. Bang, just like that." He paused, waiting for a reaction, but Wilbur was staring into the middle distance. "Or were you just boiled out of your mind and swallowed two dozen of my Nembutals for the hell of it?"

Still no reaction. Jock continued: "Whatever it was, you must've changed your mind real fast—those capsules came back up as good as new, which is more than you can say for the booze."

"Look, I'm sorry," Wilbur said. "I'll replace the Wild Turkey, okay?"

"Forget it," said Jock. "It was cheap rye anyway."

"I know," Wilbur said. A tiny but genuine grin creased his cheeks. "I was here when you refilled the bottle."

"So you were. We've been through a lot together, Wilbur."

"That's why you should get it. You of all people," Wilbur said. "Remember when you said I was the best painter you ever represented?"

"Yes. And I meant it. Still do."

"But you don't sell my stuff," Wilbur continued. "I don't mean

4

it's your fault," he continued, riding down Jock's automatic objection. "You've done your best, but it's this . . . this half-assed, watered-down, impressionistic shit that sells. If I see another view of Goleta Slough with the colors all wrong, I'll . . ." He trailed off. An expression Jock had never seen before turned his face to a mask of horror.

"What—" Jock began, but the other man held up his big hand for silence. After a long moment he spoke again, his voice hoarse.

"You know what I was going to do, when I found the sleeping pills?" Jock shook his head. "I was going to swallow them down and then, before I passed out, I was going to take that letter opener of yours and . . ." He shuddered uncontrollably. "The thing is, Jock, I'd be better off blind. I really would."

PORTOBELLO MEXICAN RESTAURANT, STATE STREET; 7:00 P.M.:
NEAL DONAHOE

Outside, the Tuesday evening farmers' market was winding down. The farmers—jeans-clad growers and bearded hippies from up in the hills—were breaking down their stands and loading the unsold organic avocados and pesticide-free oranges back into their pickups; the customers, who had moved in purposeful, antlike progression from stand to stand, had begun trailing off to dinner.

But the Portobello's narrow, dark dining room remained nearly empty. It was often nearly empty, except on those less than rare occasions when it was totally deserted. The Italian chef had fled home to Connecticut a month ago, to be replaced by a French expat who lasted three weeks and was succeeded by a Mexican recruited from Taco Bell. The printed menus had disappeared, and the carte du jour now appeared on a chalkboard in the window, between an oversize sombrero and a wooden cactus.

Seated at the Portobello's best table, in front of the nonfunctional fireplace, Neal Donahoe reflected gloomily on the mistake he had made a week earlier, when he'd confided to his regular dinner companion, Tory Lennox, that the Portobello had just about run out its string, unless there was an unseasonally heavy run of

6

German tourists, renowned for eating nearly anything and lots of it. His remark was meant to be harmlessly amusing, at a point in their relationship when neutral conversation was increasingly hard to come by.

But instead of a smile the line had earned Neal six consecutive Portobello dinners and a semipermanent case of heartburn. It wasn't the first time he'd been misled by Tory's reserved, coolly sophisticated, every-hair-in-place surface, under which lurked a fierce compassion for life's losers. That concern had been surfacing more and more frequently of late, and though Neal knew perfectly well what inspired it, Tory's career problems seemed to him a poor excuse for prolonging the half-life of another doomed Santa Barbara eating place.

Still, he wanted desperately to help her climb out of her despond, and not just on her own account. Until she was herself again, Neal's own life was marking time. There had to be some way to jolt her off dead center, but for the life of him he couldn't figure out how.

Through the course of the meal—for her, a stringy chile verde; for him, limp, greasy taquitos—her silences had stretched until he could no longer ignore them. "So what is it?" he demanded, raising his voice to carry over the TV behind the bar.

"I don't know," she said. And then, because waffling irritated her more than most other character flaws, she gave him a wry grin. "Oh, the usual. You must've had 'whither Tory' up to here by now. Heaven knows I have."

"Well, you know what *I* think you should do," he said, and took a long swallow of Negra Modelo to stop himself from telling her again: the subject of Tory's stalled Coast Guard career was an emotional minefield. She would talk about resigning her lieutenant's commission, but when Neal agreed it was the logical thing to do, she acted as if he'd suggested selling out to the enemy.

But they had had this conversation often enough, over the past couple of months, that the rest of the script was unnecessary. Tory's brows drew together in silent objection to Neal's unspoken prescription, and he could feel himself bristling at her rejection.

Christ, he thought, we're like two old married people, and we're not even married.

From the bar TV, a wave of audience hysteria washed through the nearly empty restaurant. Neal rocked back in his chair. "Irma," he called, "could you—"

"Slack off, Neal," Tory interrupted. "It's just *Making Things Right.* Give the poor woman a break—it's her favorite program."

"It's a freak show," he snapped. "Who wants to eat dinner with a screenful of geeks looking over their shoulder?"

"They're just people," Tory said. "People with problems they can't solve by themselves."

Her voice was reasoned, gently firm, adult to child. Exactly like your mother, Neal thought. But the fact that she was nearly eight years younger than he, with the face and figure of a centerfold, sometimes made it hard to take her seriously. "Sweetheart, they are in fact geeks," he said, trying to match her tone. "If they weren't making faces at a TV camera, they'd be in some carny sideshow, biting the heads off chickens."

"That's disgusting," she said, but he could tell she was only half listening, and a moment later she proved him right: "What do you know about Alameda?" she asked.

Six years in Southern California had not transplanted Neal's East Coast worldview. "Up north somewhere. In the Bay Area, I think."

"Well, of course it is," she said. "But what kind of place is it?"

"Place?" He was baffled.

"To live."

She was looking not at him but down at the congealing mess on her plate. Her short blonde hair gleamed in the dim light, and he thought he detected a slight reddening under the smooth tan on her cheeks. I am in love with this woman, he thought. "Why do you want to know?" he asked, surprised at the effort required to keep his voice level.

"We got the official word today: Eleventh District headquarters is moving up there," she replied, raising her clear blue eyes to meet his wary dark ones. "Most of it, anyway—there'll be some folks left behind in San Pedro. The Safety Detachment will still be here, of course . . ." Her voice trailed off.

"But the good jobs are going north. The two-and-a-half-stripe jobs," he said. Himself almost without ambition, he often forgot how promotion obsessed her.

She glanced automatically down at the sleeve of her blazer, as if expecting to find her lieutenant's two stripes on the cuff. Looking back up, she saw Neal was reading her perfectly. "Not that it matters," she said, managing a tight smile.

Six months earlier, Tory had let herself be maneuvered into an unofficial operation entirely outside her jurisdiction. Highly publicized success had fended off the retribution that would otherwise have swept her out of the service. But within it, her reputation was frozen in mud, and she seemed doomed to wither quietly in the Santa Barbara Marine Safety Detachment, chasing oil spills and trying to keep ungrateful commercial fishermen from destroying themselves.

To the outside world she soldiered on with no trace of resentment or frustration. Only that afternoon Neal, walking the piers in his official capacity as Santa Barbara's acting Harbormaster, had overheard her lecturing a bearlike commercial fisherman as if he were a child of six. And making him swallow it with a rueful grin.

"Smooth work," Neal had murmured, falling into step beside her. "Toto Boyle would've pitched your predecessor into the drink for talking to him like that."

She had unleashed a dazzling smile that failed to light her eyes. "Toto's a pussycat, once you get to know him," she said. A moment later she added, her lips barely moving, "My predecessor, however, is the south end of a northbound horse. And he was just selected for lieutenant commander."

Neal had had no reply, and even now all he could say was, "Just be patient. They're bound to see they can't afford to lose people like you."

"Oh, but they can," she replied. "In fact, they have to."

"The Coast Guard has to cut four thousand regulars from a

strength of thirty-nine thousand," Neal said. "You told me. What I meant was—"

"I know what you mean," she said quickly. "Unfortunately, my superiors don't see me the same way you do. Dangerously irresponsible is how I look to them. Insubordinate. And they're right."

She was quoting, Neal guessed, from the letter of reprimand she'd never let him read. "Dangerously irresponsible," Neal repeated. "Insubordinate. I like that in a woman."

"You're sweet. If only you were the admiral." This time her smile was real, and he decided to take the chance.

"I'd rather be your husband," he said.

"What did you say?" She clearly couldn't believe her ears, and he pressed in.

"Marry me. You know how I feel about you—and you've said you love me, too." But it was coming out all wrong, and he could sense her slipping away from him.

"I do love you, Neal," she said. He could see her choosing the next words with painful care. "It's just I don't know if I love you enough for marriage."

"There's one way to find out," he said.

"No," she said firmly. "That's not good enough for me—and it certainly shouldn't be good enough for you."

"After the first time, you mean?" He felt himself bridling. His divorce, years before, was something they had never discussed.

"Well, you don't want to make the same mistake twice," she replied.

"Is that different from making the same mistake over and over again?" he retorted. "That's what the Coast Guard is for you."

"Even if I thought you were right—which I don't—it's not much of an argument for marriage," she said.

He could feel the gathering chill across the table. "Marriage in general or marriage to me?" he demanded.

She took a deep breath before she replied. "Either way." And before he could say anything she went on: "Look, there's still a chance I can retrieve my career. But it means I've got to give a hundred and ten percent, and do it a hundred percent of the time."

He'd blown his chance, and the bitter realization made him snap out, "Why?"

He could see she was assembling an answer for herself as much as for him. "Why should I bother? Two reasons, I guess. The first is that I hate failure. Just *hate* it. I've never failed at anything I really put my mind to." She hesitated. "The second . . ." For several seconds she regarded him as if he were a stranger. "You'd laugh at me if I told you."

"You've got a thing for uniforms," he said. "I've noticed."

She blushed scarlet, and he suddenly recalled how she had hurled herself into his arms a few hours earlier, when he'd turned up at her apartment still wearing his Harbor Patrol uniform. "Not that way," she said quickly. And changed the subject.

They were still disconnected when they left the Portobello fifteen minutes later. Irma, the owner, was glued to the TV, tears coursing down her hollow cheeks. "Christ, Irma, what's wrong?" Neal asked, feeling for his wallet.

"It's just so beautiful," Irma said, beaming through her tears. Neal glanced at the screen, where a blotchy teenager, her face even wetter than Irma's, was clutching a tall blond man in an expensive suit. His handsome face registered deep self-satisfaction alloyed with a twinge of distaste.

"Freddy just turned her *life* around," Irma continued, her eyes overflowing. "I mean, she was ready to kill herself, and he just stepped in and fixed *everything* for her."

"I see," Neal said.

"It's like a *miracle*," Irma continued. "I don't know how Freddy hears about these cases, but he just turns up, like those Publishers Clearing House people, and makes everything right for them." She caught sight of the twenty in Neal's hand, and shook her head. "Dinner's on the house."

"Irma, you can't," said Tory.

"Sure, I can," Irma replied. "And you know why? Because this is my last night. The bank's closing me down tomorrow—one step ahead of the wholesaler and the linen service." Her gold-toothed smile, still brightening, collapsed on itself.

"Oh, Irma, I'm so sorry," said Tory, folding the other woman into her arms.

Neal stood irresolute as the two women embraced. He detested tears, yet suddenly felt his own throat blocking up. Looking away, his eye was caught by the man on the TV screen, who was looking straight at him with a knowing smile. Dropping the twenty on the bar, Neal fled blindly into the night.

ISLAND VIEW COFFEE SHOP, WEST CABRILLO BOULEVARD;
WEDNESDAY, 9:30 A.M.: LORRAINE THOMAS

"So how's it going, Lorraine?" said the man sitting across from her. "How's life treating you these days?"

He's up to something, she thought, lifting the coffee cup to her lips. She had not seen Jock Feverel for months, but she knew the faintly mocking tone, the fraudulent pleasure lighting his smooth, sleek features. A seal, she thought. That's what he looks like, with that slicked-back hair and those wide brown eyes: a seal. But a nasty seal, who can make you feel clumsy and stupid with just a smile. The sudden *aperçu*, after so many years, threw her off balance. "I'm doing okay, Jock. For someone who got shaken out of bed at three A.M."

"Ah, *mea culpa, mea maxima culpa*," he said, tenting his fingertips and rocking forward and then back in his chair. "I do apologize, but I wanted to be sure you were alone. You *were* alone, weren't you, my dear? Virtuous bed, and all that sort of thing?"

She felt her face go hot. Why had she ever confided in him? "Which of your acts is that—pimp of the realm? It needs work," she said coldly.

He beamed at her. He'd always been impervious to insult, one of his most maddening attributes. "You're still with *el doctor*, though? Even if he doesn't stay the night?"

"Why do you want to know?" she snapped, aware that any response was the wrong one. "You said this was about Wilbur. That was the only reason I agreed to meet you."

"It is about Wilbur," Jock replied. He hitched his chair forward, looked quickly around him. The motel coffee shop's other customers—camera-draped, floral-shirted, obvious tourists—were safely oblivious of them. "How would you like to be rich, Lorraine? Not massively, stinking rich, but nicely wealthy. Never have to . . . work again?"

And that, she reflected, was what kept Jock from being a truly major-league con artist: he couldn't pass up the chance to plant a needle. She took an extra breath to settle herself and bestowed a cool smile on him. "Ray pays for my apartment," she said, "and he gets what he needs in return. Which is more than the gal who staked you to the gallery can say."

It had cost her something, that admission, but she saw from Jock's suddenly blank stare that she had scored, too. Nothing could knock him down for long, though. He spread his hands, palms up, in a gesture of surrender. "My dear, I apologize. We need to be allies."

"Why?" She looked up at the wall clock. "I've got to go. The shop opens at ten, but they like us on hand early."

He could be businesslike when necessary: "How many of Wilbur's paintings do you have?"

"Twelve. You know that," she replied.

"I thought you might have sold one," he said.

"God knows I've tried. Some alimony they turned out to be."

"Think of them as nest eggs," said Jock. "Nest eggs are notoriously slow to hatch."

This is not my game, she thought. I'm not dumb, but to play with Jock you have to be totally devious. "Wilbur's been discovered?" she asked.

"He's going to be."

It was not impossible, she knew. The upper level of the art market—bred by fad, out of publicity—could be wildly mercurial. In the five years Lorraine had been married to Wilbur Andreas, she'd watched half a dozen painters no better than he rocket into the financial ionosphere, even though they never quite attained the heights inhabited by football players or rock stars. The thing was, when it came to painting, the biggest investors often knew the least about what they were buying. They could swarm like lemmings, and you could never guess what or who would turn them on next.

Jock sounded completely confident—but that was his stock-in-trade. "If you're so positive," she said, "you can buy me out now. Bargain rates. Beat the rush."

"In this case, I need your help, Lorraine," he said. Nothing about his manner had changed, but she sensed he was about to make his real pitch.

"You mean you're broke," she said, grinning in spite of herself.

"That, too." He returned her smile with interest. "But I really do need your help. And your medical friend's."

"Ray?" She was genuinely baffled. "Ray couldn't tell a de Kooning from a . . . from a Wilbur Andreas. It's one of many restful things about him."

"That's irrelevant." He looked around him once again. This time the waitress noticed him, and he made a quick writing-on-air gesture. "I said this was about Wilbur, and it is," he said, his voice dropping to a near-whisper. "He tried to kill himself last night. He was going to put out his eyes first. With that old letter opener of mine."

Her stomach knotted hard. "He's all right?"

Jock shrugged. "I was able to stop him. He's sick as a dog, is all—but you know how it is when people get an idea like that. Next time . . ." He let the words hang.

"But why?" she demanded. "And why his eyes?"

All Jock's cloying artifice had dropped away. Suddenly he was just a middle-aged man out of his depth. "Lorraine, my dear, I'm not an artist and neither are you. How can we know what goes on in his head? I mean, here's one of the most talented super-realists of our time, and you know how he's surviving? Painting trompe l'oeil flower baskets on supermarket walls. Lettering half-witty names on yachts in the harbor. And all the time he's watching other painters with less talent than him having shows, getting praise, making a living—being, for God's sake, *painters.*"

She was so shaken she couldn't even try to lift her coffee cup, and the waitress, bringing the check, gave her a quick, concerned glance. "Okay, Jock, what do you want me to do?"

"Help Wilbur go blind."

MARINE SAFETY DETACHMENT, HARBOR WAY; 10:00 A.M.: TORY
LENNOX

"I'm telling you, Lieutenant, that boat is a public danger!" Maria
Acevedo's eyes, normally heavy-lidded and watchful, were blazing.
Emotion, real or political, sent her voice up half an octave: "Somebody's going to get hurt, maybe killed. You've absolutely got to do
something about it!"

Altogether, Tory decided, the Waterfront Director seemed on the
verge of a major tantrum—and Maria Acevedo's tantrums, in the
short year she had held her office, were already legendary. But Tory
was enjoying herself. On her own figurative quarterdeck—behind
her government-issue metal desk in the Marine Safety office—she
felt in command of the situation. And there was something per-
versely delightful about pissing off a person you truly loathed.

Between Tory and Maria, a theatrically handsome woman about
Neal's age, it had been hate at first sight. Not only was Maria a
politician, and thus despicable by profession, but she ruled her department like a feudal principality, keeping her subordinates (with
the notable exception of Neal) in a permanent state of terror. Him

17

she clearly had other ambitions for—an accusation he, of course, denied (though protesting rather too strongly, Tory thought). Not that she cared, at this moment, if Neal had an affair with the Loch Ness monster, but it went on Maria's debit sheet anyway.

"Dangerous how, Ms. Acevedo?" said Tory innocently.

"What?" Maria, riding the breaker of her own eloquence, clearly wasn't listening to the actual words anymore.

"In what respect is the . . ." Tory glanced down at the pad in front of her, "is the *Prophet Jonah* alleged to be a danger? Is she in danger of sinking, or explosion, or what?" Maria's lips were moving soundlessly, and Tory decided it might be better to stop toying with her. "Look," she continued briskly, "I need to know exactly what the problem is before I can decide if it's our responsibility."

Sudden understanding informed Maria's dark eyes: they had moved from the nautical to the bureaucratic, and she was once more on familiar ground. "You're the Coast Guard, right?" she demanded. "Your office door says 'Marine Safety Detachment.' This is marine and it's safety—simple as that."

"But safety *how?*" Tory insisted. "That's what I have to know."

"Safety like that old tub is going to sink any minute," Maria fired back. "All you have to do is look at it. And there's kids aboard. Little children—you want to be responsible for the deaths of little children?"

Oh, cut the crap, Tory thought. Smiling, she said, "Of course I don't, Ms. Acevedo. But let me point out that the *Prophet Jonah* is not at sea—she's in your harbor, firmly tied to one of your piers, and if she does start to sink your excellent Harbor Patrol can handle the situation perfectly well."

Maria's face darkened, and for a long moment Tory waited for her to erupt. Instead, the woman on the other side of the desk threw back her head and laughed. It was not, Tory decided, entirely genuine but, as a demonstration of self-discipline, impressive just the same. "You don't like me, do you?" Maria said, her head cocked to one side. "Which part bugs you most—the city employee or the Hispanic?"

"Oh, come on," Tory sputtered. "I don't—"

"Or is it Donahoe?" Maria continued. Her large teeth bared in a ferocious grin. "You can tell me: we're alone."

Tory's face was aflame. "Ms. Acevedo," she said, with every ounce of restraint she could muster, "that's totally unprofessional."

This time Maria's laugh was unmistakably real, and after a second or two, Tory felt her own face stretching in an unwilling smile. "You're pretty pompous, for a kid," said the Waterfront Director pleasantly. "They teach you that back East, at your academy?"

What they teach us, Tory thought, is not to play your opponent's game. "So why do you really want the *Prophet Jonah* out of the harbor?" she countered.

Maria's eyes widened, and then the lids dropped back to their usual half-mast position. Tory had the sensation she had just passed a test. When the other woman replied, in a matter-of-fact tone, she was sure of it: "The official line is that it's complaints from the neighbors—the yachties in the slips on either side. But the truth is, it's the city versus the homeless. Again. The same old thing: city wants them out—or at least invisible, so they don't scare the tourists. The homeless want . . ." She pursed her lips, shrugged, "whatever they want."

"And where does the *Prophet Jonah* fit in?" Tory asked, interested in spite of herself. Though she had lived in Santa Barbara for nearly a year, she was only beginning to have a sense of the place. Her small apartment, near the Coast Guard's own tiny housing area, was in one of the city's dozen residential microclimates, a sprawling, self-sufficient neighborhood called the Mesa, overlooking the Santa Barbara Channel. The homeless were not a presence on the Mesa, but down on lower State Street, in the heart of town, it was a different story, and you could get panhandled—sometimes with startling belligerence—a couple of times in a block.

The harbor, however, was part of Santa Barbara only in an administrative sense. In every other way, it stood aloof from the city, its collective eye turned toward the twenty-five-mile-wide Santa Barbara Channel on its doorstep and the high-spined Channel Islands on its horizon. When the harbor thought about the city at all, it was usually with smoldering resentment. When the city remembered the harbor (so Neal said), it was only as a sheep to be sheared till the blood flowed.

And while the harbor had its own share of rough-hewn characters, from burnt-out nautical hippies to near-paranoid commercial fishermen, it didn't have homeless beggars—or none that Tory had seen.

"Those *Prophet Jonah* boat people are the first of them," said Maria, who seemed to have followed Tory's train of thought effortlessly. "That's how my bosses see it, anyway: first thing we know, the marina's going to be full of them, living in wrecked-out floating shanties. Another tourist attraction shot to hell."

"But the harbor's got a live-aboard limit," Tory protested. "A hundred boats, max—you already have to wait months for a permit."

Maria lifted her hands helplessly. "I didn't say it was logical. I just said that's what they think uptown." She laughed again. "Used to think that way myself, before I got this job."

"Look," Tory said, working it out as she spoke, "I'm assuming this family on the *Prophet Jonah*—"

"The Halvorsens," Maria put in. "Man and his five kids. I mean, *five kids*, in a space no bigger than my closet."

It would seem tight to a landlubber, Tory reflected, but Maria had never seen a sloop full of Haitian refugees, a couple of hundred in a leaky hulk smaller than the forty-foot *Prophet Jonah*. With an effort, Tory pulled her thought back on the track: "These Halvorsens. They've got a live-aboard permit?"

"Afraid so. The dimwits in the harbor office . . ." Maria shook her head.

"Have they broken any rules?" Tory pressed on. "They pay their slip fee on time?"

"*Somebody* pays it, first of every month," Maria replied.

"What's that supposed to mean?" Tory demanded.

"Halvorsen doesn't pay anything himself, as far as Accounting can tell," said Maria. "He gets the bill, but the checks come from different people. Mostly commercial fishermen."

The image of Captain Toto Boyle—grossly overweight, tattooed up and down both hairy arms, noisy and vulgar—popped unbidden into Tory's mind. He might easily throw a uniformed Coast Guard officer into the harbor, but he'd just as easily burn up a week's fuel searching for a missing buddy's boat. The commercials, Neal had taught her, lived on the ocean's sufferance and never forgot it. They could be wildly spendthrift or generous beyond reason, but seldom to outsiders.

"Why would the fishermen be picking up the Halvorsens' slip fees?" she asked.

Maria shrugged again. "I'm not sure. According to the harbor office, Halvorsen works on commercial boats from time to time. But up in City Hall, they don't think that's it."

She paused, clearly unwilling to continue, and Tory waited her out. "Frankly," the Waterfront Director said at last, "they think Halvorsen's a religious nut. And some kind of revolutionary, too." Her expression said more clearly than any words what she thought of the theory, and Tory found herself grinning. "Sure, go ahead and laugh," Maria said. "But we don't need any more headlines in Eastern papers: 'Santa Barbara—City Without a Heart' kind of thing. We had that a couple years ago, when I was in Public Works, and the downtown merchants went into colonic spasm. I must've got fifteen calls a day myself."

Now that Maria mentioned it, Tory could remember some of those headlines, on stories in the Florida dailies, when she'd been stationed in the Seventh District. She hadn't paid much attention—Florida editors lived to trash Southern California—but she supposed stuff like that looked different when you were the target. "I'm not sure I understand," Tory said. "What could Mr. Halvorsen do?"

"Who knows?" Maria replied. "He comes to City Council meetings and just sits there, taking notes. For some reason that makes them nervous. But the point isn't what he might do." She leaned forward across Tory's desk, fixing Tory's eyes with hers. "The point is what I'm going to do first, which is get him and his five kids off my turf."

21

"And you want the United States Coast Guard to do it for you," said Tory, restraining herself with an effort.

Spots of red appeared on Maria's cheekbones. "I don't care who does it."

"But why are you here?" Tory said. "You've got a Harbormaster. He works for you. Why not tell him to kick them out?"

The question had popped into her head and out of her mouth before she realized how it sounded. *That's class, Tory: Pass the buck along.* But Maria was clearly flustered. Finally she replied, addressing the desktop: "He can't. No grounds. Showed me the book." She looked up, her eyes expressionless as black glass.

"So you decided to try another book," Tory said. In the ensuing dead silence, a brief, pungent sermon began taking shape in her head. Don't say it, she thought. Don't say anything.

The silence stretched on. Neither woman moved. When it seemed the furniture might start to vibrate, rescue, in the unlikely shape of Chief Boatswain's Mate Braddock Washington, stepped through the office doorway: "Sorry, Lieutenant—didn't know you had a visitor. It's these fishing vessel inspections . . ."

"Of course, Chief." She half lunged across the desk and snatched the forms—deeply detested, often postponed—from the flabbergasted petty officer. "I'll get right on them." And to Maria: "I'm terribly sorry, but these are our bread and butter."

The Waterfront Director regarded her with sardonic amusement. "Understood," she said, getting to her feet. "But you'll at least take a look for yourself?"

"Absolutely," Tory replied, and heard herself add, "It's a promise."

And a promise, she told herself two hours later, is a promise. Even when it's accidental. Besides, the *Prophet Jonah* was right on her afternoon route through Marina I, the floating concrete walkway that stretched eastward from its locked gate, just below the Harbormaster's office, nearly a quarter-mile toward the harbor entrance. Branch piers at right angles to the main walkway, and finger piers at right angles to the branches, created some six hundred neat slots occupied by everything from rust-streaked twenty-ton drag-gers to racing sloops. It was a floating world, a minuscule seagoing universe, and Tory was beginning to feel a part of it.

The sense of belonging hadn't come quickly. At first the com-mercial fishermen had alternated between flat brush-off and sly suggestion. She saw immediately that the uniform put their backs up, while her womanhood challenged them on a more elemental level. Her instinct had been to tough it through, but a veteran Coastie from Long Beach had pointed out there were uniforms and uniforms—why didn't she swap her sharply pressed working blues for a coverall, the older the better?

She had made the switch, and the belligerence level dropped way down—but the half-heard offers, the surreptitious touches contin-ued. At last one evening, fortified by an unaccustomed three beers, Tory laid her problem on a Harbor Patrol colleague. Officer Joan Westphal—young, efficient, and almost humorless—loved noth-ing more than getting her teeth into a friend's problem, and though she had the native Californian's fondness for cosmic psychodrama, she had a cop's realism, too.

"Basically, Tory, it's the tits," said Joan, without hesitation. "They see you coming, they think it's Christmas morning."

"But I've got the damn thing zipped up to my neck," Tory protested.

"Try a jogging bra, one that'll flatten you out a little," Joan said. "Maybe a size bigger on the coverall wouldn't hurt, either."

After a week or two, Tory had managed to accept her new re-flection without wincing—if the only way to achieve a pinch-free environment was to look like a hundred and twenty-five pounds of Pillsbury's finest, then that was a price worth paying. These days, as she strode down the piers, she might get razzed or teased, but there was no edge to it. She was almost one of the family, maybe a visiting cousin. She liked the feeling. It made up, at least in part, for her growing sense of being in a professional cul-de-sac. And maybe, as she replayed last night's dinner, a personal one, too.

*　　*　　*

A hand was tugging sharply at her sleeve. An insistent female voice, with a nasal Long Island accent: "Miss! Miss! Don't you see that little boy?"

Tory, jerked back into the world, looked down at the short, round woman by her side. "What little boy?" she said.

"The one who's drowning," said the woman, pointing. "Aren't you going to save him?"

Two long strides down the finger pier, just as the tiny, sodden head vanished below the edge, and a sliding dive along the concrete, arms extended, hands grasping. A tendril of wet hair grazed her fingertips and was gone. With a grunt of effort, Tory pulled herself forward, thrust one arm down into the chill water. Cloth this time, a solid handful. She dragged it upward, thrashing and struggling: a small, chunky person with shoulder-length hair and a round face scarlet with emotion.

"Stupid fat cow! What d'you think you're doing?"

## Aboard the *Prophet Jonah*, Marina I: Erling Halvorsen

Bent double, ignoring the cramp in his calf, he had finally managed, on the seventh try, to engage the propane bottle's threaded neck into the socket when he heard a furious yell from the pier outside, in Leif's unmistakable alto: "Stupid fat cow! What d'you think you're doing?"

He jerked backward, pulling the gas bottle free and smacking his head on the locker's edge. Even half-stunned, his head spinning from the impact, he knew what he would hear next: Leif again, "I'll tell my father! You better let me go, cow lady!"

*Oh, Lord, give me strength. And patience.* He staggered to his feet and thrust his head through the open porthole. On the pier a few yards away, a dripping Leif was squirming helplessly in the grip of a tall young woman with short, golden hair. One sleeve of her blue coverall was soaked to the shoulder, and her face was scarlet with the effort of holding the struggling child. She was the most beautiful creature Erling Halvorsen had ever seen.

"You better watch it!" Leif shrieked. "I'm a cripple, you fat cow! You better not hurt me!"

Erling's patience vanished out the porthole. "Leif!" he roared. "Enough!"

The young woman dropped Leif as if he were red-hot. The boy, clearly unsure just how much his father had heard, opted for the better part of valor. He scuttled away with amazing speed, and Erling felt his heart turn over at the sight of his son's bare feet, almost hooflike in their deformity.

The woman's gaze lifted from the boy to the man. Erling was conscious only of wide-set blue eyes under brows knitted by concern. "Mr. Halvorsen?" A clear, cool, precise voice that somehow failed to cancel out the warmth of those eyes.

"I'm Erling Halvorsen, yes," he said. "I'm afraid Leif—my son—has done it again."

A slow smile lit her face. "He's a regular devil."

"No," said Erling quickly. "You mustn't say that. Naming calls, you know."

For a second she looked puzzled. "Naming calls?" she repeated. "Oh, I see. And I apologize—it wasn't meant literally."

"Of course not," he replied. "But speaking of names . . ."

"Tory Lennox," she said, smiling again. He felt his own face, stiff with dried sweat, respond.

From behind him, a warning whisper: "Father, be careful: it's the Coast Guard lady."

So this was the one, he thought. Curious he had not seen her around the harbor, but paths crossed when they were meant to. And one needed to know the messenger in order to gauge the message properly. "I think you would like to come on board," he said.

The offer seemed to fluster her. He could sense her reluctance. "It's quite all right," he assured her. "My daughter Martha is here, and of course little Anneke."

"That wasn't—" she began, but cut herself off with a shake of the head. "If you're sure I'm not intruding," she said.

"I'll be right there," he replied, pulling back into the cabin.

"Father, didn't you hear me?" Martha whispered urgently. "That's the Marine Safety woman. Captain Kerrigan told me Mrs. Acid was talking to her this morning."

There were moments, like this one, when Martha's resemblance to her mother was quite uncanny. It wasn't physical—Anna Halvorsen had been a tiny, birdlike woman, and Martha at fifteen was already nearly her father's height, with the same big-boned frame—though not, thank heaven, her father's shaggy, bearlike heft. Rather, he thought, it was the careworn, haunted look around her eyes, the permanently tightened lips, that were so familiar. They were the price of being the motherless mother to a hectic brood, as well as the keeper of a tortured father's secrets. When Erling allowed himself to realize how Martha's soul was being wrung, despair gripped his spirit.

But that was the worst sin, and presumptuous as well. If Martha was being tested, there had to be a reason—though perhaps it was he, Erling, who was being tried, through his daughter's pain. He put his big arm around Martha's shoulders. She stiffened in his grasp, and he quickly released her. For an instant, silence connected them. "Don't prejudge people, love," he said, putting a father's authority into his voice. "And her name is Mrs. Acevedo."

"Oh, *father*," Martha said despairingly. "Can't you *see*? They've sent this woman to throw us out."

Probably they—the little Caesars of the harbor—had dispatched Tory Lennox with that in mind. But a higher authority could intervene, with a little help from His servants. "Come, Martha: help me make her welcome."

"Welcome to *this*?" Martha's voice shot up to a horrified squeak.

Erling paused and took in the cabin, a rectangular box eight feet long, and not quite six feet wide—with nearly four feet of that width taken by narrow upper-and-lower berths each side. Only in the very center, under the leaky skylight, could the six-foot Erling stand erect. Forward, a faded curtain screened off the wheelhouse and, beyond it, the tiny, V-shaped cabin that was Anneke's daytime playpen and Erling's bed at night. The very after end of the cabin was given over to the galley space, which currently consisted of a leprous, thirty-two-quart ice chest, a two-burner propane stove with its guts in pieces on the floorboards, and a plastic pan for a sink, with a hose from the pier providing fresh water.

The fishermen who'd owned the *Prophet Jonah* last were young and hard-living. Two coats of white paint barely hid the graffiti in the cabin—Erling had been forced to tack a year-old souvenir calendar over one particularly gross sketch in heavy black india ink. Since there was no storage space to speak of, the children's bedding and clothes lived on their berths, mostly in tangled (and in Leif's case, dingy) heaps. The odor of old fish, from the thrice-cleaned hold at the stern, was now no stronger than the smell of old diesel oil from the bilge beneath.

Erling suppressed a sigh, saw Martha was close to tears, and gave her shoulder a squeeze. "It's not your fault, child. Our guest will understand."

Privately, he thought the trim Lieutenant Lennox might run screaming down the pier, but Martha managed something close to a smile and said, defiantly, "If she doesn't, she can help me clean it up."

He stepped past her, up two steps that flexed alarmingly under him, and into the bright sunshine of the afterdeck. Tory Lennox had taken him at his word and was balancing easily on the wide gunwale, staring with apparent fascination into the empty fish hold. "An old Monterey boat, right?" she said.

"I believe so, yes," he replied. And to her look of surprise, "I really know very little about boats."

"Oh?" She seemed to be phrasing her next question with care, and he waited. "You don't use her for fishing, then?" she said.

"Goodness, no," he replied. His eye caught the metal Fish and Game permit nailed to the wheelhouse. "Should I have taken that off? Is it illegal?"

She laughed. A nice laugh, if a little constrained. "Please, Mr. Halvorsen: relax. I'm not the Inquisition."

"I'm sure of it," he replied. "Certainly the Inquisition was never so beautiful."

The words were as much a surprise to him as they clearly were to her, and for a moment they stared at each other, mutually speechless. He was entranced to see that her ears turned bright pink when she was embarrassed—and equally entranced to observe

28

that she could be embarrassed: few young women seemed capable of it anymore. "I beg your pardon," he said. "That was uncalled for. I mean," he added quickly, "it's entirely true, but not for me to say."

His deliberate dithering, he saw, had given her the moment she needed to recover her composure. "Well, thank you anyway," she said, looking down at her coverall. "I don't feel very beautiful at the moment."

"Thanks in part to my son," Erling said. "What happened?"

"A misunderstanding," Tory replied. "Someone saw him in the water next to the pier and thought he was drowning. I reacted a little too quickly—just reached in and yanked him out."

"Ah," said Erling.

"Though he shouldn't have been swimming in the harbor in the first place," she added. "It's dangerous, with all the boats moving in and out. Not to mention the water's filthy."

She wore authority easily, he thought. What was she—twenty-five? No, a little older, but not yet thirty. He found himself glancing at her left hand. There was a ring on it, but it was not a wedding band. She was waiting for him to reply, he realized. "It was my fault, really," he said. "Leif was doing a chore for me: plugging a hole in the side of the boat where the sink used to drain out."

"Plugging a hole?" she said, her brows knitting again. "Are you making water?"

"I beg your pardon?" he said, startled, and glanced automatically down.

"Are you making— Oh, Lord." Her ears reddened again and, to Erling's surprise, she giggled. "It's a nautical expression," she said. "Is your boat leaking?"

"No, but the hole is close to the water," Erling replied deadpan. "It makes Martha nervous to see."

"Martha sounds like a sensible person," Tory said. "Your wife?"

"My older daughter. I am a widower," he said. And to forestall the inevitable, meaningless *I'm sorry*, pressed on: "So I told Leif to put a big cork into it from the outside—that way the water would push it in, not out."

"I see," Tory said. But it was clear that the solution which seemed both simple and elegant to him did not impress her. And equally clear she didn't intend to make an issue of it: "Your son's name is Life? That's unusual."

This had happened before. "It's Scandinavian: L-E-I-F. Like Ericsson, the man who really discovered America."

"Oh," she said.

"I don't mind that it sounds like another meaning," he added. "It annoys him, though."

"I suppose it does," she said. "Children don't usually like ambiguity. At least I didn't."

*No, I can see you wouldn't.* "Please, why don't you come all the way on board," he said. "You look uncomfortable, teetering there on the edge."

"What? Oh, thanks." She stepped easily from where she was balancing, across the gaping fish hold, to the small patch of worn planking.

"Welcome on board the *Prophet Jonah*," he said, holding out his hand. Hers was not small, and her grip was as firm as he'd expected. Standing on the same level, she was only two or three inches shorter than he, and she held herself so straight it seemed even less.

"Thanks," she replied, looking about her with interest. "She used to be the *Klamath Goddess*, didn't she?"

They could have told her that at the Harbor Office, but he suspected she simply recognized the boat, despite a new name and a different color of paint. "Yes, that was the name. I found it . . . inappropriate."

He had almost said *blasphemous*, but pulled himself back at the last instant. *Am I being hypocritical?* he asked himself. *Why shouldn't I say what I mean to this young woman?*

Her quick look told him she'd heard his hesitation. "Inappropriate?" she said.

"For a minister of the Gospel," he said.

"Oh. I didn't know." But she had heard something, he decided. Probably from the Acevedo woman, and therefore hostile.

30

"Not formally ordained," he said. "It's my calling, though: what I am, what I must be."

"I see," she said, though she clearly did not. What she meant was *Have it your way.* That was certainly all he could ask at this point.

"Come inside," he said. "I can offer you some of the city's own water, or a cup of truly atrocious instant coffee."

She laughed. "I've tasted the city's water. The coffee can't be worse."

The moment he led the way into the cabin, however, the disassembled stove caught his eye. He turned to apologize. She was right behind him, on the top step. Her expression, as she surveyed the cabin, was unreadable. And probably so intended. She saw him regarding her, blinked twice, and managed a faint smile. "Camping out?" she said mildly.

"Actually, this is our home," Erling replied.

Martha, emerging at that moment from the wheelhouse, snapped, "It's the nicest home we've had in a long time, and anybody who thinks they can throw us out had better think twice."

Without hesitating, Tory replied, "They'd better think three times, if it means going up against you." Edging past Erling, she held out her hand. "My name's Tory Lennox. Your father offered me a cup of coffee."

Martha stood silent but bristling, and Erling said, "This is my daughter Martha, who sometimes forgets herself."

As if the words were being dragged from her lips, Martha said, "You are welcome aboard, Miss Lennox, but there's no coffee because the stove is broken."

Tory allowed her unshaken hand to drop unobtrusively to her side. "In that case, we have two choices," she said briskly. "We can fix the stove, or we can walk over to the Minnow and I'll treat." Not waiting for Martha's answer, she dropped to one knee and inspected the pieces on the deck. "What seems to be the problem?"

"To tell you the truth, I've forgotten how the pieces fit together," Erling said.

Tory looked up at him, disbelief in her eyes. "You're not serious," she said.

"I am serious," said Erling. "Just not very mechanical."

"I suppose you think *you* can fix it," Martha put in.

"As a matter of fact, I do," Tory replied. "It's pretty straightforward." She was picking up pieces as she spoke, fitting them together with an ease that took Erling's breath away. "Hey, presto," she said after a couple of minutes. "Now, if I could borrow a wrench to tighten these connections . . ."

"We don't have a wrench," said Martha coldly. "All the tools we have are in the cardboard box next to you."

"Martha," Erling said quietly. The girl lowered her head, but Tory was looking up at him, clearly concerned. She rose to her feet.

"We seem to be off on the wrong foot," she said to Martha, and when Erling opened his mouth to object, he felt Tory's hand grasp his wrist and squeeze. "Martha," she continued, "I'm not an employee of the harbor. I'm a Coast Guard officer, but I'm on your father's boat as your guest. And it'd be easier for me to act like a guest if you acted a little more like a host."

Martha's blazing eyes lifted to meet Tory's cool blue ones. The two women eyed each other in silence for a long minute, and then Tory put out her hand again. "Truce?" she said.

Martha nodded solemnly and took the woman's hand in hers. "Truce," she said.

After three long, lonely years, he thought, I have found the one.

## Steak 'n' Brew restaurant, Camarillo; Wednesday Afternoon: Jock

"It's important you understand, Dr. Merida: This isn't about money. It's about saving a man's mind—maybe his life." Jock could hear his own voice, as if it belonged to someone else. Low and earnest, with sincerity a near-vibrato in the background. He sounded good, very good—but was he good enough to convince the middle-aged, pussywhipped *medico* across from him?

"I still don't understand what you want me to do," Merida said plaintively. His eyes kept darting to the restaurant's entrance. Jock had picked one of half a dozen interchangeable steak-and-salad places lining the freeway on the far side of Ventura, a safe forty miles from home. The clientele was mostly local, but with enough drop-in business off the 101 so that strangers never attracted attention. "I'm not a psychiatrist," Merida added. "I'm an eye doctor."

"You're not just an eye doctor," Jock said, pushing the heartiness pedal all the way down. "You're the most highly regarded ophthalmologist in the tri-county area. Exactly what poor Wilbur needs."

Merida looked to Lorraine, sitting beside him, and then once more to the door. He was sweating, and if what Jock had heard was true, he had some reason to. Mrs. Merida's jealousy was legendary, according to Lorraine, and her two brothers in the scrap-metal business worshipped her. It was hard to believe this wimp was out of his mind in love, never mind with a brittle, shopworn handmaiden to the arts like Lorraine. Maybe he had a thing for forty-year-old blondes. Jock, who had swung many ways in his day, had never let his heart lead his head, but he recognized that it happened all the time. How else could someone like Merida, with everything to lose, have wound up with a Lorraine Thomas, who had nothing to give a man but her skinny body and a certain cynical wit?

"Doctor, you know who Wilbur Andreas is, of course?"

Merida blinked. "Well, sure. Lorraine's told me . . ." He let it trail off.

"Wilbur Andreas should be the most important artist of our time," said Jock firmly. "His paintings should be worth a fortune—several fortunes. But they aren't." He leaned confidentially across the table, lowering his voice: "It's the same all through history—but of course you know that. Great artists are never appreciated while they're in their prime. It takes time for critics to learn all over again how to look at a picture. It takes time for public tastes to change."

He paused for breath, and Merida inserted a rabbity, "But what—"

"Artists are only people, Doctor," Jock said quickly. "They get discouraged. Where a man like you has the strength to press forward through adversity, an artist may be just too sensitive. Call it weak, if you will. He loses heart, gives up."

Merida was nodding sagely. *Pompous little twerp. I've almost got you.* "A man like that needs help, Doctor. If he doesn't get it, he could do . . . anything." He gave Merida a half second to absorb that one, then added, "To anybody," and let his eyes flick from the doctor to Lorraine and back again. Merida blinked, but Jock held up his hand to forestall him. "We don't want to get into that, do we? We want to be positive here—because there's a chance to make Wilbur Andreas the star he ought to be. And, incidentally, relieve Miss Thomas's financial position for the rest of her life."

The throwaway lines were often the most effective, Jock knew. Merida's eyes had lit up for half a second. *How much do you suppose he's skimming off his practice to keep Lorraine? He knows he's going to get caught sooner or later—by the IRS if he's lucky, or the brothers if he's not. But here's a way out.* Jock smiled encouragement, watching cupidity, lust, and fear alternate in the doctor's eyes, like the spinning fruit in a slot machine window.

"The rest of her life?" Merida echoed.

"She'll be free," said Jock. *And so will you.*

"So tell me what you want," Merida said.

Two minutes into Jock's pitch, Merida pushed back his chair, his face purple with indignation. "I never heard such a preposterous . . ."

Surprisingly, it was Lorraine who pulled him back. "For Christ's sake, don't make a scene, Ray," she whispered. "Just let him finish."

Jock had anticipated a first rejection. He was ready with arguments based on pity, society's responsibility to the artist, or even—shakily—the higher morality. But taking his cue from Merida's objection, he led out his trumps. "It can fly, Doctor. It *will* fly—I know how these shows work: these people are desperate for good stories, and desperate to beat each other out. This is a guaranteed winner, you can bank on it."

"But . . ."

*You want to be convinced, my friend. You really do.* "Of course they'll check, but it's a quick once-over, has to be. If all the pieces dovetail—and they will—the producers won't look further. They simply can't take the chance a competitor will pick up their ball and run with it."

"And you really think this—what's his name?—Freddy Brooks will go for it?"

"I take it you don't watch *Making Things Right?*"

"Certainly not," Merida said. "It's a woman's show."

Jock shrugged. "Well, that's true, but I've invested some time in it. Wilbur's tragic accident is exactly what the—" He caught himself, swallowed "doctor ordered," and managed to substitute "format requires" with barely a lurch. Lorraine put a hand over her mouth and looked quickly away, but Merida never noticed the near-slip.

"What do you mean?" he asked.

"It's in the title," Jock said: "*Making Things Right*. They hunt up tragedies, and then fix them. Or at least alleviate them. Now, the obvious—the too-obvious—line would be to have Wilbur lose his sight and you restore it. But there's no story in that, nothing for Freddy and his audience to do."

"Well, what *can* they do?"

Jock stifled his growing annoyance. How on earth could Lorraine have wound up with such a dope? If things worked out, he might find the time to take her in hand. "What they can do is make Wilbur famous. Make him the star of his own tragedy—and shove his paintings under the noses of thirty million people at the same time."

"And that's going to make them sell?"

"You've got it. Wilbur will start as one of those fifteen-minute celebrities, but his stuff is really good. All he needs is exposure and a publicity hook, which this will be: 'Last masterpieces of the blind young artist.' " Jock paused to acknowledge his own genius, saw Merida wavering, and pressed in for the kill: "*Last* masterpieces— that's the best part: You'd better buy one of these, because there won't be any more. It's the kind of thing that art investors knock each other down for."

His own conviction, as absolute as it was momentary, had carried the day. Or almost carried it: "One thing worries me," Merida said.

"Speak. We value your opinion, Doctor."

"Now, I don't know Wilbur. Never met him," Merida said. "But I have, you know, heard a lot about him. From everything Lorraine says, painting is his life. Now, he's going to have to stop, for good. You think he'll agree to that?"

"I knew we were right," Jock crowed. "Didn't I tell you, Lorraine, we needed a sharp mind like the doctor's?"

Her warning glance told him he was laying it on too thick, and he hurried on. "Doctor, you've put your finger on the one catch.

But there's an answer: once Wilbur's established, who says he can't be cured?"

"Well, I don't know. The kind of damage you're talking about . . ."

"Doctor, the damage is going to be what you say it is," Jock said patiently. "Make it sound permanent, but leave yourself a little loophole." He shaped an encouraging smile. "In a year, maybe two, when Wilbur's work is bringing the prices it should be, you can reevaluate the situation. Maybe an operation, in someplace far away . . ."

"Far away, yes. It'd better be far away," Merida said. "But this is still just an idea—"

"A concept," Jock agreed. "It needs fleshing out. You leave that to me, Doctor. The less you know about the details that don't concern you, the better."

Merida had the grace to look slightly guilty, but it was a thin overlay on his deep relief. "You're right." He looked at his watch, mimed surprise—just as if he hadn't been peeking covertly for the past five minutes: "I've got to run—dinner . . ."

"Of course," said Jock, getting to his feet. "We won't meet again, Doctor."

"That's sensible."

"And it'd be better if you and Lorraine sort of, well, cooled things for a while."

His pout was almost childlike. Jock risked a glance at Lorraine, read her expression. *You're ready to move on. But not quite yet, sweetheart.*

"How will you stay in touch with me?" Merida asked.

"How about I'm a prospective patient?" Jock said. He had already worked this out with Lorraine. "I've been referred by a colleague you don't see often . . ."

"Dr. Scolie, down in Ventura," Lorraine suggested. "He never comes to Santa Barbara."

"Scolie's all right," Merida said. "But why don't you come to my office?"

"I'm in Ventura, too," Jock replied. "But it's hard for me to get around, because of my eye problem. So I call to talk to you first.

37

I'm reassured, but I call a second time—that's all the contact we'll need—and then I just don't go through with it."

"That could happen," said Merida, more to himself than them. And then, quickly, "All right, but now I really have to go."

"Yes," Jock said. "So long, Doctor—until Philippi."

"What?" said Merida.

"Never mind, Ray," Lorraine snapped. "You get back to work."

MARINA 2; WEDNESDAY AFTERNOON: TORY

About two months before, it had dawned on Tory that the whole harbor knew about her and Neal. He, typically, didn't care. She did, but found her concern hard to explain.

"It's just none of their business," she had told him, annoyed at being unable to come up with anything stronger.

"That's the attraction," he'd replied—rather smugly, she thought.

"But where's the fun for them? It's not as if we were doing anything worth watching."

He shrugged. "Harbor doesn't have cable TV, so gossip's the next best thing. The uniforms make us look interesting."

The last she could appreciate, sometimes ruefully. It was a fact of life in the military, something you learned from the first day: anytime you were in uniform, you were on display, representing your entire service, living and dead, back to its beginning. You could deal with the situation in two ways—by sneaking around (which was cowardly and didn't work anyway) or by just accepting it and going about your business, which had seemed impossible at first but turned out not to be so hard.

So now, secure in her own integrity, she no longer worried about being seen aboard Neal's harbor home, the shabby, not-quite-completed ketch he'd named *Carpe Diem*. They were having lunch outside, in the big cockpit, not for propriety's sake but because Neal was halfway through changing the injectors in the old Perkins diesel that crouched under the cabin sole, and the whole interior smelled of fuel.

It was a constrained lunch by any standard. Neal was entirely silent and, instead of its usual expression of private amusement, his angular, darkly handsome face wore a distinct scowl that darkened it even more. Tory assumed last night's unresolved conversation was weighing on his spirit, but every subject that occurred to her seemed to lead inevitably to marriage, the last thing she wanted to talk about. And she couldn't even praise the food: he'd overspiced the clam chowder and burnt the toast, which was practically unheard of in her experience of his cooking.

Tory was wondering how she could slip her chowder within beak range of a gull that was sitting on the finger pier, eyeing the bowl, when Neal finally spoke: "I've got an ugly assignment this afternoon."

In any other voice it would have sounded like self-pity, or at least a bid for sympathy. For no reason, the hulking, benign image of Erling Halvorsen popped into her head. "Oh?" she said.

A grimace twisted his lips. "Maria told me she spoke to you about the Halvorsens."

*Naming calls.* "I looked at their boat."

"And found no reason to cite them."

"Not while they're at dockside," she replied.

His sidelong look told her she'd spoken more firmly than necessary. "One thing I've learned," he said. "When Maria wants something done, she can always find a way."

"What's that supposed to mean?" *Am I sounding as belligerent as I feel?* she asked herself, and saw the answer in Neal's face.

"She called Motor Vehicles in Sacramento. It seems the *Prophet*

*Jonah's* still registered to a couple of salmon fishermen." And before Tory could speak, he added, "Basic harbor rule one and a half: only the owner can live on a boat. Halvorsen told us he owns the *Prophet Jonah*, but the MVD says he doesn't—and as far as they're concerned, she's still the *Klamath Goddess*."

She could see exactly what he was leading up to: "On the basis of that, you're going to evict them."

Both his eyebrows shot upward. "Do I detect a . . . personal concern here?"

She felt dangerously close to explosion, so she forced herself to get up slowly and set the soup bowl, with exquisite care, on the seat beside her. "I met Mr. Halvorsen and his older daughter this morning," she said. "He's a good man."

"Which isn't the issue," Neal said. His face had lost all expression.

"Of course it isn't." She took a steadying breath. "I should have said I don't believe he lied about owning the boat. It's probably just a mistake."

He was looking up at her, his eyes like dark mirrors. "That's not the way my boss sees it. 'We've got him by the short and curlies' were her words. 'Tell him he's invalidated the contract,' she said."

"And you're going to do just that."

"Unless you can give me a good reason not to," he replied.

She had the feeling she was missing something, but she also knew she was too exasperated to work it through. "Thanks for lunch, anyway," she said and stepped lightly over the rail.

Her ears were cocked, as she strode down the pier, for a word from Neal. Almost any word would have done, but when she reached the corner and turned, a quick glance from under the brim of her cap showed him still sitting there, unmoving.

She heard the unaccustomed sound from forty yards away but couldn't identify it for several steps. A voice—no, several voices, singing a cappella, she decided, and then the words came clear, with one clear, pure alto rising above the rest:

*Oh, hear us when we cry to Thee*
*For those in peril on the sea.*

Tory had grown up with the hymn from earliest childhood in her family's church (the minister was a yachtsman, like half his congregation), sang it later at boarding school and of course at the Academy. Since then she had heard it less frequently, but the melody and, most of all, the words never failed to release a torrent of memories. She paused, trying to identify the voices. Erling's baritone rumble was easy enough to pick out, and the soprano, straining hard and flatting on the high notes, was certainly Martha. The beautiful alto could only be the loathsome Leif, and the piping, uncertain treble would probably be the baby, Anneke. There was another voice, too, faint behind the rest and from its uncertain register clearly a teenage boy's—another Halvorsen, she wondered, or did Martha have a boyfriend?

The chorused Amen brought her back to reality, and she rapped her class ring against the hull. "Hello," she called. "It's me, Tory Lennox."

Erling's unkempt head appeared in the companionway hatch. His face was slightly lower than hers, and she noticed, as she had not the first time, that his yellow hair was liberally streaked with gray. He was beaming—big, slightly uneven teeth bared—and her heart warmed. "Welcome back," he said. "Please come aboard."

"Thank you." She stepped to the afterdeck. "I need to—" But he was speaking again, to the watchful faces clustered at the foot of the companionway ladder.

"Come up, children, and say hello to Miss Lennox." A shuffling hesitation, and Erling said, warningly, "Children." *The voice of command. I wonder if he hears it.*

Martha was first. "Hello again, Miss Lennox." Coolly distant, but not actively hostile.

As a very junior officer, Tory had heard that tone many times, from enlisted men old enough to be her father. The one hopeless error, she had learned, was sounding anxious to please. Respect first, friendship afterward: "Hello, Martha."

42

Now Leif was standing before her, head cocked to one side, radiating charm and false humility. "Miss Lennox, I'm very, *very* sorry for what I called you."

"Don't overdo it, Leif," she said, with a smile to take some of the sting away. She saw the boy got all her meaning, then added, "Apology accepted."

Anneke, of course, was easy: all she wanted was affection, and Tory could sweep her into a hug without a second thought. Erling was beaming at the two of them in an almost proprietary fashion. *Did he set this up? No, that's ridiculous.*

From the corner of her eye, she saw a compact figure behind Erling sidling toward the gunwale: a boy about Martha's age, whose ruddy coloring and thatch of straw-colored hair mirrored his father's. "I don't think we've met," Tory said.

Erling half turned. "Oh. Erik," he said. "Come here."

He's the unseen one, Tory decided in a flash of perception. And he's got something heavy on his mind. She put out her hand. "Pleased to meet you, Erik."

He winced at her grip, quickly pulled back his dirty paw. She glanced down at her own palm, saw a faint reddish stain. The boy had jammed both hands in the pockets of his faded, patched jeans and was avoiding her eye. Martha was watching him, concern clear on her face, and Leif's too-sharp eyes glittered with malice—but their father was oblivious. Tory absorbed the scene and in the same millisecond filed it for future consideration. "Is this the whole family, then?" she asked lightly. "Somebody said you had five children."

His face turned to stone. "These are all my children."

He was not going to add anything, she saw. Something else to save for later. "Erling, I've got some bad news," she said.

"They are going to make us leave," he replied, nodding.

She was not completely surprised. For those who belonged, the harbor was one big coconut telegraph—and Erling Halvorsen clearly belonged. "That's the intention," she said. "What will you do?"

"Render unto Caesar, of course."

43

His attitude, parent to child who should know better, nettled her. But she masked her feelings. "You've got someplace to live on shore?"

"No, this boat is our home," he replied. She waited for him to explain. "Friends have arranged a mooring for us—out there." He nodded vaguely eastward, but she knew where he meant.

Fools' Anchorage it was called, the half-mile-long stretch of shallow water off East Beach. Several large oil spill cleanup vessels had secure permanent moorings there, as did a couple of barges dedicated to experimental farming of mussels and oysters. But in-shore of them a motley fleet of semi-abandoned small craft swung perilously from weed-sheathed lines made fast to barnacled floats. Mastless sailboats, cruisers with long-dead engines, a couple of commercial fishing boats whose skippers were temporarily tapped out—it was a spectacle that depressed Tory every time she saw it.

The anchorage existed partly because of the lee created by the long extrusion of Stearns Wharf to the east of it. In the prevailing westerly winds a boat was safe there, if not much fun to live aboard. The swells that swept down the Santa Barbara Channel hooked left around the end of the wharf and caught the moored boats more or less broadside as they weathercocked into the wind, rolling them sometimes unmercifully. And the occasional southeasterly storm would roar in from the other direction and transform the anchor-age into a desperate lee shore. Sun-rotted mooring lines and rusted anchor chains would snap, and the boats would blow helplessly down on the beach or into the heavy pilings of the wharf. In the former case, the sand would grip what the waves didn't destroy, making it almost impossible to drag a grounded craft off after the first critical hours; in the latter, destruction was usually faster and more complete—though the wharf's elderly pilings could be badly damaged, too.

To Tory's orderly mind, Fools' Anchorage was an abomination, made more abominable by the political back-and-forth that al-lowed it to continue. The city refused to accept responsibility for the anchorage—but, seduced by the distant possibility of milking revenue from the area, wouldn't surrender authority over it, either.

And until the city formally backed off, the Coast Guard wouldn't step in and apply the normal anchorage regulations that would turn the place into something nautically respectable.

"I don't much like the idea of you being out there," she said.

His smile could only be called indulgent, she decided. "The Lord has provided this home for us. He's certainly entitled to put it where He pleases."

Was this supposed to be some kind of Christian resignation? she wondered. "I find it hard to believe that God wants your family moored on a lee shore," she replied.

Erling could scarcely help hearing the tight self-control in her voice. "He does move in mysterious ways sometimes," he said, smiling even more broadly. "But His wonders are revealed in due course. If one is paying attention."

Enough of this, she decided. "Erling, I'd like to check out your boat, if you don't mind," she said, dropping automatically into what she thought of as the Official Voice.

"Of course, Lieutenant."

*I do believe I've just been manipulated. How interesting.*

When Neal appeared an hour later, trailed by Maria Acevedo, Tory was just climbing out of the *Prophet Jonah*'s engine compartment, notebook in hand. If you were as hippy as Maria, Tory thought irrelevantly, a skirt was indeed the only answer, no matter how out of place you looked walking a pier. The three of them exchanged stilted, formal greetings, while Erling and his family observed impassively.

The Waterfront Director was trying to suppress her feelings, but Tory could see triumph bubbling up around the edges: "So you've had a look at the boat," she said. "Turns out it wasn't necessary after all."

"Oh, but it was," Tory replied. Neal eyed her strangely—was that amusement she saw?—but Maria was intent on her own agenda.

"Mr. Halvorsen," she said, shifting her aim, "I'm afraid we must ask you to leave. Immediately."

"You'd better settle that with Lieutenant Lennox," he replied.

Maria was far too experienced a bureaucrat not to sense a trap when it was right in front of her. "Is that so?" she said, turning to Tory. "What does he mean?"

"He means this vessel is unsafe," Tory said. "She cannot leave the harbor in her present condition."

"Who says?" Maria demanded.

"I do, Ms. Acevedo. The United States Coast Guard."

MARINA 2; THURSDAY, 7:00 A.M.: NEAL

*I do, Ms. Acevedo. The United States Coast Guard.* Fourteen hours later, Tory's clear, determined voice seemed to echo off the tiled walls of the Marina 2 washroom, where Neal was dragging out his morning shave.

He could still see Maria's expression of baffled fury, too. An expression quickly veiled, since the Waterfront Director was a politician to her marrow, and she could sense the fascinated eyes and ears on boats all around them. Besides, Tory held all the cards. Briskly competent, she'd pointed out how the *Prophet Jonah*—preposterous name—might be acceptably safe while tied to a marina float, yet a clear menace when anchored a quarter of a mile off Stearns Wharf. With no two-way radio, an engine that didn't work, and several dubious through-hull fittings, the ex–fishing boat had the makings of a death trap.

Maria had retreated in as good order as possible. Even when they were back in Neal's upstairs office, overlooking the long sweep of the harbor, she didn't raise her voice. "Solve it," she told Neal.

"I don't care how, but I want that beat-up tub and those wretched people out of here by tomorrow noon."

You had to give it to Maria: she knew when to cut through the bureaucratic crap. Neal had hoped for a week's delay at least—and it was the kind of situation that could drag on for months, with no real harm to anyone, while a compromise slowly emerged. That was what his former boss, Walt d'Andrea, would have managed. Until a heart attack had sent him to the hospital, Walt was able to keep more balls in the air, and for longer, than any other person Neal had ever met. With Walt as Harbormaster, few problems were ever actually solved, but they never quite achieved critical mass.

As Walt's assistant, Neal had found existence wildly frustrating. Now that he was Harbormaster himself—acting Harbormaster, since Walt had managed to put himself on open-ended sick leave after his coronary—matters looked very different. He was only beginning to discover how many predicaments were better left unresolved. Until yesterday, however, he'd despaired of making Tory realize that summary judgments weren't always the best ones. Now the ball was back in his court, and he had the difficult job of pretending to act while actually dragging his heels—and carrying off his deception in front of someone who knew every governmental trick in the book.

"There's a way," he told his lathered image in the mirror. "I'm just not seeing it yet."

"Seeing what?" said the man at the next sink, through a foam of toothpaste. The marina washrooms were large and well-equipped, and you needed a key to enter them, but they were still public. It was like being back in college, except that most of your sinkside companions were relative strangers, people who used their boats on weekends or even less often. Neal recognized the man next to him only as an urchin diver named Sam who often slept aboard so he could get an earlier start on the forty-mile run out to San Miguel Island.

"Just talking to myself," Neal said. He stretched the skin of his cheek with his fingertips and drew the razor up it, against the grain. Even with a close shave, he'd have to scrape again by evening. But why bother? He wouldn't be seeing Tory. He focused in tightly on the tricky planes under his chin, but just as he poised the razor for a stroke, the washroom's locked door resounded to a barrage of blows, an excited voice yelling his name: "Mr. Donahoe! You in there? Hey, Mr. Donahoe, somebody's hurt!"

*Perfect.* He set the razor down, dabbed the towel at the shallow gash along his jaw, and stepped to the door. *I know that voice.*

The shaggy, ferret-faced youth outside was jabbering a mile a minute, eyes bright with excitement, face flushed. "Come on, Mr. Donahoe—it's awful!"

Junior Halvorsen, Neal thought, allowing his arm to be seized: Erling's oldest boy—a harbor hanger-out for months, always on the verge of real trouble. Junior had only to walk past a boat and something aboard vanished, usually something small, electronic, and resalable. Junior had been spiraling inevitably toward the slammer, and then a week or so ago he'd disappeared. Where's he been? Neal asked himself, remembering the rumor that was making the rounds, something about the kid moving out after a big fight with his father, but it was hard for Neal to think against the young man's nonstop monologue. He let himself be dragged to the Marina 2 gate.

"I went to your boat first, but the people in the next slip said you were up at the johns," Junior was saying. "He's down here, to the left—by that big Pacemaker. I saw it happen, the whole thing."

As Neal pushed his magnetic key into the lock, part of his mind noted the cough and roar of an engine starting up, two hundred yards or so away, on the pier where the Harbor Patrol boats tied up. "What whole thing?" Neal demanded, but saw the answer before the youth could respond.

Neal's police training had added orderly analysis to a sailor's naturally sharp eye, and his mind first photographed the whole scene, then the pieces. A heavyset figure in paint-stained overalls lay on his back on the pier, moaning wordlessly and kicking the planks in apparent agony. His hands were against his face, palms pressed to his eyes. Tory, wearing her office blues, was kneeling beside him, pale but calm. With one hand she was trying to steady his head, which thrashed back and forth, while with the other she directed a hose on his face. She looked up as she heard Neal's steps. "Acetone," she said, nodding toward an uncapped tin lying on the planks beside her. "It spilled in his eyes. This young man saw it happen."

Now Neal was aware of the sweetly sharp chemical reek. Before he could speak, the red-orange hull of *Harbor 2*, with Officer Lance Dalleson at the helm, appeared between two docked boats. "What's up?" he called to Neal. "Somebody phoned the office, said a guy was hurt."

"Man spilled acetone in his eyes," Neal shouted back. "We need the EMTs."

"You've got them," said Tory, looking past Neal and up the ramp to the parking lot.

He followed her eyes, saw the ambulance pulling through the toll gate. "Junior, go let them in," he said to the youth at his side. And to Tory, "Can you see how bad it is?"

"He won't take his hands away," she replied. "But you can smell it all over him."

Neal dropped to his knees at her side, took one of the victim's wrists. "No! No! Hurts!" the man shrieked. He rolled violently away, and Neal grabbed a fistful of coverall just in time to keep him on the float. The struggling man kicked out again, and a cupful of gold paint splashed across the planking. Neal glanced up and saw the big power yacht's stern looming above him. She had been turned in the slip, so her broad transom was against the pier. A skilled hand had traced in black the Old English outlines that read *Marti's Mink* and filled in the first word and most of the second M with gold. A six-inch golden drip, already congealing, ran down from the letter.

So that's who this is, Neal thought: the name-painter, Wilbur something-or-other. Andrews—no, Andreas.

At the head of the ramp the heavy gate clanged and three sets of feet thumped down, a man and a woman in EMT coveralls, trailed by Junior Halvorsen. The woman glanced at Neal's jaw, then to the man writhing on the float, and addressed Tory: "He the one?"

She nodded. "He was lettering the name on that boat, and the acetone tipped over onto his head. It must've run down his face. I've been trying to rinse his eyes, but he won't take his hands away."

"Right," said the woman EMT. She turned to her companion: "Ben, get the stretcher." And back to Tory: "Let me in there, would you, miss?"

"Of course." Tory rocked back on her heels, almost losing her balance. Neal was reaching to steady her when the female EMT said, "Officer, could you help Ben with the stretcher? It's kind of clumsy."

The ambulance had pulled into one of the handicapped parking slots next to the gate, and the EMT named Ben was wrestling with a folded litter. "Here, let me give you a hand," Neal said.

"Thanks," Ben replied. He was panting with the effort, and even in the moment's excitement Neal was conscious of his foul breath. "We usually use the kind with wheels, but that ramp's awful steep."

"Here, let me." Neal yanked from one side and Ben tugged at the other. The stretcher screeched open. "I'll hold the gate for you."

Before Neal could fish the key ring from his pocket, Lance Dalleson was running up the ramp to open the gate from the inside. From the pier, the female EMT called, "Hurry it up, Ben."

On the pier, Tory was standing with her knuckle pressed to her colorless lips. Neal looked past her, over the crouching EMT's shoulder, and caught a quick glimpse of the painter's face. The area around his tightly closed eyes was wetly pink, streaked with red. From ten feet away, it looked as if the skin had sloughed away, exposing the raw flesh beneath.

The EMT laid a heavy pad of bandage on the painter's face. "Is that better?" she asked.

"Oh, Jesus. It really hurts," the painter cried. "I can't see!"

"Keep your eyes closed," the EMT snapped. "Let's get him on that stretcher, guys. Quickly."

As the ambulance pulled away, Neal turned just soon enough to see Tory a hundred feet away, walking quickly in the direction of her office. *She might at least have said hello.* And then his eye caught Junior Halvorsen, drifting off in the other direction. "No, you don't," Neal said automatically.

Junior took a half step as if to run, but Lance Dalleson had moved unobtrusively to block his escape. "Hey, man, what's the beef?" the boy said. "Who was it called you guys, anyway?"

"Relax," Neal replied. "You're not in trouble—for once. I just need to know what you saw." Absently he reached up for the notebook that lived in his shirt pocket—when he was wearing a shirt. "Lance, you know Erling Halvorsen, Jr. You want to take down his statement?"

It took several minutes to convince Junior he wasn't going to be blamed for what had happened, but when he accepted the novel role of witness instead of accused, it was nearly impossible to shut him up. He'd been watching Wilbur lettering the name on *Marti's Mink*, he said. He liked to watch the painter, and Wilbur didn't object as long as Junior didn't bother him with questions. Wilbur worked freehand, sketching the letters with a carpenter's pencil, then painting the outlines in black and filling in the gold at the end. He made few mistakes, but he kept a tin of acetone and a rag handy, to wipe off drips. He'd balanced the open tin on the yacht's high stern, just above his own head, where he didn't have to bend down for it.

Wilbur had been filling in the gold of the second capital M, Junior said, when the gilt paint suddenly began to run. The painter reached up for the solvent without looking and knocked it off its perch, on the curved edge of the yacht's transom. The open tin had already been spilling when Wilbur looked up, just in time to receive a large splash full in the face. "He let out a yell you could hear clear up to the Mission," Junior said. "Started dancing around on the dock—jumping up and down, you know. Screaming like a pig."

*Most fun you've had in weeks.* "Was that when you ran over to my boat?" Neal asked.

"Like, I didn't know whether to shit or go blind," Junior said. "Wilbur, he fell down, which I figured was probably better than falling in the water." He seemed to sense Neal's impatience and hurried on. "Anyway, that's when I saw your girlfriend . . ." He was watching Neal from under his eyelashes, waiting for a reaction.

"Lieutenant Lennox, you mean," said Neal, keeping his voice flat.

"Right. The lady Coastie. She was walking right along up here, by the water . . ."

"She didn't hear Mr. Andreas screaming?"

"I guess not," said Junior, shrugging. "Like, I had to yell right at her a couple times before she heard *me.*"

"And when she did hear you, what then?"

"I yelled at her what was happening, and she came running down here. She told me to go get you off your boat."

"Which you did."

"Right, only you weren't there. I was banging on the hull, like, and the people in the next slip, they told me where you were."

"Junior pulled me out of the washroom," Neal said to Lance, who was scribbling desperately. "I was shaving."

"That's when you cut yourself?" Lance asked without looking up.

Neal touched his jaw with a fingertip. It was only slightly damp. "Right." He started to wipe his finger on his pants, caught himself in time. "I guess that's about it— Oh, Junior: one more thing."

The youth waited, clearly ready to deny everything.

"Where you staying these days? I know you're not on your dad's boat."

"I'm eighteen," Junior replied. "I can stay anyplace I want."

"If we need to ask you anything else," Neal said.

Junior shrugged. "I'm, like, around. You know the skateboard shop over on Haley? They can find me."

It would have to do, Neal decided. One Halvorsen down, one to go.

THE FEVEREL COLLECTION OF FINE ART, EAST CANON PERDIDO
STREET; THURSDAY MID-MORNING: JOCK

He could barely understand what she was saying, with the words
tumbling over each other in her excitement and her breath crackling in the phone. But the general drift was clear and perfect: Act
One (as Jock thought of it) had gone off without a hitch—even
better than expected, since the witnesses included both the Harbormaster and a Coast Guard officer.

Now Lorraine seemed to have started telling the whole thing
over again from the beginning, but Jock decided it was best to just
listen and let her burn off her excess enthusiasm. Besides, it was
good to hear her like this: she hadn't been so high since the day, five
years ago, when she thought she'd sold her screenplay. She'd been
almost beautiful then, lit up from inside, and Jock found himself
wishing he could see her now. Hold her, even.

But that would be dumb. Even this call was risky, though at least
she'd remembered to use a pay phone. She paused, and he said:
"You talked to the kid? Everything okay at his end?"

"Great," she said firmly. "Just great."

Too firmly? "Something worrying you, duck?"

"The kid was really good," she said. "A natural scam artist . . ."

54

"I could see that the minute Wilbur introduced us," said Jock. "Don't worry about the kid—I'm way ahead of him." But her concern was worth his attention. The boy was a greedo, and it wouldn't hurt to play him along, drop a hint there might be other operations he could be a part of. "Ray handled it all right?" Jock asked.

"Good as gold," she replied, laughing. "He was just outside the emergency room when we wheeled the ambulance in. Stepped up right on cue: the resident was ecstatic. Washed his hands of the whole thing without even looking at Wilbur's face—though I've got to say that red slime you cooked up gave me a turn, and I even knew what it was."

*Vaseline, Crisco, and scarlet pigment: simple is always best.* "But something's bothering you. I can tell," he prompted.

"Well, it was my partner, Vern," she said. "Aka Ben—the kid's buddy, you know?"

"Don't tell me he showed up bagged," said Jock. "Not after all the trouble we took cleaning him up."

She managed a laugh. "No, the trouble was, he was *too* sober. Shaking like a leaf. I had to pour two brandies down his throat to steady him."

"*Two brandies?* Lorraine, duckie, that wasn't—"

"You weren't there, Jock." He could hear the nerves close beneath her exuberance, and maybe she did, too. There was a second's pause, and she went on more calmly: "It's okay. I made him chew on a couple of garlic cloves. He smelled like an open grave, but not like booze."

"Clever girl," Jock said, forcing warmth into his voice. "Where'd he go afterward?"

"Who knows? He's a homeless, remember?" She sounded annoyed.

"Well, they do live someplace, even in summer," Jock insisted. "Find out where."

"How, for God's sake?"

"Get the kid to do it—we know how to find him, anyway. Tell him to keep an eye on his friend, make sure he doesn't get, you know, publicly indiscreet."

"You think the kid'll cooperate?" Lorraine was beginning to sound scared, but Jock knew the plan was still on the rails.

"He'll do anything for a buck," Jock said. "Tell him to call me at home this evening, and I'll square it with him."

"I'll have him call you from a pay phone," she said, sounding a little less doubtful.

"You've got it," Jock said. It was important to keep her up, he told himself. Confidence begets confidence. "Duckie, this is just a detail. I'll handle him, no problem. Trust me on this."

"Seems to me I've heard that song before."

"This time it's going to work," Jock said. And it would. He knew it would. It had to.

The final call was the keystone. Jock knew exactly how he wanted to sound, but boosting Lorraine's spirit had sapped his own. He needed a jump start, he told himself. A purely medicinal boost. He locked the gallery's street door, then shut himself into the closetlike bathroom and lifted the heavy porcelain lid off the toilet tank. The water inside was an impenetrable sapphire blue, the kind of color that looked as if it could eat away glass. But of course the tightly sealed bottle, suspended from the float on a thin, stainless steel wire, was intact. Jock unscrewed the cap and carefully tapped a fingernail's worth of powder on the glass of a framed miniature landscape he lifted from its wall hook. A short, thick straw that lived on the molding over the door served as an inhaler. His hand was so unsteady he forced himself to sit down and brace his forearm against the sink. "Two minutes to curtain," he whispered and bent forward.

As soon as he felt his mind begin to clear, he replaced the straw, the bottle, and the tank lid. As he stepped back into the gallery, a part of his mind noted and approved his own air of confidence. Taking his seat, he watched his hands—elegant hands, well-manicured and powerful—unfold the carefully preserved scrap of paper and spread it on the desk.

*What if they've changed the number?* It was as if someone had stabbed his heart with an icicle. He forced himself to sit straight, master of the situation. *Press on regardless.* He took a deep breath, observed his finger picking out the number.

Two rings. Three. The click made him jump. "Fixit Productions, this is Laurie."

*Curtain's up.* "Hi, Laurie. Have I got a story for you."

ABOARD THE *PROPHET JONAH,* FOOLS' ANCHORAGE; THURSDAY
AFTERNOON: TORY

She rocked back on her heels, careful not to shift position
quickly; the *Jonah*'s bilge pump intake was too high, so the last few
inches of liquid around the engine mount were never removed—
were, in fact, sloshing greasily around the ankles of her heavy
seaboots. The acrid reek of stale diesel and old bilge was lacerating
her sinuses, and she knew it was past time to get out of the engine
compartment.

From the cockpit above her, Erling's voice repeated: "Captain
Boyle said if we bled the fuel line, the engine should work perfectly."

*Easy for Toto to say, I bet he hasn't even bothered to look.* But she pasted
on a smile before looking up at the three faces regarding her with
genuine anxiety and the one—Leif's—mimicking deep concern.

"What do you think, Lieutenant?" said Erik. "Can you make it
run?"

"Well, not today, I'm afraid," Tory said. Being off duty, she
hadn't allowed herself to wear her Coast Guard coverall, but why in
heaven's name had she put on good jeans and a better-than-average
crew neck sweater, when she'd known she would wind up down

here? She reached up, groping for the hatch coaming, and Erling's powerful hand engulfed her own. She stood, raised one slippery-soled boot and placed it carefully on the exhaust manifold, and let him pull her up. "Thanks," she said, conscious of his nearness, and of the others' presence. He released her hand slowly, almost unwillingly.

Standing on the *Prophet Jonah*'s gouged and stained deck, Tory inhaled deeply. Impelled by a chill westerly, the iodized tang of sea air filled her lungs, but the diesel miasma clung to her clothes, her hair, even her skin. The *Jonah* lifted unexpectedly to a small, steep sea, and Tory swayed with it automatically, while the Halvorsens lurched awkwardly, grabbing for handholds. Erling's hand grasped—by accident?—her bicep, and this time he didn't let go.

The *Jonah*'s mooring was a good quarter-mile east of Stearns Wharf, with little protection from the metallic gray seas that swept down the Santa Barbara Channel. The narrow strip of city beach, some two hundred yards to the north, was deserted except for a handful of tourists wandering aimlessly along the water's edge, wondering where the sun had gone. Across Cabrillo Boulevard lay the vaguely Spanish sprawl of a resort hotel, with the city clustered behind it, rising into the foothills of the coastal range.

The anchorage was nearly filled at this time of year, the permanent complement of near-derelicts amplified by cruising yachts too cheap to pay for a guest slip and local mariners too poor to buy one. Just to windward a mastless sailboat about thirty feet long corkscrewed wildly, revealing heavy skirts of barnacle and seaweed with each roll. And inshore of the *Jonah* wallowed another neglected vessel, a wooden skiff on which some amateur carpenter had erected a too-large cabin. Tory was less than delighted by the *Jonah*'s location, but Toto Boyle, who'd towed the boat out of the harbor, had assured her the mooring itself was both heavy and in good condition. Tory was not about to contradict Boyle without evidence, but she made a mental note to dig out her wetsuit and have a look for herself as soon as possible.

"So what's the verdict?" said Martha abruptly. "Is it safe for us to be anchored out here?"

"Don't be rude, child," Erling snapped. "I wouldn't have brought my family here if it wasn't safe."

"But Miss Lennox said—" she began.

Erling's face darkened, and his grip tightened suddenly. Tory sensed a sudden wave of near-uncontrollable anger welling up in him, and Martha shrank back against the cabin side. The other children's faces, even Leif's, registered what looked to Tory like fearful expectation. *What on earth is wrong?* she wondered. "Easy on the arm," she said to him. "I might want to use it again."

The children's eyes, still expectant, all turned to her. "Oh. I beg your pardon," Erling said. Slowly he relaxed his grasp, his eyes still on his daughter. Martha stood as if hypnotized, eyes wide.

Unable to bear the high-voltage silence, Tory said to her, "If I wasn't confident your boat is safe out here, she'd still be in the harbor, no matter what. But the things that worried me—the holes in the hull, mostly—have all been secured."

She felt Erling start to speak, let his breath out with deliberate care, and begin again. "Miss Lennox is concerned—as a Coast Guard officer—with the safety of the boat," he said slowly, emphasizing the final word. "I am delighted to have the benefit of her . . . expertise."

*Now, what's that about?* But the crackling tension had ebbed as quickly as it had arisen. Looking past Tory, Martha said, "Look, the Harbor Patrol," in a tone that was very nearly normal.

It was Neal, alone in *Harbor 2.* With his usual crisp precision he brought the boat alongside the *Prophet Jonah* and stopped her dead ten feet away. Ignoring the others, he called to Tory, "What the hell are they doing here?"

"All the *Jonah's* defects were corrected," she replied, trying to keep defiance out of her voice. "The Halvorsens wanted to leave—and you wanted them out. So what's the problem?"

He stared at her with open disbelief. "I wanted them out?" he repeated. He shook his head slowly, as if unable to believe his ears.

She felt a dreadful suspicion forming, like a lump of lead, just below her rib cage. "I don't think this is a good place to discuss it," she said, very aware of her fascinated audience.

For a moment she wasn't sure he had heard her. "You may be right," he said at last. "When you're ready to talk, you know where I am." He turned to Erling, shutting her out as if she'd become invisible: "If you see your son—your oldest son—tell him to stop by the harbor office."

"What has he—" Erling began, then pulled himself up. "If you mean Erling Halvorsen Junior, he's no longer part of this family. By his own choice." The words sounded as if they were being torn from his heart; his face was set like stone.

Tory could see the question shaping itself in Neal's eyes, but it remained unasked. "Whatever you say," he replied. "But if you happen to run into anyone named Erling Halvorsen Junior, just give him the message." He slapped the gear lever forward and *Harbor 2* jumped ahead with a hoarse roar, spun sharply, and headed back toward the harbor entrance.

"Mr. Donahoe seems angry," Erling said. "I'd have thought he'd be pleased to be rid of us." He sounded calm, almost detached, but the children were staring at him with something close to terror in their eyes.

"Yes," she heard herself say. Her thoughts were spinning wildly. *I need to work this out. Alone.*

"Are you all right?" Erling asked, his solicitude apparently quite genuine.

"Me? Oh, sure." Suddenly she wanted to be anywhere but on the *Prophet Jonah*'s gently heaving deck. "I'd better go square things with Neal—Mr. Donahoe. Could someone run me back to the shore in your dinghy?"

"Erik will be happy to do that," Erling said. "Won't you, son?"

"Sure, father," said Erik, looking frightened and miserable in equal parts. "It's just that . . ."

As the boy's words trailed off, Martha spoke: "Father, let me do it. I'd like to—I really would."

For several seconds, Erling regarded his daughter thoughtfully. Then a singularly sweet smile lit his face. "Yes. That would be very appropriate. A good thought, Martha."

The *Jonah*'s dinghy was a filthy, eight-foot-long inflatable, more patches than original fabric. A two-horsepower outboard motor, looking as if it had been beaten with hammers, dragged down the stern. "You sit in the back, Miss Lennox," said Martha. "I'm going to row. For the exercise."

The young woman had already claimed the center seat, and she was looking up at Tory with an almost painful intentness. *Don't argue with her.* Obediently, Tory slipped down the *Jonah*'s side and into the dinghy. Two clammy, mildewed life jackets lay on the fabric floor, and Tory folded one double and sat on it, next to the outboard. "If you get tired, just sing out and I'll start the engine," she said.

Martha was strong for her age, but the dinghy's oars were too short, and the blades kept popping out of the water. After only a couple of minutes, and very little forward progress, Tory could no longer restrain herself. "You'll have to lift the handles practically up to your chin to get any kind of stroke," she said. "You sure you don't want to change your mind about the engine?"

Martha shook her head. Her face was damp with sweat, and she was breathing hard. "No gas," she panted. "Get some at the fuel dock."

Abruptly, several pieces fell into place. "Erik ran it dry, didn't he?" Tory said. *And you're covering for him. Why?*

"He didn't mean to. And he couldn't row all the way to the pier. His hands . . ." Martha's mouth clamped shut, biting off her words.

When she'd shaken hands with Erik the day before, Tory recalled, his grimy paw had left a damp red stain on her own palm. Had he torn his hands rowing? Where? The *Jonah* had been in the harbor all yesterday. But Martha clearly had something else on her mind. "What's the matter?" Tory said. "I'd like to help, if you'll let me."

"Father—" she began, just as the dinghy's bow dug into a whitecap and sent a quart of icy water into the back of the young woman's neck. She squealed and missed her stroke, both oar blades biting air instead of water. Tory reached quickly forward and grabbed Martha's wrist just in time to keep her from falling over backward. "I'm all *right*," Martha gasped, pulling free. But she wasn't, Tory saw. Her strokes were wilder, more desperately energetic. Her breath was coming in painful gasps. Tears glistened in her eyes.

On the next stroke only one oar blade immersed, and the dinghy spun broadside to the waves, lurching as it turned. *Another like that and we could be swimming.* The water temperature was in the low sixties, and a life jacket might keep you afloat, but hypothermia would paralyze you within minutes—while the inflatable, with no one in it, would blow away far faster than either of them could swim. You couldn't expect help, either: except for the immobilized *Prophet Jonah*, the boats in the anchorage all seemed deserted, and the scattering of people on the beach would probably never realize what was happening out on the water until it was too late.

Tory, a powerful, experienced swimmer, was confident she could make it to shore alone—but towing a heavy, exhausted companion was something else again. This is too ridiculous, she told herself, just as Martha burst into tears. "I can't do it!" she cried. "I just can't make this thing go!"

"Maybe I can," said Tory. "Let's trade places—carefully."

Martha, fortunately, was too wet and tired to stand on her dignity. Meekly she slid aft along one gunwale while Tory, balancing her weight, eased forward along the other. Once on the rower's seat, Tory braced her feet and began to pull, glancing over her shoulder between strokes. The dinghy was badly underinflated, and she sensed that a really strong pull on the oars might simply buckle it. To keep the boat moving she angled in toward the beach, working the dinghy into the lee of the high wharf. And since a powerful stroke was out of the question, she fell back on short, easy swipes with alternating oars, something she'd learned as a child from an old sailor who'd taken care of her father's yacht.

For several minutes the dinghy didn't seem to be making any headway at all, but at last the paired signposts on the beach marking one end of the measured mile began to line up one behind the other. "You're very good at this," Martha offered.

"You might say it goes with my job," Tory replied. She was sorting through the thicket of questions crowding her mind when Martha spoke again.

"My brother says he spoke to you yesterday."

Startled, Tory was on the point of asking Martha what she was talking about, when the answer came to her: "That was Erling Junior? On the Marina 2 float?" She pulled the young man's face from memory: *Bright and quick, but I didn't like him. Something sly about him—I bet he's got damp hands.*

"Yes."

Tory kept up the steady, rolling stroke, and after a long pause Martha continued: "Junior was very impressed, the way you were so calm."

*Calm as in helpless.* Tory looked quickly over her shoulder. The pier was less than a hundred feet away. With two corrective strokes she aimed the dinghy between a pair of massive pilings. "Well, he did pretty well himself, your brother . . . Is that what you call him: Junior?"

Martha managed a wan smile. "We all do. He hates it."

The dinghy slid into the shadows beneath the wharf. Over their heads, a car rattled the loose planking, a wooden drumroll of sound. "I'd hate it, too," Tory observed. "But why—"

"It was wrong of him to defy father," Martha said, perhaps louder than she'd intended. Her unsteady voice echoed hollowly from above.

"Defy? In what way?" With the pier planking overhead and the pilings like tarred stalactites around them to increase the feeling of isolation, Martha clearly felt able to speak. Tory kept rowing slowly, feathering the oar blades to keep the boat just stemming the current.

"A family can have only one head," said Martha. "One person to lead it, and the father must be that person."

It was, to Tory's ear, less a statement than an appeal. "That's what your father says?" she asked, willing her voice to sound neutral.

Not neutral enough. "It's what the Bible says," Martha replied firmly. "What God requires."

"I see." She waited, but Martha was silent. In the gloom beneath the pier it was hard to be certain, but her face seemed drawn with pain. "Junior had a problem with that," Tory offered.

Martha shook her head, seemingly unable to speak. Thinking the young woman had finished, Tory put a little more muscle into her stroke, aiming for an opening into the windy, gray daylight beyond the wharf. Just as the dinghy's bow came parallel with a piling, Martha said, "It was my fault."

"How?"

"He overheard." *Overheard what?* But Martha's voice was so small, so hesitant Tory didn't dare interrupt. "If I'd only been stronger," Martha continued, her head lowered, voice barely above a whisper. "Strong enough to stop him—without making a noise."

In a flash of perception Tory could see it all. "Your own brother hit on you?"

Martha nodded. "I was cleaning the little cabin where father sleeps. I didn't hear him—Junior—behind me."

It was, Tory knew, the kind of thing that happened more often than people realized. But that didn't make it any more bearable. "I'm surprised your father didn't kill him," she said.

"I think he was going to," Martha said. "He had his hands around Junior's throat. I—I had to hit him to make him let go." She drew in a deep, shuddering breath. "I was so ashamed."

"*You* were ashamed? Why, for God's sake?"

But Martha, her face hidden in her hands, only shook her head.

Tory pulled the inflatable slowly up the length of the harbor. As they passed the fuel dock, Martha finally spoke again. The young woman's eyes were red, but she seemed in control of herself. "If you could lend me a couple of dollars, I'll fill up the outboard tank," she said.

"What I'm going to do," Tory replied, without slackening her even stroke, "is buy you a proper gas container, so you can keep some fuel in reserve. Then we'll borrow somebody's pump and put a little air into this poor flabby boat, and *then* I'll stake you to the gas."

Martha managed a wan smile. "You're very bossy sometimes," she said.

Tory slid the dinghy between a couple of small outboards at the floating pier directly below the Harbormaster's office window. Neal was probably up there, looking down at her, but he could wait. "Bossy? I guess I am," she said. "But only with people who can't take care of themselves."

"Like father?" Martha asked.

Tory regarded her own capable hands as they secured the dinghy's frayed painter to a cleat. *Is that why I'm so attracted to him?* "Maybe," she said.

"Miss Lennox?" The near-desperation in Martha's tone swiveled Tory around. "You won't tell father? Please?"

She could imagine Erling's mortification. "Not hardly," she replied. "This is between us women."

Tears welled in Martha's eyes. "Thank you," she whispered. "Oh, thank you."

## Santa Barbara harbor; 8:30 p.m.: Rebecca Jardine

Over the locked gate she could just make out the crude lettering burnt into the wooden sign—MARINA 2. A steeply pitched ramp led down from the gate's far side to a floating walkway spangled with lights. In the evening breeze, a continuous rattling—metal slapping against hollow metal—floated up from the boats, along with the smell of seaweed. From the restaurant balcony diagonally across the harbor, the clatter of dishes and bursts of laughter carried clearly.

Rebecca stood beside the gate, leaning on the metal rail and considering the view below her. Down there on one of those floats was where the accident had happened. It would look very different in daylight, of course: not magical at all—just a harborful of boats, moving uneasily in their piers or docks or whatever the right word was. A camera shooting from ground level, with a wide-angle lens, would make the boats loom like predators, give the scene an overtone of menace—just the mood they'd want. Already the camera angles were forming in her mind—not that the techies would pay any attention to her. Not yet. But someday.

A figure was walking along the pier toward the ramp. A slender man in dark pants and a T-shirt. Because the walkway lights were at knee level, his chest and face were in shadow. He started up the ramp, and she called out, "Mr. Donahoe? Neal?"

He paused. "That's me." He sounded annoyed about something. But she was used to dealing with emotionally charged people. It was, after all, a basic element of her job.

As he ascended, the lights on the sea wall caught his face, and she let the visual impressions cascade over her: A thin face, wide mouth. Good bones. Hair's too short. Nice shoulders and zero flab around the middle. About thirty . . . no, older. Maybe a little Hispanic in him, in spite of the name. Didn't matter; one thing was sure—the camera would love him. Why did photography give such an unfair edge to skinny people? Not that she herself was in any way fat, but cameras added ten pounds to her appearance—and in the most unflattering places, too.

At the top of the ramp, he said, "Ms. . . . Jar*deen*, is it?"

A good try, considering how the cop on the phone had mangled it. "Jar*dine*," she corrected. "Rebecca Jardine. From the Freddy Brooks office."

"Yes." He wasn't giving an inch, but as he reached to press something at the side of the gate, just out of her vision, he said, "If you'll stand out of the way, I can push the gate open."

*Good, clear voice—we can tape outdoors: that light baritone'll cut right through background noise . . .* She caught herself, stepped back. "Sorry." And as the gate squeaked open, thrust out her hand. "Pleased to meet you."

After a long moment he took it. His own hand was cool and wet—not damp: wet. There was a difference, she decided. The contact seemed to warm him just an iota: "Officer Ortega said you were from some TV show?"

*And you think TV is shit. Well, so do I.* "A production company," she said, briskly businesslike. "We do *Making Things Right*. I'm assistant producer."

"I see," he replied, his tone clearly revealing that he didn't. Just as well, too: in the business, APs were two notches above coffee gofers; *Making Things Right* had six of them.

The sharp smell of fresh onion was coming off his clothes. "I bet I've interrupted your dinner," she said. "I'm sorry. But if I can just steal five minutes, I can explain the whole thing and get out of your hair."

Without warning he unleashed a thousand-watt smile that took her breath away. "D'you like guacamole?" he asked.

*Where did you get those teeth? Nobody's born with choppers like that.* "Guacamole? Love it," she said firmly.

Not firmly enough, it seemed: "Well, you haven't tried mine," he said. "Come on." He released the heavy gate, turned, and started down the ramp without a backward glance. She had to jump forward to keep the gate from swinging shut in her face.

A nice ass, she was thinking, just as her leather sole skidded on something squishy and she caromed off the railing. He half turned and took her by the elbow. "Easy does it." On the wooden walkway he released her, saying, "Watch the spaces between the planks. Perfectly spaced to snag—"

"—A high heel," she said. "They just did." *This is where he gallantly drops to one knee and frees my shoe, while getting a friendly feel of my pretty damn good ankle.*

But chivalry lay dead on the planking. "Don't try to kick it loose," he said. "You'll just snap the heel off."

She managed to work the shoe free. "How far are we going?" she asked.

"Only about fifty feet more. The big green ketch on the left."

She managed the distance without incident. In the diffused walkway light she had a vague impression of a high, sheer side topped by a confusion of poles, ropes, and wires. Grabbing a wire, he lifted himself with almost balletic grace up onto the boat. "Step on that box," he said. "It'd be better if you took off your shoes."

Between the shaky box and the boat's side she had an unnerving glimpse of dark and probably filthy water. "What now?"

"Put your foot on the gunwale—the edge of the boat—and grab my hand." Without perceptible effort, he pulled her across.

Cold, damp, gritty surface underfoot. *Kiss the pantyhose feet good-bye.* She made a mental note to add them to her expense account.

"Now down the ladder," he was saying. "I'll go first, just in case."

*Just in case you can look up my skirt, you mean.* But when she glanced quickly over her shoulder, his eyes met hers. She sensed he knew exactly what she'd been thinking. It was like an electrical current passing between them, so sudden and strong she blinked. *My God, you are a gorgeous man.*

"Welcome aboard," he said, when she was standing on the plywood floor at the bottom of the steep ladder.

We sure won't shoot any footage in here, she thought, her gaze panning quickly around the square, low-ceilinged chamber. You could do a low-budget fright flick in here, and call it *A Study in Squalor.* The space was about twelve feet square, with unpainted plywood walls on two sides and some kind of wet-looking semitransparent surface on the other two. At the foot of the ladder, next to her, a beautifully carpentered mahogany desk struck a jarringly opulent note. The only other pieces of furniture consisted of a weatherbeaten brass lamp—kerosene, by the smell—hanging over a stained and scarred folding card table that was flanked on two sides by unpainted, built-in settees. An L-shaped counter of raw wood seemed to serve as the kitchen area, while the visible floor was covered by about two-thirds of a once luxurious Oriental carpet roughly cut to fit the space. "You live here?" she said at last.

"Surprising as it might seem."

It *was* surprising: Even in a T-shirt and workpants he had a catlike neatness totally unrelated to this dank cavern. He stepped back behind the counter, placed an onion on a cutting board, and began to chop it with quick, precise strokes. "You won't mind if I keep on with dinner while you tell me what's going on."

"Of course." She glanced down at the settee's stained cushions, propped her rump against the chart table. "You're familiar with the show?"

He scooped the chopped onion into one hand and tossed it into a stainless steel bowl. Craning her neck, she could see chunks of avocado and something reddish she assumed was salsa. As he mashed them all together with a fork, he seemed to be considering his answer. "Not really," he finally admitted.

"Well. Where to begin?" she said, raising her eyes to the cabin overhead as if the answer might appear there. The roof seemed to be the same smooth, oddly moist-looking substance as the boat's sides, and so low she could almost . . . Before she could stop herself, she'd put up a fingertip. Stretching, she could just touch it: smooth as glass; hard and cold and quite dry.

He was watching her with a private smile she found unsettling. "Unpainted fiberglass resin," he said. "Somebody once said it looked like frozen snot."

It was so exactly right she was momentarily speechless. She could sense the interview slipping out of her control. Almost desperately, she launched into her canned spiel: "Okay. *Making Things Right* is a syndicated half hour, five times a week, mostly running against early evening cop shows. There's two segments—we call them cases—per show; part live interviews, part taped on location. The rationale is in the name—*Making Things Right*. People come to us with some unsolvable crisis, and we help them."

Unexpectedly, he was nodding. "I saw a couple of minutes of it the other night." He stopped abruptly, distaste pulling down the corners of his mouth.

His was certainly not the usual reaction, but Rebecca, to her own surprise, found herself responding: "Freaks and losers. Right?"

One of his dark eyebrows lifted in mild surprise. "You said it— I didn't." Setting down the bowl, he lifted a heavy lid built into the countertop and reached down, bringing up a pair of frosted brown bottles.

"Ricki Lake, Jerry Springer, Freddy—we all fish in the same pool," she continued, knowing she was speaking too fast but unable to slow down. "You see the kind of guests we get: your neighborhood motherhumpee, folks with the mark of Cain a foot high on their foreheads . . ."

She paused, waiting for a reaction, but all she got was an open bottle passed across the counter. She accepted it, smelling the sharp tang of serious beer, and poured a long, numbingly cold slug down her throat. "Thanks," she gasped.

"*De nada,*" he replied absently. She could almost hear the gears meshing in his head. "Wilbur Andreas," he said suddenly. "That's what this is about."

"You got it." She wasn't surprised: Donahoe was clearly no dope, and probably not a whole lot happened here in Santa Barbara.

Now he was looking at her with something like respect. "I'll be damned. The accident was—what?—only twelve hours ago. How do you know—"

"I've been in Santa Barbara four hours, long enough to do the rough check," she said quickly, hearing the triumph in her own voice. "It's a story, all right."

"Well, you know more than I do," Neal said.

It was, she sensed, as close to an appeal as she would hear from this man. And because she wanted his approval—his admiration, even—more than she liked to admit, she found herself saying more than she knew she should: "Wilbur's blinded, almost certainly for life. I talked to him, and then to the eye doctor, man named Merida—maybe you know him?"

Neal shook his head. "I've heard the name is all."

"And Wilbur's agent, Jock Feverel: owns a gallery on . . ." She groped for the street name, but it was gone. "Couple blocks off the main drag—what's wrong?" Just a momentary narrowing of Neal's eyes, but her own antennae were at full stretch. And Feverel was a schlockmeister if she'd ever met one.

"Nothing, really," Neal replied slowly. For a second or two, he seemed locked in an inner debate, and she waited for him to resolve it. "Not even a solid rumor. You might want to talk to a few other gallery owners, though."

"Thanks for the hint, Neal," she said.

"Not what you wanted to hear," he replied, with a faint smile.

Why did she want—need—to level with this guy? she asked herself. The segment would be in the can in a day or two, and she'd never see him again. But there was something about him, looks aside . . . "Of course, I'd rather hear he was St. Jock the Divine," she said. "But it's better to know the worst early on. Freddy's been stung before—not as badly as Geraldo, but it's always embarrassing." And the hapless assistant producers whose stories blew up in Freddy's face, she reminded herself, were now DJs in Armpit, Wyoming.

"I'll be straight with you, Neal," she went on. "The problem is time. We'd like to check every detail, but if it's a good case, we may be racing two or three other programs for it. It's not like the six o'clock news: with our kind of show, first on the air takes it all."

"I suppose," he said thoughtfully. "So the assistant producer's job is checking out the story?"

"That's just the beginning," she said. "If it computes, and I get the go-ahead from Freddy, then it's instant producer time—I put together a working script, line up local technical talent, and supervise the shoot. I send the footage to L.A., so my bosses can do what they call 'finding the story.' The trick is to tape somewhere between twice and three times what the show can use, to give the brains something to snip and edit, thus revealing their own genius."

It didn't come out quite as lighthearted as she'd intended, but it won her one of his quick smiles. "I think I get the idea. What do you want from me?"

*It's a little early to get into that, alas.* "First, I'd like to hear your part of the story, in your own words."

He nodded. "I didn't actually see the accident."

"I know."

"Okay. How about we eat while I talk?" But it wasn't a question: he was already out from behind the counter, the bowl in one hand, two more bottles in the other, and a crackling plastic bag of tortilla chips tucked under his arm.

The card table, she saw, had already been set—after a fashion: paper napkins, mismatched stainless forks, knives, and spoons. Set for two. *A regular companion, or what?* As he opened the bag of chips and set down the bowl—slimy green, with specks of red: *the things I do for my job*—she lowered herself gingerly onto one of the settees, unobtrusively extracted her mini tape recorder, and positioned it in her lap, below the edge of the table.

The first few times she'd felt twinges of guilt, bugging people. But she'd quickly realized how important it was to capture the fully ripened, unreconsidered version of a story. Then when your sources tried to wriggle out of it later, you had them by the electronic balls. She slipped into the mode she thought of as girlish sincere and said, "Before you begin, Neal, let me get a couple of things straight in my mind. Your title is Santa Barbara Harbormaster, right?"

He dipped a purple chip into the green guacamole, lifted and inspected it, before he said, "Acting Harbormaster. Why don't you put the recorder on the table?"

She'd been caught before and had her line ready: "It makes some people nervous—but obviously not you."

They exchanged looks of perfect understanding, capped by conspiratorial smiles, and she propped the tape recorder against her beer bottle. "Thursday, sixteen July, twenty-thirty hours," he began, speaking as if his words were being carved instead of spoken. "Santa Barbara harbor, aboard the ketch *Carpe Diem*. My name is Neal Machado Donahoe . . ."

Her quick dismay turned to amusement, when the glitter in his dark, slightly slanted eyes betrayed that it was a riff, a parody of copspeak-on-the-witness-stand. Once he warmed to the story, the artifice fell away. At the end, snapping off the tape recorder, she blurted out, "I hope to God you can do that again for the videotape."

"It was all right?" She couldn't tell if he was pleased.

"It was *perfect*. Just a hair this side of being too good entirely. We can't have you upstaging the star."

"Wilbur, you mean?" he asked, all innocence.

"Don't be cute," she replied. She could feel a grin tugging at her mouth, but it was too soon for that, and there was too much yet to do.

As if he'd read her mind, he said, "Anything else? You didn't even try the guacamole."

He was too sharp-eyed entirely, she decided. "Actually, I'm really not hungry. And I don't know if onion breath is a good idea for my next interview."

"Now? At nine P.M.?"

"At nine-thirty," she said, glancing automatically at her watch. "A colleague of yours—Lieutenant Victoria Lennox, of the Coast Guard."

No single muscle of his face moved, but it was as if he'd turned to stone before her eyes. *What's this—professional enemies? No, this is personal. Interesting.*

He walked her to the gate at the end of the pier, shook hands, watched till she'd unlocked her car and gotten in. Not till she'd started the engine and stuck the Post-it with the directions to Lt. Lennox's apartment onto the dashboard did she remember the second place setting on the folding card table.

ABOARD THE *PROPHET JONAH*, FOOLS' ANCHORAGE; 9:00 P.M.:
ERIK HALVORSEN

He lay curled up in his berth, the single blanket covering him completely and tucked in all around, except for one small opening for his nose. After much experimenting, Erik had decided this arrangement was the only way to keep the heat in while still allowing him to breathe. Most nights, it got so warm under the blanket he didn't even need his nightshirt, which he hated wearing, only father insisted. Tonight he'd kept his jeans on under the nightshirt, rolling the legs up so no one would know.

All around him were the noises of the boat—creaking wood, the gurgling slap of waves against the outside of the hull, rattle and click and rattle again of something small rolling back and forth in a galley drawer. And smells. He started listing them in his head, to keep his mind from settling on the thoughts he feared: first and strongest, the stale smell of his old wool blanket; sour odor of the damp mattress under him; and the boat itself, of course—bilge and diesel oil and an almost sweet smell that father said was dry rot in the deck.

Father. The looming image derailed his thought. At prayers, just before bedtime, father had included Lieutenant Lennox, and Erik had looked quickly, under half-closed eyelids, at Martha. Her eyes were tightly shut, and her lips were moving quickly—too quickly for him to read. She scared him sometimes, especially late at night when she would sob so hard Erik's berth, just above hers, shook with it, and yet she never made a sound. She was awake now, he was sure—asleep, she whimpered (though Erik had never told her so), and sometimes called out, but never to anyone by name.

Across the cabin, Leif was snoring softly—and Anneke, above him, was, too. Slowly and carefully, Erik pushed his head out of hiding. No sound from the forward cabin. Unable to contain his anxious impatience, the boy thrust a skinny leg over the edge of the berth. Martha's strong hand grabbed his ankle, and her faint whisper drifted up to him. "Not yet."

He pulled his foot back under the blanket. She had sharper ears than he did. Suddenly her head appeared over the edge of his berth, a ghostly silhouette that made him start. "What?" he breathed.

"I know where you're going," she whispered.

"I have to."

"I know." A shapeless blob appeared beside her head, plopped on his mattress. "Gloves," she breathed.

It was just the kind of thing she'd think of. All at once he felt the tears welling up, choking him. As if she knew—probably she did—her hand patted his. Then clamped down almost painfully. "Erik, will you do something?"

"What?"

He thought she hadn't heard him, was on the point of repeating his question, when she whispered, "Pray for me. Please."

"Okay," he said. It wouldn't do any good, he knew. God didn't listen to him.

A soft, heavy thump from up forward. Martha's head and hand vanished, and Erik retreated under his blanket. A softly heavy tread in the wheelhouse. The *Prophet Jonah* dipped slightly to one side, then straightened up. Erik felt rather than heard shuffling footsteps down the middle of the cabin. Footsteps that stopped level with his head. *The gloves. Please, God, don't let him see the gloves.*

His toes were curled tight with tension, and his right foot began to cramp. He set his jaw against the pain, knowing that if he moved he would certainly cry out.

The whisper, when it came, was from only a foot away at most. "Are you awake?" *Not me, God. Pleasepleaseplease.*

"Yes, Father." *Thank you, Martha. Oh, thank you.*

"We must pray together, child."

"I'm so tired, Father. Please can't I sleep?" Even her whisper couldn't hide her despair.

"You must help me, child." A pause, and then an agonized, "I am in torment."

She didn't answer, but a moment later Erik heard the sounds of her getting out of the bunk. Consumed by shame and fear—and most of all relief—he lay motionless, barely breathing, until he heard the flimsy door to the forward cabin close. Now that it was safe to move, he had to drag himself out of the bunk. He pushed his own lumpy pillow under his blanket and added Martha's for good measure, molding the pile into what might look like a curled-up small boy, if you weren't paying attention. Not that he had to worry much about his absence being noticed, any more than his presence. Mostly he tried to feel grateful, *did* feel grateful. But every once in a while he wanted to stand up in the middle of everybody and shout, "Look at *me!*"

On the afterdeck, he realized he'd forgotten the gloves Martha had given him. Even though he knew rowing would be impossible without them, he had to force himself to go back. When he crept back below, he couldn't help hearing his father's low murmur from the forward cabin, but he deliberately shut out the words. Even so, the tone gave away the meaning; once and once only, Erik had eavesdropped. The memory of what he'd heard would never leave him.

On deck again, he dragged the dinghy up close under the stern and slid into it. He'd forgotten about the oars, but someone—Martha, of course—had left them wedged under the seat. He let the breeze push the little boat away a few yards before he set the oars in the row locks. The first pull was agony, the second even worse. By the time he'd gone two hundred yards the pain in his palms was like a flame right up to his elbows, but it was something he could set his jaw against. At last he judged it was safe to start the outboard. It caught on the second pull, and its high whine sawed across the night—Junior said it sounded like a giant metal mosquito.

Erik crouched next to the motor, huddled against the night chill. With his free hand he felt for the small wad of money in his pocket. To keep himself from thinking about Martha, he recited the list of items he was to buy. It didn't do any good, and when he tried to pray for her, that didn't work, either: No one was listening. No one ever would be.

APARTMENT #3, 200 ELISE WAY; 2125 HOURS: TORY

She held up the uniform blouse, trying to consider her reflection with professional detachment. No, she decided, it would be too much, like some kind of audition, and every time she thought about *Making Things Right*, Neal's less favorable comments kept forcing their way into her head. Geeks, she thought. What have I done?

The Public Affairs lieutenant in Eleventh District headquarters hadn't had any doubts, though: "Tory, you'll be great. You've got real star quality."

*Star quality: I don't think so.* He seemed to think he'd made the phrase up himself, but it was clear that an appearance on *Making Things Right* had her superiors' unqualified blessing. At this point, if half an hour with a creep like Freddy Brooks made her look good in Long Beach, it'd be worth it. And besides, she reminded herself, it might help poor Wilbur Andreas.

Downstairs, the doorbell rang. Tory folded the blouse, careful to preserve its freshly ironed creases, and laid it on the counter. She threw one quick glance at the mirror: the black cotton jumpsuit might be too informal for a normal business meeting, but this was

80

after hours in her own apartment. And with someone in show business, too—a child, judging by her tiny, breathless telephone voice.

She was halfway down the stairs when the bell rang again. On the sofa, Atrocious the cat was sitting bolt upright, ears laid back, her single, malevolent green eye fixed on the door. A nautical cat, Atrocious had spent most of her combative life on piers or boats, learning two basic lessons of survival: sudden loud noises meant trouble, and every visitor was a dog until proven innocent.

"Nice kitty," said Tory, brushing past. Atrocious got slowly to her feet, jumped loose-jointedly to the floor, and stalked off, tail waving. *Why did I let Neal unload her on me, anyway? She'd be better off on his boat.* A look through the door's peephole revealed the usual weirdly distorted image—perceptibly female, but that was about all Tory could be sure of. Fixing a welcoming smile to her face, she opened the door. "Ms. Jardine?"

"Hi, I'm Rebecca," said her visitor, extending her hand—small, plump, and neat, just like the rest of her. She was wearing an unfashionably tailored tan suit, and her frilly blouse only accentuated a bosom that needed no assistance. Her face was half-elf, half-pussycat—knowing eyes, a sharp, inquisitive nose, a surprisingly full mouth. *Not a child at all, and very female indeed.* Her voice sounded entirely different in person—insinuating, Tory decided, as if she was about to share some slightly disreputable secret.

"Come on in," Tory said, wryly aware of her Easterner's reluctance to lower the first-name barrier too easily. "Would you like some coffee? It's fresh."

"Coffee would save my life." She followed Tory into the living room and stopped short, staring around her. "Hey, this is like total elegance. Is this all yours, or did you rent it furnished?"

"Most of it's family stuff," Tory replied. It was her stock answer—and narrowly true, if you went only by the number of pieces: her parents had contributed the unnecessary glass-topped table and four chairs that crammed the dining alcove, though she herself had commissioned the two custom leather couches, teak-wood coffee table, and standing lamp. The original oil—a New

England sea scene—over the fireplace did not, she felt, count as furniture, though its current market value was about twice that of everything else in the room.

Like the rest of her family, Tory had always bristled at being called rich—"comfortable" was her euphemism of choice—but she'd quickly given up pretending she lived on her lieutenant's pay. In Santa Barbara's minuscule Coast Guard community, comprising the crew of the eighty-two-foot cutter *Point Hampton*, the personnel of her own Marine Safety Detachment, and their families, that kind of deception would've been doomed at takeoff. At the same time, she made a careful point of never rubbing in the fact that there were very few of life's necessities (including her condominium apartment) she couldn't write a check for.

Rebecca Jardine was clearly having some difficulty swallowing her curiosity, and while there was some amusement in watching her try to put a price on the place without actually whipping out a calculator, Tory had a strong disinclination to talk about money, especially her own. It was definitely time to take charge of the conversation: "So you've been in town since this afternoon. Who've you talked to so far?" she asked, stepping into the tiny kitchen.

"Pretty much everybody," the other woman said. "One more interview after you, and then I can start blocking in a script."

"Ah," said Tory, measuring coffee into a filter. She poured near-boiling water over the grounds, then looked up. "I hope you like French roast: it's all I drink, but we can dilute to taste."

"French roast is fine. Black—and maybe a little weaker."

"Here you go." She led the way into the living room and sat down. "Now, what can I tell you?"

From her shoulder bag, Rebecca produced a small leatherbound notebook and an even smaller tape recorder, which she set on the coffee table. "I'm sure you won't mind this," she confided, clicking it on. "I'm just hopeless without it."

Watching the tape spool revolve, Tory realized that she minded a good deal. But that, she told herself, was just remembered pain from a previous assignment back in the Seventh District, where drug smugglers, Cuban refugees, and injured manatees made Public Affairs virtually a combat assignment. The one thing you had to remember was that a taped interview might sound like a conversation, but it was really a minefield where the interviewer had the only map. "By all means," Tory said, pasting on her most agreeable smile.

Rebecca flipped backward through the pages of her notebook until she found what she wanted. From across the table it looked like a list of names, with all but two checked off. Ceremoniously, Rebecca placed a mark next to a name that might have been Lennox and turned to a page with half a dozen lines scribbled on it. "Okay," she said, "now why don't we start with you telling me exactly what happened. In your own words."

*You mean you don't want official prose. Fair enough.* "About seven this morning," Tory began, "I was walking along the harbor, just passing Marina 2—you know what that is, I'm sure?—and a teenager came running up the ramp, very excited . . ."

Three minutes later, with barely a hesitation, she concluded, ". . . I told the female EMT exactly what I'd done and why, and I saw I wasn't needed anymore. So I went on to work. That's about it—until your office called."

Rebecca's mouth, which had been slightly open for the previous minute and a half, closed. "Did you rehearse that?" she demanded. "I mean, nobody talks that way, off the top of their head."

Cautiously pleased, Tory said, "Well, I figured you'd ask me what happened."

"But how did you *feel?*" Rebecca demanded suddenly. "I mean, when you saw his eyes."

Nettled, Tory replied: "I didn't see his eyes, not really. He had his hands over his face the whole time, and even when I could see between his fingers, his eyes were squeezed shut."

"But you saw, like, where the acid got on his face," Rebecca insisted. "Was it all burned and awful? Did it make you feel sick?"

"First off," said Tory, now seriously annoyed, "acetone isn't acid. It's a solvent—like paint thinner, only stronger. It won't actually burn most people's skin—"

"Look, Victoria," Rebecca interrupted, "you've got to help me out here. I mean, I can appreciate a professional attitude, but what we need is some human feeling, a gut reaction."

But his skin *was* burnt, Tory was thinking. Or if not burnt, kind of melted. She summoned up, past memory's barrier, a picture of Wilbur Andreas's face, as he lay writhing and moaning at her feet. Between his fingers, weirdly stained with black and gold pigment, she'd seen—what? Streaks of blood, a sort of pinky red mush around his closed eyes. Or was that stuff his eyeballs, liquefied by the acetone? An involuntary shiver shook her shoulders, and she heard Rebecca's triumphant voice: "That's right, Victoria! I want you to feel it!"

"No." In Tory's ears, her voice was flat, harsh. She reined in her anger with an effort. "I'm sorry, but my personal feelings aren't for TV. All I can tell you is what I saw."

"What you *didn't* see, you mean," Rebecca said. She looked poised for another attack, then seemingly thought better of it. "Well, don't worry about it. Too much sensitivity probably wouldn't help someone in your job." Her condescending smile was a small masterpiece, Tory thought.

"You're absolutely right," said Tory, getting to her feet. "Those Coasties who aren't born with thick skins simply have to develop them." Tory could still remember her first corpse, a baby about eight months old, washed up on a Maryland beach. And the hard-bitten chief petty officer, cradling it in his arms with the tears running down his face. *Neal was right: these people are awful.*

Rebecca had risen, too, and picked up her notebook and tape recorder. "We'll probably be taping day after tomorrow," she said. "I know your Public Affairs guy wants you in the shoot, but . . ." She let her words trail off.

She had already made her decision: "Be happy to," she replied. "I'll do my best not to be too affectless."

Rebecca threw her a startled look but allowed herself to be led to the door. Halfway there, she said, "One small question, Victoria: What on earth were you doing down at the harbor at seven in the morning? Jogging?"

She hadn't readied herself for this one, and it took her a second to respond: "Just a walk to clear my head, before a day in the office." *And the chance I might run into a particular guy on the way to or from the Marina 2 shower.*

UPPER STATE STREET; 10:00 P.M.: LORRAINE

As her car came abreast of the La Cumbre mall she began to slow, ignoring the obvious impatience of the driver behind her. Up ahead on the right, the plant nursery's tall logo, with its distinctive Oriental crossbar, stood out and immediately beyond it the smaller, lower sign—CHUCK'S OF HAWAII. Without Jock's directions, twice repeated, she would have missed the narrow driveway between the two. Even so, she had to brake sharply to make the turn.

A sharp left at the end of the driveway, through the parking lot and past the ATM behind the restaurant. Right in front of her, as Jock had promised, a sloping access drive led up to another lot, this one in near-total darkness. She pulled into one of the left-hand slots and had just set the parking brake when a figure materialized on the passenger side. Her heart skipped a beat, but before she could react the car door opened and the dome light revealed Jock, who slipped into the seat without a word. The light picked out unsuspected seams and gullies in his face, adding ten years and a note of character she'd never suspected.

It seemed completely natural, as the door closed and the light went out, to reach for him. In her arms, he was as hungry as she, his mouth clamped on hers, his hands exploring, clutching, rubbing her body. But he was the one who pulled back first, breathing hard. "Hey, Lorraine. Hold it, darling," he gasped. "You said we had to talk."

He wanted her, though. She could tell. That somehow made it easier for her to assume a coolness she was far from feeling. "We've got a problem," she said.

"Problem?" he said. "What problem? We have liftoff: the taping here in town's tomorrow morning—"

"I know," she interrupted. "That gal producer wants me down at the marina at bloody *dawn*. With the ambulance."

"Oh, Christ," Jock breathed. "Can we get the ambulance again?"

"No, but Ray's renting one for us. Two hundred and fifty bucks—"

"Two hundred and fifty? That's extortion!"

"—With the driver," she continued, riding down his objection. "But the ambulance isn't the problem. Vern is."

"Vern? Vern who?" His bewilderment sounded genuine, and angered her all the more.

"Vern the homeless. The lush with the killer breath who played the other EMT."

"Oh, him," said Jock dismissively. "We don't need him anymore. Let him disappear."

Her hands were clutching the steering wheel so hard her fingers had begun to cramp. "He doesn't want to disappear," she said, between gritted teeth.

"What's that supposed to mean? He's been paid. He's history." Jock's righteous indignation was so perfect it aroused her instant suspicion.

"That's not how he sees it," she said. "He thinks this is some kind of insurance scam, and he wants a piece of the pie. Or else," she added, as Jock began to sputter.

His silhouetted head, black against dark gray, snapped around to face her. "Or else what?" he said quietly.

His bluster had vanished completely. He sounded only mildly interested, but his calm unsettled her. This was not the usual Jock reaction. "Or else he'll blow the whole thing," she said. "Jock, he knows my name, he knows Wilbur's injuries are faked . . ." She could hear her own voice rising, feeling the gathering alarm under her breastbone. "Even if he doesn't understand what's going on, he could ruin everything."

"He could indeed," said Jock, as if he were speaking to himself.

"We can still get out of it," she blurted. "We'll tell them it was a gag. Or we'll go to another network—no, to the newspapers." Panic was sweeping over her, and she found herself eager to submit to it. Words poured from her mouth in a torrent: "We'll still get publicity for Wilbur. You'll see—maybe not as much . . ."

"Stop it, Lorraine."

". . . but when they see how Freddy Brooks fell for our act, he'll be the fool and we'll—"

His hand exploded against her cheek, slamming her head against the window. Through the blur of pain his voice was thoughtful. "Just shut up, darling. I need to think this through."

She waited, her head spinning. I feel grateful, she thought. Why is that? But she knew the answer perfectly well: he had taken the burden from her. It was his problem now.

At last he asked, "Where is this Vern person?"

"I don't know," she replied. "The kid Junior Halvorsen's got him stashed away someplace. I talked to him on the phone."

"Then we'd better get hold of Junior."

HARBOR PARKING LOT; MIDNIGHT: ERIK

Every time they met, Junior seemed to have a new gizmo, and next time it'd be gone, replaced by something even newer. Tonight's toy was a cellular phone, with a panel that flipped open to reveal the tiny keyboard, each key lit from behind. "So where did you get it?" Erik demanded again. "I mean, those things must really cost." He wasn't sure he wanted to hear the truth, but fascination made him ask.

"Cost? Where you been—outer space? They give these phones away for a penny, to get you to sign up for the service." That was the thing about Junior: he always had the answer, the angle. But if Erik admired his brother's savvy—and he did—it was the older boy's nerve he envied: of all the family, only Junior had stood up to their father, nose to nose—okay, just out of reach—and defied him. These days, Erik's fear of his parent was more than matched by awe of his older brother. Tonight, though he couldn't figure out why, Junior actually seemed to want him to hang around.

"Well, I bet using it costs a bundle, then," Erik said. They were sitting side by side in the shadows of the harbor parking lot, sheltered by a commercial fisherman's flatbed truck which was stacked high with homemade wire lobster pots. On Junior's far side the man called Vern, who smelled almost as bad as the traps, had passed out leaning against a tire.

"I don't know about that," said Junior absently. "I don't keep them long enough to get a bill." His brother's attention, Erik realized, was on the toll gate at the parking lot entrance. Even this late at night, cars and trucks pulled in and out of the lot, and every time one entered, Junior squeezed back into the darkness, never taking his eyes off it until it had parked and the driver had gotten out.

"Hey, is she ever going to come?" Erik asked. He shivered as a small, searching gust knifed straight through his thin shirt, damp and stiff from spray. "I got to get back to the boat before father . . ." He let it trail off, unsure how to finish, but Junior knew what he meant.

"The old man's up forward with Martha, right? You've got time."

"I guess," said Erik doubtfully. "He was talking a streak when I left."

"Talking, yeah," Junior repeated, in what Martha called his wiseguy voice. But before Erik could pursue the thought, his brother's hand closed hard on his arm. "There! That's Lorraine's car."

The battered light-colored Corvair was rolling slowly along the drive beside the water. "Somebody's with her," Erik said. He could see the thin-faced blonde woman in the driver's seat quite clearly, but the man beside her was only a shadow.

His brother wasn't listening. He was shaking Vern, first gently, then really shoving him back and forth. The man's head wobbled loosely on his skinny neck, struck the tire with a dead-sounding thud. "What? Whatsit?" Vern mumbled. "Lea'me 'lone."

"Wake up, Vern," Junior snarled. "They're here. Wake your dead ass up, you drunk."

"Hey, listen," said Erik, "I better go. I really better—"

"No!" Junior spun around. "Don't run out on me, man. I need somebody I can trust, and you're the only one."

In the course of his fourteen years, Erik Halvorsen had been bullied by his brother, praised (once or twice) by Martha, harangued, belittled, and—mostly—ignored. Before tonight, no one had ever appealed for his help. Scared as he was, Erik found himself unable to refuse. "Sure, I'll stay—long as you want."

But Junior had turned back to Vern, who was sitting up now, rubbing his eyes. "They're here, man," Junior was saying. "You remember what to say?"

"Who's here?" Vern asked groggily. "Hey, I need a drink."

Junior darted a quick glance over his shoulder, to where the woman he called Lorraine had slid her car into a parking slot next to the Marina 3 gate, about twenty yards from them. The man with her had got out and was standing on his side of the car, scanning the darkened, mostly empty lot. A stocky man with slicked-back hair, Erik saw, wearing a fancy leather jacket.

"Come *on*, Vern," Junior whispered urgently. "She brought a guy along—they must be ready to deal."

With a groan, Vern heaved himself to his haunches, grabbed the truck body, and pulled himself erect. He stood for a moment, rocking slightly, one hand on the truck, then called out, hoarse and a little slurred, "Lorraine: that you?"

"Vern? Where the hell are you?" The woman's voice went with her face—tense, harsh, frightened.

"Right over here, honey." Vern seemed to gain confidence from Lorraine's nervousness, but when he let go of the truck and took a step forward, he staggered and nearly fell.

"*Shit!*" said Junior under his breath. He scrambled up and stood behind Vern. From where Erik crouched under the truck, he could see his brother's hand under the man's elbow, steadying him. With the streetlight full in his face, Vern looked about a thousand years old, a nose like dried-out putty and little blue and purple veins crisscrossing his cheeks. His new khaki pants and shirt were still creased, but already stained with food and booze in front and grease behind.

"Who's with you?" Lorraine called out. "That you, kid?" She was out of the car, staring hard toward them. Her companion had moved around to her side. He hadn't spoken, but Erik could tell he was the one in charge.

Just like Junior was in charge of Vern—in charge and, Erik saw, wishing he weren't. "It's me, Lorraine. Vern and I need to talk to you," Junior called.

Now, as if he'd finally got the whole picture, the man at Lorraine's side stepped forward. "That's what we're here for: to talk," he said. "But not in quite so public a place." A smooth voice, Erik decided. Confident, in control—though there was something under the buttery smoothness that Erik couldn't define.

"Where you wanna go?" Junior said, trying to sound rough and tough. His voice—to Erik's ear, anyway—wasn't quite steady.

"Anyplace you like, just so it's not spotlighted," the man said easily. "Right down on this pier's fine—if you've got a key to the gate."

"There's people asleep on some of those boats," Junior said. "Let's go to the launch ramps, through the gate at the end of this drive. Nobody there this time of night."

"That's cool," the man replied. "Hop in, we'll give you a lift."

"Be right there," Vern replied, taking an unexpected, lurching step forward, out of Junior's grasp. He seemed a little steadier, but Junior quickly closed the gap, standing just behind him and to one side. "Don't tell me you're chickening out," Vern said, in a grating whisper.

"Hell, no," Junior replied.

"Let's get this show on the road, then. There's drinkin' to do— and I need the bucks to do it with." Straightening his back, Vern stepped out without a backward look.

Junior's reluctance was plain for his brother to see. Tucking his head down, he whispered, "Wait for me at the dinghy," and followed his friend.

Some kind of payoff, Erik thought. But for what? He watched his brother and Vern fold themselves into the Corvair's backseat— Vern's head hit the door frame, hard, but he didn't seem to notice. The Corvair, sagging on its springs, moved slowly down the drive, and Erik gave it a good fifty yards before he detached himself from the truck's shadow. It was easy, with the lot mostly empty, to run from lane to lane, but a lot harder always to keep a parked car or truck between him and the Corvair.

In the hedged-off end of the lot reserved for trailers there were enough vehicles and boats to provide good cover. Erik paused behind an urchin diver's boat, watched as the Corvair angled into a slot near the ramp. Lorraine and her friend climbed out, followed by Junior and, with much grunting and half-suppressed cursing, Vern. After some more milling around, the three males started down toward one of the launch ramp finger piers, unlit floating sidewalks that extended from shore into the basin, flanked by the charter boat pier on the left and the final row of marina slips to the right.

Lorraine climbed back in the driver's seat of the Corvair and locked both the doors—Erik could hear the *snick* of the locks from where he stood. A part of him wanted to stay where he was, out of sight yet able to keep an eye both on Lorraine and the pier. But Junior had told him to go back to the dinghy, which lay wedged between two cruising boats on the floating pier of Marina 4, the last gate before the launch ramp area. Irresolute, Erik began to drift slowly in the direction of the gate while trying to keep the car in sight.

Out on the pier, the three figures were a single, dim clump. Erik was conscious of their muttering voices, and the rhythmic noise of music coming from Lorraine's car. And then, abruptly, one of the voices—Vern's—was yelling angrily. Erik froze, listening hard. A blur of movement, followed by a flat, meaty *whack*. Part of the clump detached itself and fell, with a muffled splash, into the water next to the pier.

Erik took one instinctive step forward, then stopped in his tracks as another instinct kicked in. The indistinct shape on the finger pier seemed to be doing some kind of slow, awkward dance, its two voices grunting an accompaniment that raised the hairs on Erik's neck. As he watched, helpless, a yell of anger and pain split the night, followed by the thudding of light footsteps. Junior burst into the light at the pier's landward end, running for his life, with a wet, red stain down one side of his face.

"The dinghy! The dinghy!" he screamed.

The pure terror in his brother's voice galvanized Erik. Without conscious thought he was sprinting for the Marina 4 gate, which he had wedged open with a slip of wood. He hurled himself at the heavy steel wire gate, slipped through the narrow opening. He could hear Junior's steps only a few yards behind him, and he forced himself to stop and hold the gate open. Junior sailed through without even slowing, skidded on the ramp, and slid all the way down to the pier.

A few yards away, Lorraine's friend was running hard toward the gate, waving what looked like a two-by-four in one hand. Erik dragged at the gate, pulling desperately against its friction brake. It was closing, but far too slowly. The running man, wide-eyed, scarlet-faced, gave a wordless roar and leaped forward, free hand clawing for the steel frame. With every ounce of his strength—far more than he thought he possessed—Erik pulled at the barrier, heard the bolt click closed an instant before the man slammed into it, shaking the entire frame with his weight.

For a long moment, Erik and the stranger stood staring at each other, separated only by the wire mesh. Mad fury was draining from the man's face, and from the pier behind him, Erik heard the dinghy's outboard motor roar. "Come on!" Junior's anguished voice cried out. "For Christ's sake, don't just stand there."

Beyond the wire mesh, the man bared his teeth in a smile. "I'll know you again, kid," he said.

The voice was like a trigger. Erik took a step backward and, finding he could move, spun around and hurtled down the ramp. The inflatable dinghy was already six or eight feet from the pier, but he never paused. His wild leap landed him on the little boat's bow, and he bounced straight up, but Junior snagged him in midair and dragged him down. With the engine whining at full speed, the dinghy fled into the night.

At the harbor mouth, Erik turned the dinghy east, toward the anchorage where the *Prohpet Jonah* wallowed at her mooring. Junior, who had huddled in the bow, shaking and silent, lifted his head. "No. Not there. I can't go there. I gotta find a place I can hide out."

Erik slowed the outboard. "Hide out—from that guy?" And when his brother didn't respond, said, "What happened, anyway? Where's Vern?"

"Don't ask!" It was half command, half appeal. "Don't ever ask!"

*He saw me, too: "I'll know you again, kid."* Erik shivered, but he waited for his brother to find the angle, take charge, the way he always did. The inflatable circled twice, the motor just purring, before Erik found he had to speak. "We're going to run out of gas, we keep doing this," he offered.

"Shut up," Junior snapped, but there was no force behind the words, and his "I got to think" sounded almost like an apology.

Another slow circle. Into the wind, the spray resoaked Erik's thin shirt, and his shivering was almost uncontrollable. At last, Junior asked, "I don't suppose you've got any ideas, lizard-breath."

"Places to hide, you mean?" It was hard to think when you were so cold. And so scared. "Where'd Vern live, before you guys got the motel room?"

"Vern? Mostly that lot off Cabrillo, with the dead trucks and stuff. The jungle near the railroad tracks. Sometimes gullies up in the hills—he had a tent."

It was funny, Erik thought: Santa Barbara was a rich town, but it had a whole layer of invisible poor people under it. They were everywhere, if you knew where to look, and before the *Prophet Jonah*, the Halvorsens had been part of them, living in an old school bus that could just limp from one part of town to another, about fifteen minutes ahead of the neighbors' complaints. But a place to really hide, that was something else . . .

The answer came to him all in one piece, as if he'd planned it out. "I know," he said, turning the dinghy's bow as he spoke. In the darkness, he could just see the outline of Junior's head, turned toward him. "Tonight, you can sleep in one of the caves under the

95

bluff, just west of the harbor. You'll be safe there." He paused, because this was where Junior always interrupted his ideas, pouring scorn all over them. But not this time.

"What about tomorrow?" Junior asked.

"You remember the gully that runs up from the beach, right near the caves? It widens out up at the top of the bluffs, but it's real deep and overgrown. You could find a place to camp in there."

"I suppose," said Junior slowly.

"I'll go by the motel tomorrow morning," Erik said quickly. "Bring you Vern's tent—and that food I bought you guys."

"Yeah, but what do I do when that runs out?" Junior said. His question had an edge that would usually have stopped Erik cold, but not now.

"How should I know?" he heard himself say. "We'll figure that out when we have to."

STUDIO CITY; SATURDAY, 6:28 P.M.: NEAL


Wilbur Andreas, his eyes bandaged, stood awkwardly oblivious as the camera dollied in on him. At his side, one arm draped protectively across the artist's shoulders, Freddy Brooks was swinging into his peroration, as the text scrolled across the TelePrompTer: ". . . According to what we've heard here, Wilbur, there's little or no chance of you regaining your sight. As a talented artist, cut off on the threshold of success, how does that make you feel?"

"If it was me," whispered Neal to Rebecca, standing next to him at one side of the set, "I'd throw up all over your boss."

But Wilbur had been well-coached. His head swiveled slowly toward the star of *Making Things Right*, and he said, "Well, Freddy, I just don't know." Suddenly he seemed to choke up. He shook his head and added, hoarsely, "Without my eyes, I'm not sure . . . I don't know if I can go on."

The studio audience sat in frozen silence. Several women and a couple of men were openly in tears. A technician near the front of the set was making a spinning motion with her forefinger.

"Wilbur, does this tragedy make you bitter?" Freddy asked, oozing solicitude. "Would this blow have been easier to bear, if you were famous?"

Rebecca, under her breath, said, "Clock's running, Freddy. Don't milk it too long."

"Bitter?" said Wilbur. "Not really. The work is what counts, and I feel good about what I've done." A gallant smile lit his round face. "I can still see them, my paintings. They're all in my mind—forever."

On the huge studio monitor, Wilbur's face dissolved into a panning shot of his works, hung side by side across the back of the set. As the camera moved past them, Freddy's voice, with a faint echo laid on it, intoned, "Would it be too much to call these . . . masterpieces? Maybe it's just too soon. But one thing is sure: What you're looking at are"—pause—"*all* the paintings of Wilbur Andreas."

The show's theme—a choral arrangement of "You'll Never Walk Alone" sung by massed funeral directors, boomed out, and the monitor flicked to the studio audience, bawling its collective head off.

Freddy Brooks, gleaming through his makeup, hurried off the set. He paused as he saw Rebecca waiting expectantly and lifted her off her feet in an embrace. "Honey, that was *fine*," he said. "I mean, that's grade-A tall Niblets. Keep up the good work." His voice, Neal noted, sounded half an octave higher than when he was on camera, and he seemed to have picked up a faint mid-South accent.

Rebecca was beaming as her employer set her down, but the expression vanished as he moved away. "Something wrong?" Neal asked.

She pasted on a smile that contrasted harshly with her bleak eyes. "It's better than a poke in the eye with a sharp stick, but he still doesn't remember my name," she said.

"So what happens now?" Neal asked. The audience, he saw, was still busy mopping itself; Wilbur and a man Neal recognized as Jock Feverel were looking bewildered among a handful of technicians packing up.

"What's to happen?" Rebecca said. "That show's history." She took his arm possessively. "Let's get out of here before we're stuck with Wilbur and his slippery guru."

In the first bar they went to, Rebecca was greeted with cheers by the customers, all of whom she seemed to know. Neal quickly saw it was her moment to preen before her colleagues, and he docilely allowed himself to be introduced to a dozen or so people who barely glanced at him, then marooned on a barstool. After a few pro forma congratulations, the group—led by Rebecca—got down to serious business, tearing the show to ribbons.

The consensus, as far as Neal could tell, was that Wilbur had been great—"*this* far from over the top, sweetheart!"—but everybody else in the segment had been terrible. "You weren't totally bad," a female technician in black leather assured Neal. "Great teeth."

"What about the Coast Guard lieutenant?" he asked.

The woman shrugged. "She photographs okay, for a full-bodied dame. But she hated being interviewed, and it showed."

He was still digesting the remark when Rebecca grabbed his arm. "Our mission is accomplished. Let's get the flock out of here."

Halfway to the door, he saw Jock and Wilbur in a booth. Jock, looking tense and pale under his too-smooth tan, was talking earnestly to a hard-faced young man with a ponytail. "Somebody from the show?" Neal asked.

Rebecca, following his look, shook her head. "Different style of bottom-feeder. Maybe from the ad agency."

Two bars later, or maybe three, the evening seemed to be following a fairly obvious script. Rebecca's elfin face was becoming more attractive with every sip, and the look in her eyes suggested it was mutual. Maybe more than mutual—Neal had the uncomfortable feeling he was at least partly a trophy, and he was surprised at how much it annoyed him. Besides, having spent most of the 1980s in the Caribbean, he still felt like a stranger in the California world of foreplay with AIDS overtones.

They were dancing to something slow and raw when Rebecca suddenly said, "You people up there in Santa Barbara are pretty blasé, you know?"

Neal, who'd been thinking how little he missed bar-hopping since he'd begun going out with Tory, said, "Blasé how?"

"Like practically nobody wanted free tickets to the show. Even that kid Junior, for Christ's sake. Not to mention the eye doctor and the EMTs . . . and your friend the lady lieutenant."

Yes, he thought, this is indeed a test. He fudged his answer: "None of them wanted to come?"

"You'd have thought I was giving away ringside seats for the Black Plague," she said. And a calculated moment later: "So what is it with you and the lieutenant?"

"I thought we had something going, but I guess I was wrong," he replied.

"Want to talk about it?"

"Not really."

CENTURY PLAZA HOTEL; 8:45 P.M.: JOCK


The ornate, anonymous suite was chilled to meatlocker temperature, but neither the tall, gaunt man in the dark suit nor his ponytailed acolyte, who called himself Felix, seemed to notice. "I saw the show," said the gaunt man. "I liked it." Behind the glass-topped desk he leaned back in his armchair, regarding his two guests with open calculation. Wavy gray hair, lined gray horse's face, silvery tie with a pattern of black lines woven into it. The suit was clearly expensive, new yet very old-fashioned.

"Thank you," Jock replied cautiously. It seemed a safe response to a gambit that could mean anything or nothing, and it was the best he could come up with. After a night of panic—was that a patrol car pulling up outside? Someone watching his house from the shadows across the street?—all morning he had been swept by successive waves of exultation and terror. By show time, though, he'd managed to rationalize last night's horror out of existence: God knew he hadn't mean to hurt Vern or whatever his name was—actually, the drunken bum had attacked him, he'd only been defending himself; it was really an accident, and nobody cared about one

101

dead homeless more or less, even if they found him; and the two kids would be too scared to make trouble, anyway. But Jock's surface calm was like a barely cooled lava crust over the red-hot, boiling magma of fear beneath, and his brain felt as if it had been microwaved in his skull.

Exhausted as he was, he sensed the man across from him was the kind of negotiator who wouldn't be hurried, despite the fact that his invitation—or summons—had come within minutes of the show's ending, when the ponytailed Felix had materialized at Jock's side. He glanced down at the business card he still held: "T. Celeste," in featureless sans serif caps, and under it, slightly smaller, "Investor." No address, not even a phone number.

Felix tried to make a joke of it: "Don't call us; we'll call you— that's all it means." But when Jock asked what the initial stood for, Felix's tight, unconvincing grin vanished. "Never mind about that," he said. "It's Mister Celeste to you." That had been the moment, Jock now recalled, when he began to suspect the breed of tiger he was dealing with.

He decided, against instinct, to venture a question: "You invest in art a lot, Mr. Celeste?"

His eyes fixed on the man opposite him, Jock felt rather than saw Felix go suddenly still. Mr. Celeste's beautifully manicured right hand made a small, dismissive gesture. "Some," he said. "It's a new area for me, but I've been . . . lucky."

"Is that so?" Jock said.

Beside him, Wilbur stirred for the first time since he'd been guided into his chair. Before he could say—inevitably—the wrong thing, Mr. Celeste continued: "That's probably the word you'd use, 'lucky.' I don't know anything about art . . ."

Jock was sure his well-schooled face betrayed nothing of what he felt, and then he looked into Mr. Celeste's hooded eyes and was not so sure.

". . . But I've got an instinct," the other man said. "My instinct says this kid's stuff is going to take off. Straight up."

You couldn't be too scornful of a man whose opinion matched your own, and Jock forced warmth into his voice. "I agree, Mr. Celeste. It's something I—and Wilbur, too, of course—have been expecting for quite a while."

"Quite a while," Mr. Celeste repeated. "Yes. You've been pushing this loser for fifteen years." He regarded the stricken Jock for a long, silent moment. "You want to know what else my instinct tells me?"

Jock's mouth opened, but wit—indeed, speech—had deserted him.

"It tells me you're what my friends back in Brooklyn used to call a goniff," Mr. Celeste observed calmly. "You know the word?"

He paused. Jock's brain, briefly paralyzed, reengaged. *He didn't get us up here just to say we're thieves.* "What do you want?" he croaked.

Mr. Celeste's lips, what there was of them, drew back. His teeth were big and yellow, very straight. "Wilbur, how many paintings have you done? All together?"

Wilbur shrugged helplessly, turned to Jock. "About a hundred and forty finished canvases," Jock replied. "Maybe twenty are scattered around Santa Barbara. The former Mrs. Andreas has twelve, and my gallery—"

"This thing is going to move fast," Mr. Celeste interrupted. "If we're going to stay on top of it, we've got to move faster. Felix will drive you boys back to Santa Barbara tonight, and I'll come up tomorrow, about noon. I want you to have an inventory when I get there: every painting, what it is, and who owns it. Then we'll set up our marketing operation."

"What d'you mean, *our* marketing operation?" Wilbur suddenly demanded. "Who the hell are you, mister?"

Mr. Celeste laughed, a dry rustle like the breeze in long-dead leaves. "I'm the man who's going to make you boys rich," he said. "That's all you need to know, Wilbur."

"Hell you say," Wilbur snarled. "You can't—"

He got no further. Jock heard Mr. Celeste snap his fingers, but Felix was already in motion around the desk, knocking Jock over with a splintering crash. By the time Jock pulled himself clear of the broken chair, Wilbur was halfway out the open window, hammerlocked and squirming desperately.

"*Basta!*" snapped Mr. Celeste, his voice cutting through the fear and rage that filled the room. They froze—Wilbur, Felix, and Jock—at the authentic voice of absolute command. From far below, the traffic noises of Los Angeles floated through the window. In the gasping silence, Mr. Celeste observed calmly, "A live blind artist would be best, but an unhappy suicide's good enough. Your choice, Wilbur."

"All right. Jesus," Wilbur whispered. Mr. Celeste nodded, and Felix pulled his prisoner back into the room and heaved him, without visible effort, into a corner.

"I want to be sure we understand each other," Mr. Celeste said. "From here on out, I'm in charge. Any objections?"

There were none.

EAST HALEY STREET; SUNDAY, 9:55 A.M.: TORY

With practiced skill, Tory slipped the Honda neatly into a spot along the curb. Handling a car well was something that gave her pleasure, even though her Accord was only a stand-in for the 325i Beamer convertible of her daydreams. She'd settled on the Honda—neat, clean, middle-aged, and unobtrusive—because it went with a lieutenant living on her salary. Like so many hypocrisies, it fooled nobody who mattered. Still, the car had served her faithfully, like a boring but devoted nanny. Now that she looked around her at the neighborhood in which she'd parked, she felt a distinct reluctance to leave it unprotected.

Probably, she told herself, it was because Santa Barbara's East Haley Street reminded her a little of the area around Opa Locka, the Coast Guard airfield north of Miami—grim, dusty, one-story commercial buildings, shabby homes, and the occasional depressed palm. Miami, of course, was potentially dangerous anytime for a single Anglo female, while Haley was best avoided only after dark, when the druggies and the streetwalkers owned it. Besides, if you once started to let fear dictate where you went, pretty soon you'd never go anyplace. Still, she found herself thinking, as she got out of the car and locked it, she certainly had dressed to call attention to herself. The demure print dress that seemed so appropriately Episcopalian at her uptown church stood out down here like a ball gown in a saloon.

The street number Erling had given her was painted freehand on the door of a nondescript one-story structure with a small cupola on the roof. As Tory walked up the steep flight of cracked concrete steps from the street, she realized that what she'd thought was gray-stained siding was in fact a total absence of paint. The only touch of elegance was an elaborately carved mahogany door, which an inept hand had ruined by burning in the words CHURCH OF THE APOCALYPSE.

Oh, dear, Tory thought. For a moment she was poised for flight, but she had accepted Erling's invitation—and she found herself curious to see him in his role as preacher.

The door opened as she reached for the knob, and he was standing before her, beaming. "You did come," he said. "I should never have doubted."

She felt her face grow hot, wondered if he saw. "Of course I came," she said firmly.

He was nearly bursting out of a suit made from some shiny artificial fabric, a white shirt with a frayed collar, and, to her astonishment, a stained and wrinkled New York Yacht Club tie. "It's all from the Goodwill," he said. And then, following her startled gaze, "Do you like the tie? I wore it for you—I thought it looked somewhat nautical."

"It's very nice," she murmured. The last NYYC tie she'd seen had been around her father's neck, when he'd taken her to dinner in the club's vast dining room, designed to look like the captain's cabin of a square-rigger. Despite the frayed shirt and the dreadful suit, the tie looked somehow more appropriate beneath Erling's rugged, weatherbeaten face than it did under her father's, with its Wall Street pallor.

"Well, come in, come in," Erling was saying. "We're holding up the procession."

She looked over her shoulder, right into the baby blue eyes of Captain Toto Boyle, standing on the next step down, trailed by a worn-looking blonde and—she counted twice, to be sure—six little Boyles. By some genetic trick, the three girls were shorter, less chunky versions of their father, while the boys had their mother's limp blonde hair and air of exhaustion. The male Boyles wore faded sports shirts and jeans, the females uniformly unbecoming skirts and blouses.

"Hi, Tory," Toto said, grinning. "Glad to see you here. Folks, this is Lieutenant Lennox, the Coastie." He sounded as if he really was pleased, though Mrs. Boyle looked less than overjoyed, and all six children regarded her with wary expectation, as if she were an unpredictable performing animal.

"Good morning." *I wonder what he's told them about me.* She waited to be introduced, but that social nicety seemed to have passed Toto by.

"Could we take our seats, Toto?" Erling said from behind her.

Past the tiny vestibule, the building opened into a single bleak room, bare walls of tongue-and-groove pine stained an improbable mahogany, its only furniture a dozen rows of ill-assorted folding chairs facing a plywood lectern that looked as if it had come from a cheap hotel's meeting room. The window glass was painted over, and on the wall behind the lectern hung a fringed purple drape with a tarnished cloth-of-gold cross stitched onto it. As she stepped across the threshold, the congregation turned as one to stare at her. Tory recognized a handful of harbor faces, mostly commercial fishermen. All of them were sitting in the first four rows. Behind them and separated by an aisle was a mixed bag of women and children.

*This is the most depressing place I've ever seen,* Tory thought, and the audience doesn't help. Dutiful and guilty in equal parts, her conscience added, *But of course the Lord doesn't mind.*

Resolutely, she marched toward the front row, only to be stopped by Toto: "You sit here, Tory."

"I beg your pardon?"

"I'm afraid it's one of our rules," Erling said. "We ask the ladies and the youngsters to sit behind their menfolk."

"It mirrors the proper structure of the family," said Mrs. Boyle, acid dripping from every word.

When in Rome . . . Tory told herself, but it didn't help. Seething inwardly, she allowed herself to be placed in the first row of the women's section, at one end of the line of Halvorsens.

"We saved this seat for you, Miss Lennox." It was Leif, fine-tuning the ingratiating smile that made Tory want to put him over her knee.

But she managed a thank-you and a wave to Anneke, beyond him. Erik, looking pale and frightened, gave Tory a curt nod, but Martha, farthest down the line, stared straight ahead. *She looks as if she'd spent the night in hell.*

Erling had taken his place behind the lectern, and from some-place out of Tory's sight came an electronic chord that brought the congregation straggling to its feet. "Eternal Father, strong to save . . ." filled the already airless room.

Rise above, Tory told herself, and picked up the second line. She had been born with a love of singing and a powerful soprano, countered by an occasional difficulty in hitting exactly the right note. After several teenage mortifications, she restricted her vocalizing to church, where she presumed the Almighty would accept a willing spirit in lieu of perfect pitch. As always, the music, the other voices (many of them perceptibly worse than her own), the fellowship of sound combined to sweep her away.

When the collective Amen boomed out, she sat—back poker-straight, ankles crossed, hands folded in her lap —ready to hear just what apocalypse Erling preached.

It was the spray, a solid dollop full in the face, that brought Tory back to herself. For several seconds she continued to paddle automatically, as her senses accepted the brightly hazy sky, the steep little white-capped seas, the rising westerly into which she was driving her plastic kayak with all the strength and skill at her command. A free-floating strand of kelp embraced her paddle blade, and she slipped it free with a twist of her wrist, never losing the rhythm of the stroke.

Off to her right, tan, gullied bluffs underlined Shoreline Park; to her left, the glittery sweep of the channel lost itself in a blurred horizon well short of the islands. A pleasant summer Sunday afternoon, the kind of seascape that should have made her heart sing. Instead she felt empty, drained, defensive.

*What if he's right?* The question had been struggling upward through layers of denial ever since she had walked, stunned and dazed, from Erling Halvorsen's little church. Erling had gone to some trouble to sugarcoat his message, she guessed, but he was too honest to deny what he so clearly believed. "God has made man and woman partners from the beginning," he'd said, looking straight into her eyes as he spoke. "But not equal partners, because there is no such thing."

She could feel the congregation's attention on her, like a physical weight, and she'd forced herself to freeze rigid in the folding chair. Although her face was quite numb, she knew she was wearing a tight-lipped half smile.

"In every human relationship, there has to be a leader and followers, a captain and crew," Erling continued. The mostly shaggy heads in front of her nodded solemn acceptance, but Erling's brown eyes—gentle, infinitely understanding—were sending his message straight to her, with a subtext: I have no choice but to tell you this truth, even if you hate me for it.

"I'm not saying man is more important than woman," Erling said. "No. Not at all. Woman gives man the strength to lead. She provides the example of purity he can—he must—aspire to . . ." At that moment, she now recalled, Martha had buried her face in her two hands, and Tory had felt the thread between herself and Erling tighten to the breaking point.

He gave her no time to think, pouring out what sounded like biblical references and quotations of famous men, words she'd often heard or read, but presented now in contexts that at first outraged and then confused her. The message was always the same: man led, supported—and deferred to—by woman. No questioning, no debate were possible for the believer. This was God's command: take it and be saved, reject it and be damned.

As a cadet and then a junior officer, Tory had had to submit silently to superiors' opinions she totally rejected. She found her fingers itching for a pad on which she could scribble down at least a couple of the citations, for refutation later. But Erling was no snotty lieutenant commander whose extra half stripe had eroded his brain. The man facing her, rumpled and sweating, was in deadly, humble earnest. He didn't even seem to enjoy what he taught, but she was convinced he believed it utterly.

What derailed her composure almost completely was the way he was speaking only to her. Though he never referred to her by name or even implication, his eyes remained locked on hers. At first she told herself she was imagining it, but then she'd glanced sidelong left and right, saw the fascinated stares of the other women, watching how she took it. At the ends of the rows ahead, men's heads were swiveling quickly. *No question, sweetheart: this one's for you.*

Condescension she would have laughed off; superiority she could have brushed away, but Erling's humility was hard to get a grip on. He was subjecting her to this, she suddenly realized, out of love—for his God and for her. She felt her throat lock up. The avid, greedy eyes of a woman halfway down her row caught her own. *She's waiting for me to crack. Damned if I will.*

It had been a close-run thing, and the Halvorsen children had nearly been the collective last straw. The closing hymn, "Fight the Good Fight," was the kind of rouser Tory could usually cut loose on, but not today: if she opened her mouth, she knew the only sound to emerge would be a sob. As she stood at rigid attention, her gaze focused on the spot halfway between herself and Erling, she felt a small hand pluck at her dress. It was Leif, angelic beyond belief, holding up his hymnbook for her to share. Beyond him, Anneke was watching with huge, serious eyes, and Martha was staring at the floor, the tears streaming down her cheeks.

So what's become of Erik? Tory thought, when she saw a flick of faded plaid shirt going up the aisle. The boy glanced back at the same instant, and his eyes went suddenly dark with fear. Three minutes later, the hymn thundered to its slightly discordant climax, and Tory realized the service was ending. *Can I face these people? Can I face Erling? No and no.* She fled.

This time the hoarse roar of a toppling wave crest provided the wake-up call. Two steep seas, crossing at a narrow angle, had combined into a single angry breaker rolling right down on her. Tory leaned all her weight into consecutive strokes, right and left, that punched her kayak straight through the white water. "All *right!*" she heard herself exult, as she shook the saltwater from her hair. But it wasn't all right, she saw: the Santa Barbara Channel, in its treacherous fashion, had suddenly overlaid a hard sou'wester across the afternoon's brisk northerly. As the kayak mounted another big sea, Tory got a panoramic view of whitecaps all around, clear into shore.

"Time to go home," she said aloud. *Past time.* Not that she was unduly concerned—she was a strong, experienced ocean paddler, she'd taken the fourteen-foot sit-on-top kayak through worse seas than these, and even if the boat was swept by breakers, she'd still be warm for hours in her wetsuit. No, it was a question of example: if your job was pitching boating safety to the public, then you had to live it, too.

The kayak rose to the crest of a wave, and just at the top she spun it around, ready to catch and ride the next sea toward the harbor. For the instant her boat sat poised eight feet above the surrounding sea, she had an incomparable view in every direction. Her eye was caught, just as the kayak began to shoot forward, by an unnatural burst of spray near shore. Even as she rocketed down the wave's slope, feeling the kayak planing like a bobsled, her interior computer was evaluating what she'd seen. That spray, she decided, had been tossed up by a wave hitting another boat, rather than a buoy; a westbound boat, small enough to be hidden by the seas and—judging by the shape of the spray—blunt-bowed. Probably an outboard-powered inflatable.

The wave she was riding dropped her reluctantly, and she felt the kayak sag back in the grip of the next. A quick glance over her shoulder told her this one was much bigger, cresting, the kind of breaker that could provide a long, stirring ride. She leaned back in the cockpit, moving her weight aft, and let the wave seize her little boat as its stern rose. A couple of quick, sharp strokes were all it took to shoot her forward, and then a light drag with the paddle to keep the kayak lined up at a slight diagonal down the wave's face. Now the cresting sea was doing all the work—or all but a very little. At the same time, she was completely conscious that the smallest mistake in balance, the smallest misalignment of the trailing paddle blade, could roll the kayak, spill her into the chill blue water.

*Life on the edge.* The words jumped into her head, and she knew they were true. This was the kind of thing that made all the dull bits bearable. Up ahead, she saw a roller from the secondary wave system bearing down from starboard. Where it collided with her wave there'd be an explosion of water—not the place to be. Reluctantly she braked with the paddle, let her sea escape from beneath her. As it did, lifting her stern-first into the crisp gusts of the westerly, she again saw the odd-shaped burst of spray to port, but much nearer now. Near enough so she could see, this time, the gray of the inflatable's hull, and as the little boat slammed up and over a breaker, a pale, tense face over an unmistakable plaid shirt.

*Erik Halvorsen, by God. What's he doing out here?* He was, she saw, in no danger—handling the inflatable with a teenager's quick reflexes, swinging the outboard first one way and then the other to send his stubby little craft angling over the crests, like a high-jumper taking the crossbar. For a moment she was sure he'd seen her, but whether he recognized her in wetsuit and hood was another question. He didn't wave, and she decided not to risk it, and in seconds they had passed, small boats on a bright afternoon.

Approached from the west, Santa Barbara Point was almost invisible until you were abeam of it, but the steep cliff, cutting in sharply a hundred yards or so to a flat beach, created the natural windbreak that had given the town its nineteenth-century existence as a port. The big, rolling seas lost much of their drive east of the point, but Tory's mood held as she paddled the remaining half-mile to the harbor entrance. The sight of a thirty-five-foot sloop coming in from the south under working jib and double-reefed main raised her spirits even higher, especially when the large crew—the large, all-male crew—made a total hash of lowering sail in the entrance channel.

"Second to *none*," she yelled at a startled Officer Taffy Hegemann, waltzing *Harbor 1* slowly back and forth just outside the dredged channel.

The last fifty yards were the longest, even though the sheltered cul-de-sac around the launching ramps was nearly breezeless compared to the sea outside. Now the wetsuit was hot and sticky and constricting, and her face felt as if the skin might crack completely under all the dried salt. Even her hands, hardened by regular paddling, had developed painful swellings at the bases of her thumbs. Still a good afternoon, she told herself, grabbing at the floating concrete finger pier. A good antidote to Erling.

She tied off the kayak's bow and, shifting her weight carefully, swarmed up out of the cockpit and across to the float—only to freeze halfway. "Oh, my God," she heard herself say, her voice unnaturally harsh. The kayak's stern started to swing away from the pier, leaving her straddling air. Instinct and an ungraceful scramble saved her, and a moment later she was on hands and knees on the concrete, breathing hard.

No time for thought, or she might lose her resolution. She dropped to her belly and reached down into the still water beneath the float to let her fingers confirm what she'd glimpsed. One touch was more than enough. She sat up slowly, aware of a fisherman and his young son at the shore end of the float, watching her with clear concern. She constructed a smile that at least turned their faces away and pulled from her drybag the handheld VHF transceiver she always carried. Punching in channel 12, she keyed the transmit button. "Harbor Patrol, Harbor Patrol. This is . . . Tory's kayak. Channel one-two."

Behind the flat acknowledgment—"*Harbor 1*. Go ahead."—she could hear Taffy's curiosity.

"*Harbor 1*, kayak. I'm at the launch ramp. Right-hand finger pier. I think you'd better get somebody over here right away." She hesitated, then added, knowing there was no point to it: "And an ambulance. Out."

A little light-headed now, she leaned back against one of the float's concrete support poles. Sweat was pouring down her face, and she swung her legs over the edge to cool them in the water. The heels of her wetsuit booties touched the water's surface, but she couldn't force herself to immerse even her feet.

Oh, come on, she admonished herself. Dead men don't bite, as Cap'n Silver used to say.

But Long John hadn't seen that gaping mouth, those blackened teeth. Or the little crab working its way methodically along the swollen lips.

As he pushed open the heavy wire gate to Marina 2, Rebecca clattering not quite breathlessly at his heels, Neal could see two strobes—one on an SBPD black-and-white, the other on *Harbor 1*—flashing down by the launch ramps. From Cabrillo Boulevard an ambulance siren wailed and, in the distance, a police cruiser answered. *Trouble big time—and Tory in it.*

"Do you think somebody's dead?" Rebecca panted. She sounded hopeful, and he wondered if she just didn't know any better or if she were some kind of media ghoul.

"We'll see in a minute," he said over his shoulder. They'd been sprawled in *Carpe Diem*'s forward cabin—an upholstered triangular platform three feet above deck level—nibbling chips and drinking beer, when Tory's strained voice had come out of the transceiver speaker, screwed to the bulkhead above them.

For Neal, hearing her crystallized the guilty distaste that had been growing ever since he'd awakened, with gummy eyes and a mouth like the bottom of a crab pot, to find the lushly naked Rebecca lying on her stomach with her chin cradled in her hands, watching him. Though the overhead hatch was cracked open, the forward cabin was stifling, with a dizzying, almost visible miasma compounded of stale smoke, stale rum, and stale lust. But even postcoital disgust amplified by a brutal hangover hadn't postponed round two for more than a few minutes. In the midst of it, with both of them sweat-slick and straining hard, she'd grinned up at him and panted, "Oh, my. We're just horny as hoptoads—and I do mean we."

She had got it mostly right. Lacking both Tory's physical elegance and her skillfully controlled passion, Rebecca was still a young, attractive woman, and her convulsive hunger would've galvanized any man (Neal told himself)—not to mention, of course, the novelty of unexplored terrain. Apparent insatiability, too, if you counted that as an asset. Only the promise of a brunch-and-shopping tour of State Street had bought Neal enough time to recoup for the afternoon assault.

In broad daylight, without makeup, her hair matted, her brand-new souvenir T-shirt hopelessly wrinkled, she looked to Neal's jaded eye exactly like a woman who'd been screwing her head off for the past twelve hours. And her death grip on his trailing forearm would make it clear to anyone with eyes just who her partner had been. For his own part, when Tory's call had come through he had the unfair advantage of preparedness: as always, a fresh khaki uniform shirt with the top two buttons undone hung on the bulkhead, next to a pair of dark blue shorts and the heavy belt with the tools of his trade weighing it down. A headlong dive-and-wriggle up into his shirt, a squirming tug on his shorts, a button-tuck-zip, and he was dressed—while Rebecca was still struggling with her bra.

He slipped his bare feet into Top-Siders, and thoughts of escape were just beginning to form as she looked up and said, "You can wait till I'm dressed, or I'll follow you like this." He could see in her eyes that she would, too.

Taffy Hegemann was standing at the shore end of the floating finger pier, next to an SBPD cop, both of them more or less soaked. Beyond them on the float, a soggy bundle under a tarp. Tory was standing over it in her wetsuit, staring down hard, as if to prove her toughness. ("I just unfocus my eyes," she'd confided once. "Then I can look at anything.") Next to her slouched the familiar skinny shape of Steve Merriam, a police lieutenant with whom Neal had formed a tentative, spiky friendship.

Taffy's eyes widened, then went blank as she saw Neal and Rebecca approaching. "What's up?" Neal demanded, when they were face-to-face. "I picked up Tory's call and your response, but that's all I know."

"A floater," Taffy said, pointedly not looking at Rebecca. "Tory saw him, stuck under the pier, when she pulled her kayak in. She and I and the officer here got him out. Ambulance should be along any minute, but it was too late a couple days ago."

Relief washed over him. It was nothing very unusual. A fair number of people, many of them drunk, managed to fall in the harbor every year, and two or three drowned. The floating piers were only a foot or so above the water, but hauling yourself out, especially when you were weighted down by soaked clothes, wasn't easy. By the time you realized your situation was more than just embarrassing, the cold was already beginning to get to you. And even if you yelled your head off, the lines of boats in their slips made it almost impossible for a searcher to see more than twenty or thirty yards without an obstruction. Assuming there even was a searcher: for hours at a time, and not just at night, the harbor was surprisingly empty of human beings.

"He's not a regular," Taffy added. "You want a look before they take him away?"

*Not really* was forming on Neal's lips when Rebecca, beside him, said, "Of course we do." He was still blinking as she dragged him forward. The street cop, a solid middle-aged man who'd seen it all, only raised an eyebrow, but Taffy looked genuinely scandalized.

Tory was saying something to Steve Merriam as Rebecca led Neal down the pier toward them. Tory's statement, probably, because Merriam was taking it down. Or just finishing: he capped his expensive ballpoint and slipped it into a loop in the gleaming leather notebook whose appearance was ruined by his habit of overstuffing it with calling cards, notes to himself, meal receipts, and newspaper clippings. Merriam was a native Santa Barbaran, one of the few Neal had met, and a longtime spokesman for the SBPD faction lobbying to take over the Harbor Patrol. In spite of that, Neal respected him as an honest, efficient cop, and liked him, too. There were times when he could even imagine himself trusting Merriam.

But a death at the harbor put the two men automatically into subdued competition, and Neal felt wariness drop like a curtain between them. Wariness tinged with malice on Steve's part: "Going to introduce your friend, Neal?"

Tory, poker-faced, chose the moment to blindside all of them. "Lieutenant Merriam, this is Ms. Jardine, from the *Making Things Right* staff. Rebecca, Steve Merriam of the Santa Barbara PD." It was what Neal thought of as her grande dame voice—every syllable diamond-etched and frozen solid—and it sounded even more inhuman coming from a tousled, statuesque blonde encased in dripping black neoprene.

Merriam, with the advantage of detachment, threw Rebecca a lascivious grin and a cheery, "Welcome aboard, even if it's not my idea how to spend a Sunday afternoon." He gestured toward the tarp-covered bundle. "Help yourself, Neal."

Neal squatted by the tarp and gingerly lifted one corner, hearing a quick intake of breath, presumably Rebecca's, from above and behind him. *Early middle age? Hard to say—the bad teeth make him look older, and the rummy nose. Dent in his forehead: a right-angle V, like the edge of . . . what? Piece of timber, maybe.*

Rocking back on his heels, he said, "One thing this guy isn't is a floater. He hasn't been in the water long enough—two days, max."

"That's right," Tory's voice, cool and remote, put in. "When I found him, his shirt was snagged on the underside of the float. As soon as I got him loose, he started to sink."

"How dreadful for you!" Rebecca exclaimed. "You're a lot braver than I am, Lieutenant."

Her solicitude sounded real enough to Neal, but he knew from experience that women who hated each other had a special frequency they communicated on, inaudible to everyone else.

"Brave? Hardly," Tory replied. And in a quite different tone, professional to professional: "There's no ID on him—pockets completely empty. But the khaki shirt and trousers made me wonder if he might be someone who works around the harbor."

Neal pulled the tarp down another foot, leaned forward until his face was a few inches from the dead man's shirt. "Could be. Shirt looks new, but it's stained." He flipped the tarp all the way back. "Same for the pants."

"Stains are what labs are for," Steve Merriam put in. "What about those sneakers? They're definitely new: the soles are barely scuffed."

Annoyed with himself for not immediately noticing something so obvious, Neal said, "Of course. And they don't make much sense for somebody working around boats."

He paused, framing his explanation, but Tory was ahead of him: "Those treads are fine for hiking, but they pick stuff up—pebbles, bits of hardware—the kind of thing boatyards are full of. And they don't provide much traction, which is the whole point of boat shoes."

Merriam looked over his shoulder. "Meatwagon's here. But Neal—you said this guy might have worked around the harbor. Have you ever seen him down here?"

"Not to put a name to," Neal said slowly. "But I could swear I've seen him, and not long ago."

"It'll come to you," Merriam said. And then, deadpan, "Why don't we adjourn to that boat of yours? You could treat us all to a beer—and your memory might slip back into gear."

Neal opened his mouth without the slightest notion of what he was going to say, only to be rescued by Rebecca: "I'm afraid he can't. We've got an important appointment." Seeing Neal's bewilderment, she continued: "You can't have forgotten already—the Feverel gallery, to see Wilbur Andreas's paintings."

THE FEVEREL COLLECTION OF FINE ART, EAST CANON PERDIDO
STREET; 5:45 P.M.: JOCK

"All set, Jock," said the caterer, a big, hard-faced woman with
curly red hair. As she slipped the gold links into the cuffs of her
dress shirt, she scanned the dimly lit gallery with weary satisfaction.

Following her eye, Jock had to agree; the gallery virtually trem-
bled with anticipation, from the improvised bar with its triple-deep
row of Firestone whites and reds, its palisade of pale green Perrier
bottles behind the sterling ice bucket, its glittering pyramided wine
glasses; to the neighboring counter topped with wheels of Camem-
bert and Brie, crisply fresh loaves of French bread whose aroma
filled the room, crystal plates piled with expensive nuts and choco-
lates. People might not come to an opening for the food, but what
you served set the tone, and the tone here was every inch class: no
scrimping, no substitutes. It had been a long time since Jock had
been able to stage a show where cost was literally no object, and it
was exhilarating—almost worth the menacing presence of Mr. Celeste and his associates.

Around the draped walls Wilbur Andreas's paintings hung each
in its own perfect pool of light—an extraordinary effect, like

120

standing in a darkened house looking out a succession of sunlit windows. Two framers and an exhibitions man from L.A. had worked all afternoon, squabbling sotto voce under Jock's demands for perfection. Perfection was what he'd got, too. Wilbur's work had never shown so well; the disparate canvases seemed to form a visual symphony, building from the smallest—the harbor entrance at dawn, barely a foot on a side—to the huge, panoramic *Southeast Gale: Fools' Anchorage*, which occupied ten linear feet of the gallery's longest wall.

Even Wilbur himself had a place in the composition. Cleaned up, dinner-jacketed, his eyes bandaged in black silk that echoed his lapels, he was enthroned at one side of *Southeast Gale*, ready to receive admirers. Though the ponytailed Felix had been given the assignment of keeping Wilbur presentable, Jock suspected his old friend was already quietly stoned. Well, that might be best, Jock thought. Wilbur was finding blindness more of a drag than he'd expected, and he'd been jumpily unpredictable all day. From the corner of his eye, Jock saw Wilbur's head sag, then jerk back upright. Good, he thought. A passed-out guest of honor would be slightly embarrassing, but there were far worse alternatives.

Surveying his gallery, Jock found himself beginning to believe the show might fly. Mr. Celeste certainly seemed sublimely confident, and the two gray suits who'd come up with him from L.A. didn't look like the kind of men who'd be associated with failure. "You just keep a cool tool, dude," one of them had said. "By six-thirty, you'll see a famous faces riot in here."

The other, the dark one, had looked up from the fax machine in time to catch Jock's quickly erased incredulity. "Mr. Celeste tells them to come, they come. You'll see," he said.

Their quiet confidence was contagious, and Jock had started to feel a little better, to the point of adding ten percent to each of the picture prices. Then Mr. Celeste, who'd been outside in his limo, making phone calls, appeared. He took one look at Jock's price list and said, "Jesus Christ."

"You think I'm a little high?" Jock had asked quickly.

"I think you're going to die a penny-ante grifter," Mr. Celeste said, shaking his head. "For something like this, you need vision. You got no vision. And you need balls. You don't have them, either."

For a lunatic moment, Jock was on the verge of exploding. *Balls? I killed a man two nights ago. With my bare hands, almost. Don't talk to me about balls.* He pulled himself back from the abyss, but his expression had betrayed him. He saw, for almost the first time, a glint of appraisal in Mr. Celeste's eyes. Not even the ghost of a threat in that calculating stare, but Jock felt as if the floor beneath him had suddenly flexed. An almost uncontrollable urge to gabble swept over him, but he managed to fight it down.

And this, too, Mr. Celeste apparently saw. "That's better," he said. "If you don't have anything to say, don't say it."

"But if—when somebody wants to buy one of Wilbur's paintings . . ." Jock began.

"You just let Michael and Leon handle that," Mr. Celeste said, nodding toward the two suits. "It's all arranged."

And so it was. The evening's first guest appeared five minutes before the official opening time, making his entrance through the gallery's back door. His shiny sateen bomber jacket was thrown over his shoulders like a cape, and his face was shadowed by the bill of a baseball cap, his eyes barely hidden by sunglasses whose round, nearly black lenses were not much larger than quarters. But there was no masking the grossly simian physique, biceps as big around as Jock's thighs, the brutal Neanderthal features that had stared down from a hundred movie house screens.

He stood in the doorway, head lowered and swinging from side to side, like a bull selecting a toreador, then spotted Mr. Celeste and trotted swiftly to him. "I only heard a couple hours ago," he said, voice incongruously high and precise. "Figured it was better to come the way I was."

"I appreciate it," Mr. Celeste replied evenly.

Leon, the dark suit, glided up without a sound, and the newcomer said to him, "Which one?"

"Right this way," Leon replied.

The questions in Jock's head were still fighting for priority when he heard a quick rat-tat-tat on the glass of the front door, a few feet behind him. He spun and found himself confronting an explosion of blonde hair framing two huge, hungry dark eyes and a wetly carnivorous scarlet pout, all set into a perfect ivory oval. It was last month's *Vanity Fair* cover come to life, and all Jock could do was gape.

"Open the door," said Mr. Celeste.

Moving as if he were underwater, Jock unlocked the door and stepped aside just in time to avoid being knocked down. The blonde hair, rigid as wire, sailed past him in a pungent cloud of makeup, hair spray, cognac, and perfume, but not so fast that Jock's trained eye failed to notice the networks of lines, hairline cracks in the ivory, around eyes and mouth, the stretch marks at her temple and along her jaw. My God, she must be seventy, he thought.

But the famous voice, purring Italian into Mr. Celeste's ear, sounded as warm and vibrant and sensual as ever. Then she turned, surveying the pictures, and suddenly cried out, "*Ecco!* That one! I must have it!" her voice like a trumpet.

"Michael," said Mr. Celeste, but it was unnecessary.

The other suit was already at the blonde's elbow: "May I help you, *serenissima?*" he said, taking her arm.

"Like I said, it's all arranged," said Mr. Celeste.

In his nervousness, Jock had issued invitations of his own, calling in every social and business debt he'd squirreled away over the years. By normal gallery standards, he'd done well—a good two dozen members of the Montecito squirearchy, giving off the aura of what in Southern California passed for old money; the more presentable members of the Santa Barbara art community, always ready to turn out in support of a colleague; even the local media's second string—the society lady from the *News-Press*, a jowly aesthete from the weekly *Independent*, and a downy fledgling from KEYT, trailed by her cameraman.

But they were swamped by the seemingly endless parade of Mr. Celeste's clients. Show business faces mostly, but several professional athletes Jock barely recognized and some silent, gray-skinned financial types who set the Montecitans to genuflecting uncontrollably. By now, the street outside was nearly blocked by stretch limos, chauffeured Mercedeses, and a fire-engine-red Ferrari of shattering vulgarity. The cars had drawn a crowd of their own, faces pressed to the gallery's windows, eager for a look at the presumably rich and famous, and maybe even a grope as they entered and left.

But the real point was that Mr. Celeste's people were buying, and buying big. Every few minutes, to the spatter of applause, a painting would be lifted reverently from the wall and carried off into the back for wrapping. As if by magic, a new work would appear in its place, only to vanish in its turn. Jock had never seen anything like it, though when he tried to follow a triumphant purchaser into the back room, he found himself blocked by the ponytailed Felix. "Don't you worry, Mr. Feverel. It's all arranged."

Celeste must be giving the damn things away, Jock thought suddenly. But why? Slowly he let the circular movement of the crowd carry him toward the gallery desk behind its folding screen, where Michael and Leon had set up their headquarters. The view, or lack of it, was maddening: the discreet flourish of checkbooks, punctuated by the muted metallic slam of a credit card machine, but never a number could he see.

At last, a snatch of conversation slipped through a momentary gap in the hubbub: "Thirteen big ones? Hell of a lot for something the size of a legal pad," said a rasping voice that came, incongruously, from the pastel-tinted mouth of a redhead with marzipan skin, scrawling laboriously on a check.

Leon, standing over her, beamed down. "Think of it as an investment," he said, then bent quickly forward and whispered something else in her ear—something that made her laugh aloud.

*Thirteen big ones.* Surely he'd heard wrong, but he had to know. Taking his courage in both hands, he stepped forward quickly. Leon turned, fast as a snake and a half-second late. His hand scooped the check up and away, but not before Jock had got a perfect, heart-stopping look. Thirteen big ones. Euphoria, held at arm's length for hours, swept him into its embrace.

At last he had the definite sense the crowd was thinning. New faces were still arriving, but nearly all of them were just tire-kickers—locals taking an after-dinner stroll and drawn by the gallery's activity. Mr. Celeste's clients or victims or whatever they were had long since disappeared, purchases in hand. Wilbur was still on his throne, but he'd been unconscious for an hour. Jock found himself suffused with unaccustomed benevolence and no one to share it with. Surveying the room, he settled on a face, topping a zaftig figure, that he'd seen before: the *Making Things Right* producer, what was her name? Rebecca something.

She was hanging on the arm of a slender, dark, vaguely familiar young man whose well-worn blazer and gray slacks looked from a distance like the carelessness of money. Jock prided himself on being able to define a couple's relationship after a minute's unseen observation; it didn't require that long to see this pair was a non-starter. Her still-possessive grip on his elbow said it all: *Il y a toujours l'un qui baise, et l'un qui tourne la joue.*

He poured himself a quick refill and ambled toward them. With each step he was more positive he'd seen the young man recently, though in some very different setting. And equally positive he'd been wrong about the money: there was casually shabby rich and just casually shabby; this guy was the latter, for sure. Beautiful tan, though half of it looked to be genetic. A surfer, more than likely.

The two of them had come to Wilbur's magnum opus, the immense *Southeast Gale: Fools' Anchorage.* The painting hadn't been bought, but at least two wealthy local collectors had been circling gingerly around it, and Jock felt definitely hopeful. Rebecca's escort seemed to have definite opinions about the picture, Jock saw—or maybe it just represented a safe topic between two people who had nothing more to say to each other. He moved soundlessly up behind them, just in time to see Rebecca stiffen and turn quickly to the man beside her. "That's impossible!" she snapped. Flustered and even a little frightened, he decided. Why?

The young man shrugged. "I could be wrong," he said, clearly meaning *I'm not—but I'm not going to argue, either.*

Her last name came to Jock then, and he said, "Rebecca Jardine: how nice to see you."

Startled for only an instant, she seemed relieved to see him: "Jock—what a super show. How on earth did you put it together so fast?"

Not a question he felt like addressing. "I'm glad you're enjoying yourself, Rebecca. Especially since you made it all possible." And to her escort: "Good to see you again."

The tanned young man unveiled a dazzling smile. "We haven't actually met, but we're both creatures of Rebecca's imagination." He extended a big, muscular hand. "Neal Donahoe. I'm the Harbormaster."

"Of course—you were on the taped segment," Jock replied. Something was gnawing at the edge of his well-being, but he ignored it. "What's your expert opinion of Wilbur's work?"

"It's amazing. I can damn near recognize the individual pelicans," Donahoe said. He had an engaging grin, Jock thought. "What do you call his style? Super-realism?"

"That's the term. But Wilbur's taken it to a new level."

Donahoe nodded, clearly about to say something else. Rebecca, her chin thrust out, interrupted: "Jock, when was this painted?"

Mystified, Jock pointed to the painting's lower right corner, just below the sprawling signature. "Like it says: October last year. Nine months ago," he said.

"You see?" Rebecca hissed at her companion.

"Sure," Neal replied. "Hell, I remember Wilbur painting this. He was standing on that little shoreward extension of Stearns Wharf. His hat blew off."

"Then what . . ." she began.

"All I was saying is he's touched it up since then," Neal said. He leaned forward, pointing. "This boat here, the dismasted *Catalina 25*, was in a slip in Marina 2 till late December."

The faintest chill rippled down Jock's spine. "Wilbur does . . . did change things in some of his works," he said quickly. "That little boat you were talking about really adds something to the composition. See how it extends the line of the wharf?"

"Sure," said Rebecca dismissively. She turned to Neal: "But that wasn't what you were saying a minute ago. You said Wilbur must've added that little purple thing, that flag, just yesterday."

And now, as if in a nightmare, Mr. Celeste had materialized at his elbow. "What's going on?" he said quietly.

For almost the first time in his life, Jock was without words. He looked helplessly from Rebecca to Neal Donahoe. The Harbormaster's grin, so engaging a minute before, had faded to a tight half smile.

"Well?" said Mr. Celeste. Across the room, at the desk, the two suits looked up sharply.

"It's nothing," Rebecca said abruptly. "Neal's memory must've played a trick on him."

*Of course. She had a stake in this, too.* The realization galvanized Jock's nerve. "Happens to the best of us," he said.

"Neal who?" Mr. Celeste demanded, ignoring him. "That you, friend?"

"That's me," Donahoe replied.

"You were on the TV show, right?" Mr. Celeste continued. "So how do you fit in here?" The two suits were on their feet, Jock saw. But where was Felix?

"Just another art lover," Donahoe said. His dark eyes flicked to something—or someone—over Jock's shoulder and back to Mr. Celeste. Donahoe's stance was easy, even relaxed, but Jock had the sense of a cat ready to jump in any direction.

"You've got a problem with this picture?" Mr. Celeste said softly. "Lots of people are saying it's a masterpiece."

Without warning, Donahoe's grin reappeared. "It's . . . miraculous. Could be a masterpiece."

Rebecca looked sharply at Donahoe, but Mr. Celeste seemed to take his words at face value. He nodded. "Time will tell—and I'm betting in favor."

"Well, it's none of my business," Donahoe said. "You seen enough, Rebecca?"

*She doesn't want to leave,* Jock thought. Suddenly she looked directly into Jock's eyes for a long second, then turned to Donahoe.

"I suppose so. Yes. And it's a long drive back to L.A.: I'd better be rolling."

Clearly, that was fine with the Harbormaster. "I'll walk you to your car," he said.

"Thanks. Just let me make sure I've got the keys." She pawed in her purse, nodded. "All set." To Jock: "Nice to meet you again." Her hand was extended, palm down as if she expected him to kiss it.

He bent over it, just touching her fingertips with his, and palmed the oblong of cardboard she was holding. *"Enchanté,"* he said, slipping it into his pocket.

"He's wearing a badge on his belt, that Donahoe," observed Mr. Celeste a few minutes later, as the two suits urged the last guests out the gallery door. "Is he some kind of cop?"

*Cop.* Jock's stomach tightened momentarily. "He runs our Harbor Patrol. It's not exactly the FBI."

But Mr. Celeste's mind was clearly elsewhere. "Something I want to say, Feverel, and I'm only going to say it this once." He turned on Jock, his hard face inches from Jock's own. "Tomorrow, when word gets around about this sale tonight, Wilbur's paintings are going to skyrocket."

"Maybe we shouldn't have sold so many of them," said Jock. But his feeble joke seemed only to annoy Mr. Celeste.

"Sold?" He shook his head. "Jesus, you're stupid. Anyway, that's not my point. You know what's making these paintings take off?" It was so obviously a rhetorical question that Jock didn't attempt a response. "Because they're the last works of a blind genius."

"Well, of course—" Jock began, but Mr. Celeste hadn't finished.

"The operative words are 'last' and 'blind,' " he said, stabbing Jock's chest with a bony forefinger.

"What d'you mean?" Jock heard himself croak.

Mr. Celeste sighed. "Don't try shitting me. Not ever." He half turned, considering Wilbur's slumped form. "You pitched a blind artist to those TV people, and they bought it. Hell, the whole world's buying it. Now all of a sudden it seems your tiger's tired of being blind. Well, that's out."

"Look, I can handle this," Jock said.

"I hope so."

"I'll—I'll tear a strip off Wilbur. Really read him the riot act. Straighten him—"

"No." Mr. Celeste's tone was calm and final. He walked over to Wilbur, grasped a handful of his damp hair and raised the bandaged head. "You promised me a blind painter. Tomorrow you deliver."

Leaning on the seawall railing, Neal stared absently down at Officer Gaspar Ortega untying *Harbor 2*. After a couple of minutes, Ortega looked up. "Morning, Maximum Leader," he said, grinning. "Want to take a little spin?"

"Why not?" Neal replied. In fact he was glad of an excuse—any excuse—to get out on the water and away from his own thoughts. He'd spent a brutally uncomfortable night on *Carpe Diem*'s main cabin settee (the lingering odors in the forward cabin were more than he could handle), trying to think of a way he could retrieve his relationship with Tory. He was still rerunning that hopeless exercise—she would never forgive him, he was sure of it—when his exhausted brain switched automatically to Wilbur Andreas's huge painting of Fools' Anchorage.

Among the speckling of moored boats occupying the picture's middle ground, the *Prophet Jonah*, ex–*Klamath Goddess*, dominated, her straight bow plunging into a nasty roller. The boat's presence certainly matched the time of the work's original composition: the *Goddess* had been on a mooring for a couple of years—hadn't moved into the harbor until just before her previous owners had skipped town. But in all the time she'd sat offshore, there'd been nothing hanging from her spars. No streamers or plastic owls to scare the gulls and pelicans off, certainly not a purple banner with what looked like a gold cross on it.

The banner had appeared when the Halvorsens moved aboard in the harbor, something to do with Erling's screwball religion. The more Neal pressured his memory, the more certain he became. And unless someone else had taken to touching up Wilbur's works, that left only one conclusion. Outside the gallery he'd tried to explain his reasoning to Rebecca, in a furious whisper, but she didn't want to listen. *Really* didn't want to listen, as if hearing Neal out would be the same as agreeing with him.

"Some journalist you are," he snapped, as she got into her rented car.

"Go screw yourself," she'd snapped back, and slammed the door.

He hadn't tried to stop her. This morning he could even admit he'd been glad to see her drive off. But what now? On the one hand, the cop in Neal resonated to the presence of an obvious major bad guy in Jock's gallery. On the other, Neal wasn't sure Jock or Wilbur had committed any crime—not, at least, until somebody filed a complaint. And when you came right down to it, what harm had been done? Wilbur Andreas might be blind as a starfish or visually intact, but his paintings were the best of their kind Neal had ever seen . . .

"You awake up there, boss?" Gaspar called.

A typical July morning: outside the breakwater, the fog lay on the water thick enough to choke you, and even inside the harbor you could barely see the big blue-sided floating drydock, less than a hundred yards from the Harbor Patrol's pier. Southern California summer mornings—damp and gray, week after week—were the tourist board's dirty little secret. Visitors came here expecting the weather to be like *Baywatch*. What they got, at least till lunchtime, was the Grand Banks.

Gaspar cast off the boat, looked inquiringly at Neal. "You want to drive?"

"You take it." He felt and ignored Gaspar's quick appraisal. The patrol crews all knew Neal was uncomfortable aboard any boat he wasn't handling himself: he seldom tried to hide it. Today, though, he needed to just let the harbor—his harbor—chill him down. Gaspar idled the boat right along the main channel's axis, the engine murmuring wetly. As they approached the harbor's east end, the fog seemed even thicker. Focusing on a high, dark hull in an end-tie slip, Neal could see the light-colored streamers of fog ghosting past on the faint easterly breeze.

Gaspar saw them, too: "Still coming in off the channel. Bet it'll stay like this till noon."

Conversation over even an idling engine was an effort Neal disliked making. He grunted agreement—or disagreement, if Gaspar wanted to take it that way. At the moored bait boat marking the channel's turn to seaward, Gaspar spun the wheel. "You going outside?" Neal asked, mildly surprised. The normal procedure would be to double back, poking *Harbor 2* into each row of slips to make sure no mooring lines had chafed through in the night, no boat had sprung a leak.

His words were bitten off by the foghorn at the end of Stearns Wharf, the first catarrhal bleat of its two-blast pattern. Gaspar waited for the second, then said: "Some busybody called in, said a couple boats are fouled on each other, out in the anchorage."

"Surprised he could see them," Neal replied. "Was he on the beach?"

"That's what he said."

Neal grunted again. To port, the black pilings of Stearns Wharf loomed high over *Harbor 2*. Low tide—a new-moon low, Neal thought. Not that it made much difference to an outdrive like *Harbor 2*. "Where're these two turkeys supposed to be?"

"The way the guy described it, they're off the quarter-mile markers, just outside the swimming area buoys."

Well, that was precise enough, Neal thought. If true. Gaspar eased the patrol boat around the wharf's seaward end, keeping about fifty yards away. Even on days like this, fishermen festooned the end of the pier from dawn to well after dusk. Given half a chance, they would try to bean you with a sinker, and their transparent monofilament lines could foul a prop or slash through a rubber outdrive seal.

Bobbing ahead of *Harbor 2* the first of the white cylinders that marked the outer limit of the East Beach swimming area eased into view. Gaspar swung the boat to run parallel to the dimly seen shore. "Guy must've been standing right at the low-tide mark," he said.

Neal, peering ahead, could barely make out the next buoy, only fifty yards away. The fog was definitely thicker out here, but then it usually was. Another buoy, and another. *Harbor 2*, running in less than fifteen feet of water, passed the west end of the measured nautical mile, marked on shore by a pair of rectangular signs, one behind the other, each with a thick black line down its center. The quarter-mile markers, white rectangles with wide red lines, came sooner than he expected, and Gaspar throttled back to neutral.

"Well, I don't . . ." Neal began, and caught himself: "There, to starboard." Two sailboats were lying alongside each other, scraping noisily as they rolled. The one without a mast was still made fast to its mooring buoy; the other, having chafed through its line, had seemingly drifted into it. From a distance it looked as if the dismasted boat's lifeline stanchions had fouled in the other vessel's shrouds; if so, the two could break free anytime.

"Want to take her in?" Gaspar asked.

"Why not," Neal replied, knowing that even if they were able to trace the owner, his phone would probably be disconnected; and even if they got hold of him, he'd have a dozen excuses for not taking responsibility. It was the kind of situation that offended him almost beyond bearing. A boat was—or should be—like a member of your family, not some goddamned disposable box you walked away from when you got bored with it.

Neal, who was dressed for a morning meeting up at City Hall— blue slacks with a crease in them and a freshly pressed uniform shirt—took the helm while Gaspar wrestled the boats apart and got a towline on the drifter. Neal swung *Harbor 2* away from the shore in a wide, easy half-circle that took them just past the stern of the moored *Prophet Jonah.* Her cabin hatch was open, and he could hear what sounded like a hymn, sung by several voices.

Gaspar, sponging seagull droppings off his uniform shirt, looked as if he were about to say something clever, when his eyes widened in surprise and he gasped. "Christmas! It's Tory."

Neal, who had been looking over his shoulder, gauging the towed boat's swinging circle, snapped around. Gaspar was right: she had just emerged from the cabin, dressed in dark slacks and a sweatshirt. Her hand was raised, as if to flag down the patrol boat, when she saw Neal and froze. For several seconds, he was motionless, too, his brain spinning. "I think she wants a lift," said Gaspar diplomatically.

"I think you're right." Tory half turned, as if to retreat down the companionway, stopped, and swung back to face them, her spine rigid. Neal could sense her reluctance from thirty yards away, and in a perverse way it stiffened his wavering resolve. "We'll ease up on the *Jonah's* port side," he said. "Touch and go."

"I'll handle the towline."

"Right." He cut the throttle, letting *Harbor 2* glide alongside just as the singing in the cabin ground to a discordant Amen. He groped for some neutral greeting, said, "We're taking this poor old tub in to the pier, if you're going that way."

She was pale and drawn, dark circles beneath her eyes. Her clothes looked as if she'd slept in them. Instead of speaking she simply nodded and stepped aboard, with a neat economy of motion that made his heart turn over. Behind her, the massive shape of Erling Halvorsen appeared in the *Prophet Jonah's* hatch. He, too, looked tired and tense, but there was no mistaking the sincerity in his voice: "Just think it over, Tory," he called. "We need you—all of us."

*He's in love with her.* "Stand by, Gaspar," he said. For the first time in months, he pushed the combination throttle–shift lever too hard, and *Harbor 2* leaped forward. "Sorry," he said automatically, as Tory snatched at a grabrail. "You okay, Gaspar?"

"No sweat," Gaspar replied. His wooden expression was more expressive than any words.

Only the patrol boat's muttering outdrive and the double blast of the foghorn broke the silence for the next five minutes. Tory, at Neal's side, might have been three states away, and Gaspar clearly had no intention of coming forward from the towing bitt without a direct order. As *Harbor 2* cleared the end of Stearns Wharf, another boat materialized out of the fog—a small outboard-powered inflatable coming at them from the direction of the breakwater. "That's one of the Halvorsen kids," Neal said, before he could stop himself.

"It's Erik," Tory replied. "He was supposed to run me in to shore." She paused, seemingly on the verge of adding something, shook her head.

Unwilling to let communication die, Neal asked, "You want to let him know you're here?"

Clearly she did, but something was holding her back. At last she said, "If it's not too much trouble," in the detached, polite voice she might have used to ask a cab driver to wait.

"Not at all." By now, the inflatable and *Harbor 2* were nearly abreast. Erik was huddled in the little boat's stern, his back to the patrol boat. "People always think if they're not looking at a cop, it makes them invisible," Neal observed to no one in particular. He keyed the siren, and Erik straightened up as if he'd been stung. He looked around, miming surprise. Neal drew a finger across his throat, and the boy obediently cut his engine. "Smarter than the average bear," Neal said, swinging *Harbor 2* in close.

Tory ignored him. Leaning outboard toward Erik, she called, "You were missed this morning."

"I'm sorry, Miss Lennox. I was busy." *Not sullen, like a lot of teenagers. More . . . what? Oppressed, maybe, as if he had the world on his back. And scared.*

"That's okay," Tory said. "But your father's very . . . concerned about you."

The boy's tanned face paled by two shades, so the freckles across the bridge of his nose stood out starkly. "I better go," he said, yanking at the outboard's starter cord. The engine roared and the inflatable leaped ahead, its stern sagging under the pressure of the motor.

"What's that all about?" Neal asked. He waited a few seconds for her answer, and when it didn't come eased the throttle forward. *Harbor 2* slowly picked up speed, and Gaspar, pointedly looking over the stern, fed out the towline.

"There's something wrong with that family. Something terribly wrong," Tory said suddenly. "I just don't know what it is."

He responded, without thinking, to her tone more than her words: "Are you sure you don't?" *A second chance, and I blow it.*

Amazingly, she didn't bristle. Or maybe not so amazingly: she had the rare ability to look at herself with complete detachment. It was, he realized, one of the things about her he loved. When she spoke, it was as if she were talking to herself: "He loves them, I'm sure of that. And they're terrified of him."

"All that righteousness have something to do with it?" Neal suggested.

"He's not righteous, not in the way you mean it."

*You think I'm unfair to Halvorsen. Maybe you're right.* He saw he'd taken *Harbor 2* past the entrance channel turning mark and cut the wheel sharply. Behind the boat, the towline looped slack and the towed sailboat lost way. "Okay, I withdraw the righteousness," Neal said.

"He's actually a very humble man," she went on. "He never stops seeing how much he falls short of his own ideals."

*Sounds like a guy with a lot to be humble about.* The towline, coming taut, yanked the sailboat's bow around. Neal found himself glad Tory was too preoccupied to notice. "Falls short how?" he said.

He had struck a nerve, he saw. But her startled expression evaporated, replaced by reserve. "I can't say—yet," she replied.

The silence between them lasted until Neal brought *Harbor 2*, with the sailboat now strapped neatly alongside, into the patrol's pier. Without being asked, Tory stepped across the towed boat and onto the float, securing the sailboat's bow with its frayed mooring line. Neal saw she was waiting for him, and he turned to Gaspar: "Finish things up, would you? Get the owner's name from DMV."

"Right," the young officer replied. "I'll chase the sucker down, too. Give him a piece of my mind."

Neal paused, standing by the sailboat's shrouds. Below him Tory knelt on one knee, tying a figure-8 stopper into the end of the ragged line. She didn't look up as he jumped lightly down to the floating pier beside her. Her voice, when she spoke, was coolly neutral: "I don't see any reason we can't work together. When there's a reason to."

"I hope we're both professionals—I mean, I know *you* are," Neal said. He wanted desperately to say something about Erling Halvorsen, realized the self-styled preacher was off limits between them until she brought him up. "I'll see you," he said.

SANTA BARBARA CHANNEL, OFF LEDBETTER BEACH; 0745 HOURS: TORY

She drove the kayak paddle fiercely into the water, dragging it back hard. The little boat jumped forward through a wavetop that cascaded back along the deck and into the open cockpit. The water was cold right through her wetsuit, but she barely noticed.

What's happening in the *Prophet Jonah?* she asked herself for the fifth time in half an hour. What in God's name is wrong?

Tory had gone back aboard the trawler against every inclination, dragged only by Martha's telephoned dinner invitation—more plea than invitation, it seemed to Tory, delivered from the depths of near despair. And the meal itself might have been designed to erase the memory of Erling's sermon: the old boat scrubbed until the reek of ammonia quite blanketed the odor of bilge, the children gleaming with cleanliness and good manners, the food predictably dreadful and the portions far too small. Tory found herself treated like minor royalty by Erling; to her deep relief, the church service might never have happened—though she was asked to say grace be-

138

fore the meal, and her memory had obliged with a long-forgotten blessing from her boarding school days.

Afterward they sang, of course: mostly gospel songs that didn't figure in Tory's Episcopalian repertoire, though she hummed along with the familiar tunes. The evening might even have been relaxing, except that she had the constant feeling of being watched—with proprietary tenderness by Erling, with nervous calculation by Erik, with what she could only define as hopeless hope by Martha. When, about half an hour before sunset, she insisted she had to leave, meaningful glances darted between the two teenagers, and she was not entirely surprised when Erik announced (avoiding her eye) that the dinghy's outboard wouldn't start.

From the sound of it, as he pulled and repulled the starter cord, Tory suspected he'd somehow blocked the fuel line. She could probably fix it; she could even row the dinghy to shore and walk back along the beach. But something told her to go with the flow, whichever way it was running. A little skirmishing, obviously rehearsed, put her in what was normally Erik's berth, inboard of and below Martha's, while he retreated, grumbling, to the deck. But *what are they up to?* she'd asked herself. *Have I stumbled into some fifties sitcom, where the kids set up a romance for dad?*

Then Erling had suggested she sleep in his curtained-off cabin forward, while he took Erik's berth. The effect was like a silent bombshell, emotions suddenly cascading in every direction and quite swamping Tory's ability to sort them out. All she knew was that the thought of being isolated—cornered, to put it bluntly—up in the *Prophet Jonah's* bow was simply out of the question. "No," she'd said flatly. "That's very generous, Erling, but we girls will sleep together. And Leif, of course."

In the night she waked twice. The first time Erling had been standing over her, motionless in the moonlight streaming through the port. He had whispered, quite distinctly, "Thank you, Lord." And had padded forward to his cabin. When he had vanished through the curtain, Tory heard Martha, in the berth above, release her breath in a long sigh. She fell back asleep considering what it had meant.

Much later, just before dawn, she became aware of movement on deck. Erik, presumably, but she couldn't quite identify the sounds—until five minutes later she'd heard the dinghy's outboard, a hundred yards away, suddenly roar.

At breakfast, with Erik and the dinghy missing, Erling had been rigid with barely contained wrath, making the trawler's cabin so uncomfortable Tory had gone on deck simply to escape—and to find herself confronting Neal Donahoe and *Harbor 2*.

And now the kayak lifted to a swell and she saw, scarcely a hundred yards in front of her, the low, familiar bright orange hull with the big white 2 on its gray steering console. The patrol boat was broadside to the seas, and a single uniformed, black-haired figure was bending over the far gunwale, his back to her. At her first thought—*it must be Neal*—she felt her stomach tighten. *I'm not ready.*

But then the man straightened, and she saw it was Gaspar Ortega. Relief and, surprisingly, disappointment flooded through her, followed by curiosity. A dozen quick, deep strokes brought her kayak up in *Harbor 2*'s lee just as it swung, revealing a half-deflated rubber dinghy alongside. Erik, sopping wet, was bailing desperately with a child's toy bucket. The little boat's stern air chamber must have sprung a leak, she decided—the gray fabric looked flabby and limp, and the dead outboard on its bracket sagged almost completely underwater.

"Come on, tiger—leave that stuff and get aboard." Gaspar sounded annoyed, and no wonder: a good part of every bucketful Erik threw over the side was dousing him. But the boy ignored him, and the expression on his pale, blue-lipped face was desperate.

Wedging her paddle under a bungee strap on the kayak's deck, Tory grabbed the patrol boat's gunwale with her free hand. As Gaspar spun around, nearly losing his balance, she said, "Good morning again, Officer." And just loud enough for him to hear, "Let me talk to the kid."

"I don't know . . ." Gaspar began, but Tory was already unclipping the kayak's bowline from its cockpit fitting.

"Take this, please," she said, passing him the end. Automatically he accepted the line from her, and a half-second later she followed, swarming ungracefully over the gunwale and into his arms. He staggered backward, lost his footing, and dragged her to the deck on top of him.

"Holy shit, Tory!" he gasped, as she rolled off.

"I *am* sorry, Gaspar—are you all right?" she said and burst into helpless laughter.

"I guess," he replied. And then, his dark eyes snapping, "Hell, you can jump on me anytime."

"*Pas devant l'enfant*," she replied, without thinking. "Easy does it." She stepped to the gunwale. Erik was still bailing, but with little effect: the dinghy's stern was now so low that every second wave washed right over it, replacing the water he'd just heaved out. In the bow two big, wet brown-paper bags had split, spilling their contents onto the wooden floorboards . . .

*The wooden floorboards?* The Halvorsens' dinghy didn't have floorboards. Didn't have this boat's inflatable seat, either. Tory dropped to her knees, leaned over the patrol boat's side, and began grabbing at cans and boxes. "We'll get this stuff," she said. "But then you come aboard, and we'll tow her in. Agreed?"

Still scooping water over the dinghy's stern, the boy looked up at her and nodded. His eyes were red, she saw. And defiant.

She swept up another armful: spaghetti dinners, canned hash, bags of candy bars, a six-pack of sodas. So, she thought: Erik, like his older brother, was running away from home.

Back in the harbor, tied up to the patrol's float, Officer Ortega pulled out his pad of citation forms. Erik, whose color had begun to return, lowered his head as if to receive a blow. Tory felt her heart go out to him.

"You didn't have a life jacket aboard," said Gaspar, uncapping his pen. "I've got to write you up for it."

"Oh," said Erik, sounding dazed. He peered cautiously at the patrolman, and Tory suspected he might be holding his breath.

Without quite knowing why, she said, "That's funny. When I was in the Halvorsens' dinghy, it had two PFDs."

His wide, frightened eyes told her he'd caught her real meaning, but he wasn't going to give up without a fight. "Must've left them behind," he said.

"Live and learn," she said.

"I guess so," he replied. While Gaspar finished writing the citation, Erik never took his eyes off Tory. When they were alone, he said, "Why'd you do that?"

She was feeling chafed and hot in the wetsuit. Also conspicuous: fifty yards away, the rail of the *Point Hampton* was lined with blue-uniformed figures pretending not to stare; on the old Navy pier to which the cutter was tied, a dozen commercial fishermen and as many early-morning tourists watched with undisguised interest. "I'll tell you when I've got some answers," she said. "Why'd you steal the inflatable?"

"Father took ours. Left me on the *Jonah*. Urchin diver gave me a lift to shore." The sentences dragged out, one word after another, and then the dam broke: "I was going to put it back, honest. I just needed it for an hour, but it sprung a leak, and then the motor quit . . ." He shrugged, and she saw from the brightness of his eyes he couldn't trust himself to continue.

"So where'd you take it from—the dinghy float?" she demanded. He nodded. "Here's what you're going to do: You'll put it back, with a note saying you damaged it by accident and you'll pay for any repairs. You'll put my phone number on the note—and, believe me, I'll follow up. Okay?"

"Okay."

He wanted to trust her, she was sure of it, but something was holding him back. *In for a penny, in for a pound.* "What about this food? Most of it's still all right."

Clearly he had forgotten the soaked containers stacked on the pier behind him. "Miss Lennox . . ." he began, but it trailed off. She waited, saw the decision click into place. "I've got to . . . deliver this somewhere," he said.

*You mean to Junior?* was on her lips, but she saw his face close and changed her question just in time. "Has to go by boat?"

"No," he admitted slowly. "It's too late, anyway. Later I can carry it."

Her eye caught movement behind the second-floor windows of the Harbor Patrol office. Neal? Probably. "Later *we* can carry it," she said. "Now, I've got to get to work."

After the first uncomfortable month, Tory had begun to accept the unsociability of her principal subordinate, Chief Boatswain's Mate Braddock Washington. A short, stocky ex-Marine, the chief could be scrupulously polite, but he had no small talk whatever. He never brought his personal life to the office, and if he had any curiosity about Tory's, he didn't let it show. Probably (she suspected) because he already knew: knowing everything was part of a chief petty officer's job description, and in a service as small as the Coast Guard, personal reputations spread far and fast.

Once Chief Washington had decided Tory was serious about their mutual job, and once Tory had realized that taciturn wasn't the same as hostile, they managed to hammer out an effective working relationship. They occupied catty-corner desks in the same twenty-foot-square office, and entire mornings would pass, to the bewilderment of their shared clerk, YN2 Graziano, with no more than a half-dozen elliptical sentences exchanged between them. In the field, whether surveying oil spills or accident sites, they divided the work with automatic ease: the chief handled the heavy lifting and Tory shoveled out the endless snowstorm of forms and reports.

Today, however, she found herself needing to confide in someone, and Chief Washington had the obvious qualifications: old enough to be her uncle, if not her father, he was married to a woman Tory's own age and had a teenage son and daughter from his first marriage. But the wall of impersonality between them was high and thick. She could see no way to breach it.

"Helo's laid on for noon," the chief observed, without looking up.

"Oh. Right." She knew the context: a yachtsman had reported an oil spill near one of the dozen drilling platforms out in the

Santa Barbara Channel. A preliminary reconnaissance from the air was the best way to start investigating it, and the oil company was responsible for providing transportation. Normally, the prospect of a helo flight would have lifted Tory's spirits—she loved the un-trammeled view out the bubble nose, the sensation (if you could ignore the hellish racket) of unassisted flight. But not today.

Voices in the outer office interrupted her thought. One was Graziano, of course, though she couldn't hear the words. A second later a familiar head poked itself around the door frame. "Got a couple minutes?" asked Steve Merriam.

"For you, always." And as she took in his appearance, "What on earth happened to your face?"

He grimaced. "Keratosis. The old surfer's penance. I have to have 'em frozen off every once in a while."

It should've been no surprise: fair-skinned, almost pasty, Steve Merriam burned after a few minutes in the noonday sun, any time of year. And as he came into the office, she saw he was wearing a loose white shirt with long sleeves. "There, too? Does it hurt?" she said.

"Stings, mostly. Like a jellyfish bite," he replied. "How's it going, Brad?"

The chief shrugged. "Holding up. You guys want to be private?"

"Actually, I want both of you to hear this," Merriam said. He dropped bonelessly into the chair in front of Tory's big desk. "That guy you found in the water yesterday—somebody bashed him before he went in."

Memory of wet, cold, too-soft skin against her fingertips. She suppressed a shudder. "Couldn't have been an accident?"

"Not from the way he was popped: a blow more or less straight down, from in front, by someone a little taller."

"What else?" she asked.

Perhaps Steve heard her distaste: he threw her a quick, apprais-ing look before going on: "One hard swing. Our victim is stunned. He drops to his knees—onto concrete, from the way his pants and skin are roughed up—then falls or gets pushed into the water. Where he proceeds to drown."

Her imagination, shifting into high, sketched the scene as the police lieutenant spoke. Chief Washington broke the ensuing silence. "Any ideas about the weapon?"

"Matter of fact, yes," Steve replied. "Pine, probably a two-by-four, rotted enough to leave little chips embedded in the wound."

"A piece of scrap wood, you think?" said Tory, thinking out loud.

"Could be," Steve replied. "Assuming he was killed here at the harbor, there must be lots of that kind of stuff around."

"Less than you'd think," Tory said. "You couldn't expect to just grab something suitable off the ground. Plenty of scrap lumber just across Cabrillo Boulevard, though—in those empty lots where the homeless camp out."

Steve nodded. "It's got possibilities, but there's holes, too. First off, the homeless don't usually bash—they cut. And they don't move the casualties around. They just evaporate and leave the victim on the ground. Sure as hell they don't cart him two blocks to the harbor and dump him in."

"This guy was a homeless, you think?" asked Chief Washington.

"That," said Steve, "is the question. Let me lay out what we know so far, and you tell me." He glanced up at the wall clock and added, "If you've got the time."

"I've got the time," Tory said. *Especially since it's a problem that doesn't really involve me.*

"Okay. Dead guy's middle forties, average height, skinny but flabby, an alcoholic of long standing—before he fell in the drink, his liver could've burst into flame by itself."

"Lovely," said Tory.

"Anyway, it's the guy's skin that's unusual. Old dirt ingrained in the folds of his body: navel, armpits, buttocks—"

"I get the idea. He didn't wash," Tory interrupted.

"Oh, but he did," said Steve triumphantly. "He did wash parts of himself, practically scrubbed the skin off."

"I have a feeling I'll be sorry I asked," Tory said. "What parts?"

"Head and neck. Hands and forearms to above the elbows,"

Steve said. "He had a fresh haircut, but a two-day beard. And a very careful manicure, but his toenails were—"

"Unspeakable," said Tory firmly. "So what do you think—a job interview?"

"Or jail," the chief put in, then quickly corrected himself: "No, they'd just hose him down, not scrub him raw."

"What about his clothes?" Tory demanded. "I remember he was wearing work clothes—khaki shirt and trousers. Anything in the pockets?"

"No ID at all. One crumpled dollar bill, two matchbooks from State Street bars, and a clasp knife," Steve replied. "The clothes were more interesting: shirt's from Banana Republic; pants are from King's."

The chief's dark mahogany face had assumed the withdrawn look that Tory knew meant he'd lost the thread but wasn't about to admit it. The two times she'd seen Washington out of uniform, he'd been wearing jeans and a T-shirt, and there was no reason to suppose he'd ever been in Santa Barbara's more elegant clothing stores. "That's about a hundred and fifty bucks," she observed, as if thinking aloud. "Plus what for those cross-trainers he was wearing—another fifty?"

"If he bought them new, yes. And the sneakers were new, or nearly—fifty-five at Outfooter, where he probably bought the socks, too. The pants and shirt, we're guessing secondhand. They've been worn, but they don't quite fit our corpse. But the underwear . . ." He paused, grinning. "Let's just say the underwear is old, cheap, and dirty."

"Thank you," said Tory.

"Once we've got the guy's picture circulating, I'm hoping it'll all fall into place," Steve said.

"You haven't got a photo yet?" the chief said, not bothering to hide his surprise.

The police lieutenant shrugged. "You know how it is, photographing corpses—or maybe you don't. Sometimes they look so goddamned dead it throws witnesses off. You've got to touch the shot up before you can use it. That's what happened with this guy, even though he was only under for two days, just like Neal said."

The way Steve pulled himself up, and the quarter-second hesitation before Neal's name, told Tory everything. She felt her face go hot, but she forced herself to ask, "Didn't Neal think he recognized the body?"

"Neal thought he'd seen the guy around the harbor fairly recently, but he couldn't be any more precise than that," Steve said. "I'm hoping somebody else down here can do better—and I'm hoping you can help us check out the ID. Some of the folks down here are a little reluctant about talking to cops."

"Some of the folks down here are reluctant about talking to any uniforms," Tory corrected him. "But we'll do what we can."

From the helo it was obvious that the oil sheen—an oval patch two hundred yards in length that gleamed and glistened with every sunlit heave—could not possibly have come from the drilling platform a mile downwind.

"A seep, d'you think?" Tory asked. Oil had, after all, been seeping from cracks in the Santa Barbara Channel's floor for hundreds of years—the Chumash Indians had caulked their canoes with the tarlike crude. But Tory doubted it in this case, and the company technician agreed.

"Not a chance." The relief in his voice came through Tory's headset clearly. "Dumped from a ship in the westbound traffic lane—that's my bet. If you like, I'll check the platform's radar log."

"I'd appreciate it," Tory said. Down below them, the afternoon's carpet of whitecaps marched eastward toward Ventura, but as the helicopter closed the coast, the sea looked nearly flat beneath the high bluffs.

He heard the footsteps on the outside stairs—two pairs of feet—and looked up from the computer screen as the door opened. Tory was wearing what she called her office uniform—dark blue skirt, light blue short-sleeve blouse with ribbons and shoulder boards, officer's cap with its gold eagle. Its crisp lines, the shades of blue highlighted with touches of gold seemed to him precisely designed to set off her cover-girl blondeness. *Tropical Blue Delicious*, he'd called it once, and they'd both laughed.

"Hi," he said now. *Pretty smooth, Donahoe.*

She met his eyes and colored slightly. "You're busy. May we interrupt?" What he thought of as her Katharine Hepburn voice: the essence of cool superiority. When he'd told her so, her smile had lit the room. "Years of practice pay off," she'd said.

"Of course. What's up?" As he got to his feet, he saw the Halvorsen boy—Erik—sheltering behind her. *Fight or flight, he's ready for either one.*

Tory's glance flicked around the office and back to Neal. He read her thought as clearly as if she'd spoken, and she was right: the

148

low-ceilinged room, full of municipal desks and communications equipment, was too cold, too official-looking. "Let's move down the hall to my place," Neal said, opening the barrier to let them past the counter. "We can leave the door open, in case anybody comes in."

When Neal was appointed acting Harbormaster, he'd cleaned out the big end office his predecessor, Walt d'Andrea, had kept in a state of wild disorder. But because Walt was still on extended sick leave, Neal used the room mostly for meetings and interviews. It was a cheerful place, with big windows overlooking the harbor on two sides and a huge satellite photo of the channel and its islands covering one wall. Even the metal shelves crammed with regulations, edicts, and records looked harmless.

Neal waved Tory and Erik to seats by the larger window and dropped into the swiveling desk chair. Tory, as always, sat perfectly straight, hands in her lap, and almost made it look natural. Erik, however, was crouched on the very edge of his chair, watching her anxiously.

"This was my idea," she said. "Erik has gone along with it."

*But you leaned on him pretty hard.* Neal nodded, keeping his eyes on Tory.

"We—Erik and I—have an errand to run, and we need an escort," she continued.

"I see," said Neal.

The ghost of a grin shaped itself and was gone in an instant. "Maybe I'll explain anyway," she said. "You know Erik's big brother . . ."

"The invisible Junior. I know him," Neal said.

It was, her eyebrows told him, the wrong thing to say. "Junior," she repeated. "He's run away from his family." Neal nodded. "But you know that, too. Well, for reasons I won't go into, Junior's hiding out."

Neal's ears pricked up, but he saw Tory didn't want him to interrupt. "Erik's been buying food for him," she continued. "He brings it to a meeting place near Junior's . . . near where Junior's staying."

*And he brings it by boat. Except this morning the delivery misfired.*

"Yes," Tory said, and Neal saw she'd read his expression again. "Well, Erik knows another way to get the food to Junior, but it has to be after dark, and the route is a little . . ." She turned to Erik: "A little scary? Is that fair?"

The boy colored. "Maybe a little," he said.

Neal, who had mentally been matching the details of Gaspar Ortega's report to his own knowledge of the shoreline, wondered just how much the boy had told Tory. "So you want somebody to ride shotgun for you, is that it?" he said.

Erik opened his mouth, but Tory waved him to silence. "More or less," she said quickly. "We—Erik doesn't want you to actually appear, though. Just stand by in case you're needed."

"Ah," said Neal. "And not in uniform, right?"

"That would be better," Tory said.

"Suits me," Neal agreed. "We can meet at your place."

"My place? Why there?"

*So Erik hasn't told you where Junior's hiding.* "Because it's so convenient," he said.


"You're early," she said. He couldn't tell if she was annoyed or pleased, but she stood back to let him in. She was wearing a blue coverall, one of the older ones that failed to hide her figure, and a pair of hiking boots.

"Couple of things we need to square away before Erik turns up—*if* he turns up."

"He'll turn up." She led the way into her high-ceilinged living room, overlooked by the balcony with the bedroom behind it. Over the fireplace *Sailing Day*—*Nantucket* beamed down like an old friend, and on one of the leather couches Atrocious sat bolt upright, her head tilted, surveying him with her single baleful eye. The apartment, he realized, had become more like home to him than *Carpe Diem* ever had, and he was surprised to find it unchanged: for some reason he'd expected it to look different.

Atrocious jumped down and sauntered over to him, rubbed her side against his leg. Neal bent down and scratched just behind her large, slightly frayed ears. "Sounds like she needs a valve job," he observed and added, "You're saying Erik wanted me along?"

"She missed you. You were my idea."

"I've missed her." He straightened up. "We've got ten minutes, if Erik's on time. What the hell is all this about?"

"I'm hoping Junior will tell me," she replied. She was standing by the fireplace, apparently focused on the painting above it, but Neal knew she was organizing her thoughts. As if she'd suddenly come to a difficult decision, she turned to him. "Neal, there's something terribly wrong with the Halvorsens."

*With Erling, you mean.* He sat on the nearer couch, and Atrocious promptly jumped into his lap. Her claws—eighteen scimitars—sank into his thigh. "Tell me," he said between gritted teeth.

"At first I took things pretty much at face value," she began slowly. "I do that, you know."

"I've noticed."

She managed a quick grin. "All right, it was the kind of situation I'm a sucker for: good, well-intentioned man and his helpless kids being harassed by the city bureaucracy."

"We were harassing them, all right," Neal said. *But because sometimes you're the bureaucracy, too, you were glad to find yourself on the other side.*

"And they welcomed me—made me feel like part of their family," she said, her eyes locking on his. "That's really important to me, a family."

"I know," he said, aware as he spoke that he really didn't. Three thousand miles was barely enough distance between him and his parents, and if there was anything he shared with his older sister, he'd forgotten what it was. But Tory's affection for her own family—and theirs for her—was so clear it couldn't be overlooked.

"Anyway, when I got to know the Halvorsen kids, I could see they loved their father, but they're terrified of him, too." She paused, shook her head. "That's not putting it quite the way I mean. They're terrified of something *about* him, but none of them will talk about it. I'm hoping maybe Junior will tell me something—he at least had the nerve to break free."

He'll more than likely tell you something, Neal thought. But as a disinterested witness, Junior's no prize. "I understand Halvorsen's a real authoritarian," Neal offered. "D'you think that might be the problem?"

He touched a nerve, he saw. For a second he thought she was going to burst out, but when she finally spoke, her voice was fully under control. "You're not at all religious, are you?"

"Not even a little," he said, but of course she'd already known that.

"I've always taken it for granted," she said, more to herself than him. "Now—"

The doorbell cut off her words and, apparently, her train of thought. She seemed adrift, and Neal said: "I'll let myself out the patio, come to the front door in two minutes. How's that?"

"That's good," she said. And then, "Damn the Ephesians, anyway."

## LA MESA PARK; 2015 HOURS: TORY

"This way, Miss Lennox." Erik's voice, tense and unsteady, was coming from only a few feet ahead of her, but thanks to the twilight and the thick shrubbery he was nearly invisible. The narrow, twisting path wound sharply downward, switchbacking across the ravine's steep side. They might, Tory thought, have been miles away in the Los Padres forest, instead of a mere hundred yards from her own door.

The ravine, which began as a shallow gully somewhere up in the hills behind the city, was a streambed during Santa Barbara's brief winter rainy season, carrying storm runoff down through culverts and past backyards, disappearing under streets and reappearing again, picking up lesser streamlets and gradually gouging a deeper path until finally it pitched over the bluffs and spilled into the sea. But the other eight or nine months of the year it was dry, its sides overgrown with bushes, grass, and weeds until it was virtually invisible from Tory's apartment or from the city park next door.

She had known, vaguely, that there was some kind of deep furrow in the waste ground between her condo complex and the next

153

one. A family of foxes lived there—she'd seen them one morning, just after dawn, burrowing in the park's trash bin. But she had never realized how deep the cut ran or how much wild space there really was, tucked in below the homes that seemed so closely set.

Erik stopped to let her catch up. Despite the two big plastic bags he carried, he slipped easily through the underbrush, with only the occasional crackle of dead leaves crushed underfoot. "This is where they used to camp," he whispered. "The grass and stuff is all dead where they pitched the tent."

In the quickly gathering gloom, the flattened area in a little clearing beside the path was gray and spectral. A faint odor of human waste hung in the air. "So where'd they go?" she asked. "And who's *they?*"

Erik jumped as if he'd been stung. "Junior, I should've said. I don't know where he moved the tent—someplace down there," he added quickly.

Tory was conscious that Neal, who seemed able to move through the scrubby woods like a wisp of smoke, had materialized just behind her right shoulder. "Can you find him?" he asked.

"Sure. Maybe. You better wait," the boy replied. "He's only expecting me." He began to sidle off as he spoke, but Tory stepped forward and took him by the arm.

"Why don't you leave the food here? That way he'll have to come up here to get it," she said. She could sense Erik's reluctance, but after a moment he set down the two bags.

"It'd be better if Junior didn't see . . . him," he whispered, angling his head toward Neal.

"I'll take care of it," Tory replied and heard a ghost of a chuckle from behind her.

When Erik had vanished down the slope, she said, "I never imagined all this was here. How do you suppose Junior found it?"

Neal, a lean shadow, had moved up beside her. She felt an almost overpowering urge to touch him. "Junior didn't find it," he said quietly. "His buddy did—the other half of 'they.' " He took a cautious step into the clearing. "Probably a homeless—they camp around the edges of city parks a lot, because of the water taps and the bathrooms."

"Do you think Junior's . . . friend is out there someplace?" she asked. The idea didn't frighten her, she was interested to note, but it was a factor to bear in mind. She wondered if Neal was armed—her own handgun, the .32 her father had given her, was still in the drawer by her bedside.

"He might be," Neal said, and then: "They're coming."

A second later she heard the footsteps farther down the slope. Erik was saying something. She couldn't hear the words, but it sounded as if he was pleading with his brother. She half turned, but Neal had vanished. She took two steps into the clearing, where she could easily be seen, stood with feet apart and both hands visible, inhaled deeply to steady herself.

Two shapes, the taller one behind, appeared on the path. "Come on. She won't bite you," Erik whispered.

"Shut up, buttbreath." The older boy's tone was weary, nearly drained of emotion.

*He's made up his mind, one way or the other.* "Thanks for coming," she said.

"You got my food?" Junior demanded, a trace of belligerence creeping back into his voice.

"Right by the tree," she said.

With a wordless growl, Junior elbowed his brother out of the way. Crouching over the plastic bags, he rummaged first in one and then the other until he came up with a narrow box Tory recognized by its shape—cookies—and tore it open. By the sound of his crunching, she decided, he must have stuffed two or even three in his mouth at once. The cookies were followed by an entire Coke, swallowed down in a series of spasmodic gulps. At last he raised his head in Tory's direction. "What do you want?" he said.

She had tried to prepare a coherent argument, but it disintegrated as she opened her mouth. She heard herself say, "Something terrible is going to happen to your family. I think I can stop it—if you'll help me."

Five seconds' silence, broken only by Junior chewing. "Sure, you can stop it," he said at last. The sneer was audible, even if she couldn't see it. "And you already know how."

Her face went hot, but in the back of her mind a voice was saying, Don't boil over: he's testing you. "The one I'm most worried about is Martha," she said, surprised at her own calm. "And if—when—she snaps . . ." She let the words hang.

"Martha!" He managed to put a world of angry scorn in the name. "Didn't father tell you about me and Martha? Why should I give a shit about her? I got serious stuff to worry about."

She nearly snapped back at him, managed to pull back at the last instant. She stood unmoving, feeling the storm inside the youth who faced her.

"All right," he said suddenly. It was his first voice again, only even more exhausted. "Erik: get lost."

"What the hell—"

Genuine outrage, she decided, underlaid with relief. "Do what he says, Erik. Please."

The boy retreated up the path past her, grumbling as he went like a small, retreating thunderstorm.

"So what do you want to know about our wonderful family?" Junior said.

"Everything," she replied.

An hour later, back in her apartment, she said to Neal: "Do you believe him?"

He was standing by the mantel, looking up at the painting as if there were some secret hidden in it. After a moment, he said, "Yes." And added, "Most of it, anyway."

It was the answer she'd expected, but she felt herself swept by apprehension. "Sure—the excuses we can ignore," she agreed, keeping her voice even with an effort. "But even so . . ."

"What's left is pretty ugly," Neal said, nodding. He turned to face her. His dark eyes were withdrawn, as though he were still hearing Junior Halvorsen's halting confession, but he twisted his wide mouth into a wry grin. "The question is, what do we do now?"

*We:* for him, anyway, the team was clearly back in business. "We have to go to the authorities—Children's Services, whoever," Tory said. "This kind of thing is outside my experience. Thank God." Another thought struck her: "How could we let Erik go back to the boat? Maybe we can still catch him."

She had taken one step toward the door when she felt his hand on her arm. "Hold it." His certainty stopped her. "That was Erik's decision, and Junior backed him up—"

"But they're just children!" she exclaimed.

"In a family like that, you grow up fast," Neal replied. He paused, and she sensed he was sorting his thoughts, putting words to something that was, for him, transparently obvious. "When a kid has parents who're . . . unstable, he learns how to—what's the word?—manipulate them. Maybe not all the time and maybe not completely, but he gets to know which levers to pull."

"What if he pulls the wrong lever?" she demanded. "What then?"

He was looking right past her. "Then he gets belted, if he's lucky. But he bounces back."

"And if he's a she?"

The question brought him back, she saw. He seemed to search for an answer, then shrugged: "I don't know."

"I don't either," Tory confessed. "But I have the feeling Martha's about at the end of her rope."

"If she goes over the edge, so does Erling," Neal said. His absolute conviction terrified her. And she knew he was right.

"Maybe we can call . . ." Tory said. Two steps to the little kitchen. The phone book was on the counter. She flipped to the government pages at the front, and after a minute looked up. "Nothing under 'Children' or 'Family.' Maybe I should try 911."

"What would you tell them?" Neal said. "I'm a peace officer, and I sure couldn't justify emergency action based on the unsupported word of a teenage runaway with a juvenile record half a yard long—especially now he's disappeared again."

She saw at once he was right, and it infuriated her. "You'd just let it happen? Let Erling do that to Martha?" she demanded.

"Well, I won't." She could hear the unsteadiness in her voice, and it made her even angrier.

"What d'you mean?" He sounded alarmed.

"I'm going out there—out to the *Prophet Jonah*. And if you won't take me, I'll find someone who will."

"That's a terrible idea, and you know it," he snapped. She wanted to object, contradict, but she let him continue, his concern ringing clear: "He'll think you've come to submit, the way a woman should. Then you don't; you turn him down—in front of his children, the ones he's promised you to . . ." He shook his head. "If Erling's as tightly wound as Erik and Junior say, a disappointment like that could snap him."

"All right, all right," she said, holding up her hands in defeat. "But I've got to do something. I can't sit here and think of that poor girl . . ."

"You're right. Somebody's got to be out there. But who?"

The answer popped into her head so suddenly and so fully formed she could only gasp. Neal read her expression instantly. "Tell me."

"Erling's parishioners," she said. "Toto Boyle, MacInnes, Harris—the other fishermen. They'd be perfect."

"You think you can convince Toto that his hero's a lunatic who's been raping his own daughter?" Neal's disbelief was total, but she was already at the telephone, dialing.

"I know someone who can," she said to him.

The phone at the other end rang three times before someone picked it up. "Yes?" The voice was harsh, suspicious.

"Mrs. Boyle? Tory Lennox here. No, I don't want Toto. You're the one I need to talk to . . ."

## Harbor Office; Tuesday, 11:30 a.m.: Neal

"This version looks a little more human," said Steve Merriam, tossing a 5x7 glossy on Neal's desk. "See if it rings any bells."

The man facing the camera looked a lot more lifelike with his eyes closed, Neal thought. Even airbrushed, though, no one would take him for anything but a corpse. "I've definitely seen him. Around here, and recently," he said, feeling more annoyed than he'd expected to. "But I still can't pin it down."

"It'll come to you. Especially if you don't try to force it." Merriam dropped into the armchair beside the desk. "I've got a bunch more of these to pass out," he added. "And we know who the guy is—not that it tells us much."

"A homeless?"

Steve nodded. "Name's Vernon Benjamin. Been around town about a year. At least that was the date of his first arrest."

"For what?"

"Threatening a tourist. It didn't stick: she was going back to Germany in two days. Wouldn't press charges." He sighed. "Prob-

159

ably wouldn't have flown anyway—broad daylight, middle of lower State, her word against his. And the goddamned free speech thing."

Neal nodded sympathetically. Ever since a California appeals judge had declared that panhandling was an expression of political opinion, the street cops' hands had been tied. Tourist towns like Santa Barbara had seen an explosion of street begging, and even though most of the panhandlers were harmless, too zonked to do more than mumble at passersby, there were a belligerent few who scared the daylights out of elderly visitors. Upset some who weren't elderly at all, Neal recalled. "You have to be a woman to understand," Tory had said. The thing is, you never know, he reflected. Take Erling Halvorsen. "Listen, Steve," he said. "We've got a potential problem of our own—"

"If you mean the floating minister," Steve interrupted quickly, "Tory's already been at my throat about him. Nothing we can do, but I steered her to a couple of people who can at least tell her what she needs to back up a formal complaint."

It was better than nothing, Neal decided, and it lowered his own level of guilt a notch or two. "About this Benjamin. What were his other arrests for?"

"Little stuff," Steve replied. "Two fights outside bars. Woman caught him peeing on her Bentley in the Paseo Nuevo lot. No hesitation about filing charges that time," he added, grinning. "Tom Argent in the City Attorney's office had some trouble convincing her it wasn't a capital offense."

"Seems to me we're talking about a belligerent dummy. The kind of guy who might get in one fight too many," Neal offered.

"Something like that. Oh, there's one other thing: Benjamin made a big thing about being a Vietnam vet, but he wasn't—at least not under that name."

"Benjamin who?" said Tory's voice.

Neal, who had been facing the window, spun his chair so fast that he nearly lost his balance. She was standing in his office doorway, wearing a soberly dark blue suit he'd never seen before and a plain white blouse. *She didn't sleep last night.* "Your floater," he said after a moment. "He's a homeless named Vernon Benjamin."

"This is him," Steve added, passing her a glossy. "Better than the first shot."

"A thousand percent," she agreed, taking the photo.

"About this morning," Steve began, but Neal, seeing her expression, waved him to silence.

She turned the glossy first one way, then the other, her lips pursed. "Yes," she said to herself, then raised her eyes to Neal's. "Don't you recognize him? One of the EMTs when Wilbur Andreas had his accident?"

"Jesus! Of course it is." Neal picked up his own copy of the shot. *How could I have missed that?*

"You're positive?" Steve asked.

"No question."

"But when you helped pull him out of the water . . ."

She grinned shamefacedly at Steve, and her haggard face turned a shade of pink that sent a chill up Neal's spine. "It's my way of dealing with really unpleasant sights," she said. "I seem to be looking right at them, but I just unfocus."

"Wait a minute," said Neal, whose mind had been racing ahead. "Steve, this guy Benjamin couldn't have got a job as an EMT, could he?"

"Sounds impossible to me," said the police lieutenant, regarding Neal closely. "What don't I know here?"

The words wanted to tumble out of his mouth; it was all he could do to restrain his excitement: "The other day, when Wilbur Andreas—the artist, you know?—spilled acetone in his eyes, Tory was the first on the scene. In fact, she phoned for the ambulance—"

"No, I didn't," Tory interjected. And as both men turned to stare, added, "I thought you did, before you came down the ramp."

She seemed on the point of saying more, but Neal held up his hand. "Whoever called it, the ambulance was there in a couple of minutes," he said. "There were two EMTs—a woman and this Benjamin. I remember he had awful breath . . ."

"Booze?" said Steve.

"I'd have said garlic and tooth decay," Neal replied. From the corner of his eye, he saw Tory's moue of distaste. "But the woman was in charge."

"Definitely," Tory agreed. "And I think she called him Ben."

"Did Ben have a name for her?"

"Not that I remember," Tory said.

"But there's something else," Neal said. "Wilbur's accident . . ."

He paused, and Steve, smiling faintly, said, "I did wonder about that, at the time. My wife said I had a nasty, suspicious mind."

"What about Wilbur's accident?" Tory asked, and her tone told him she'd heard his reluctance.

There was no way to fudge it, he decided. "Sunday evening, I went to Wilbur's big show, at Feverel's gallery." And seeing Tory's raised eyebrow added, "I went with Rebecca Jardine, the gal who produced Wilbur's segment of *Making Things Right.*" He waited for Tory to say whatever was clearly on the tip of her tongue, but when she didn't, he went on: "The biggest painting there was the one called *Fools' Anchorage*—"

"*Southeast Gale—Fools' Anchorage,*" Tory murmured.

"Right. Anyway, in the picture there's a trawler right in the center foreground, Erling Halvorsen's boat, back when she was the *Klamath Goddess:* the name's right on the bow."

"That's right," said Tory.

"Only somebody's added a little purple-and-gold banner at the masthead. And that wasn't on the boat till the Halvorsens moved her back out to the anchorage—after Wilbur's so-called accident."

"Oh, my God," Tory whispered.

"I think I see," Steve said.

"Wilbur does have a reputation for touching up his work after it's done," Tory said. And in response to Steve's unspoken question added, "I was thinking of buying one for myself. So naturally I did a little research."

"Naturally," said Steve, his eyes flicking to Neal, but not so quickly that Tory missed it.

"He really is good," she said, coloring slightly. "As good as Stobart, only of course Wilbur's subjects are all contemporary."

"Out of curiosity, what does a Wilbur go for?" Steve asked.

"Well, they were asking one eighty-five for *Southeast Gale* yesterday afternoon," Tory said. "Up twenty from Sunday night."

"That's one hundred and eighty-five thousand *dollars?*" Steve asked, pronouncing the number with meticulous care.

Tory nodded. "It's much the most expensive, though. Figure fifty on average—and rising fast."

"I'm impressed," Steve said. He did not, Neal noted, ask the obvious next question. Instead, he heaved himself upright and continued, "The point, however, is that one of the players in what may be a major swindle has got himself murdered."

"Puzzly puzzle, wonder why," murmured Neal, not quite under his breath. "It's a line from a John Lennon book," he explained, seeing their startled expressions.

"It's a good question, whoever asked it," said Steve. "What's wrong, Tory?"

The near-exhaustion had vanished from her face. "I just remembered: when Wilbur was hurt—or whatever—the person who supposedly saw it happen was Junior Halvorsen."

"So if something's going on, he's part of it," Steve said. "Only you said he's faded back into the boonies."

"That's right," Tory replied. Neal could see her mind was racing. She turned to face him: "When I was talking to Junior last night, about his family, do you remember what he said? 'I've got serious stuff to worry about.'"

"Something like that," Neal agreed. "Steve, I think there's a better place to start."

*"Back in half an hour,"* Steve read aloud. "Half an hour from when?"

"Nobody inside," said Neal, his cheek pressed to the window.

"That sign's been there two hours. At least," said a man's angry voice from behind them.

Tory turned to see a well-dressed couple—maybe a little too well-dressed—on the curb. The man had an angular face on which his oddly thick lips seemed out of place. He looked to Tory like someone who pouted a lot. The woman at his side—short, round, pink—was clearly his buffer, the one who absorbed his tantrums and scattered apologies in his wake. "We had an appointment with Jock at ten," she said. "Are you waiting for him, too?"

"Drove all the way up here from Santa Monica, just to look at this damned blind painter's stuff," the man put in.

"Everybody says his work is just wonderful," the woman added.

"I don't care if he's the next Grant Wood. I've had enough," the man snorted. He stalked down the street toward a vast black Mercedes, fumbling with a key case as he walked. Clucking dolefully, the woman trotted behind him.

"What do you think?" Neal asked, staring after them.

"They look like serious buyers to me," Tory said. "I don't see Jock passing up people like that unless he had to."

"Agreed," said Steve. "I'll call headquarters: get his home address."

"It's on Alameda Padre Serra," Tory said. "Wait a minute." She pulled a card case from her handbag and extracted a slightly over-size cardboard rectangle. "Here." And in response to Steve's raised eyebrow added, demurely, "I'm almost a customer. I've got an open invitation to examine his private collection."

From the corner of her eye she watched Neal's face turn to stone. Steve followed her look, and his lips twitched. "Does his private collection include etchings?" he asked.

"I wouldn't be surprised," Tory replied.

"Well, this must be the place," she said dubiously, braking to a crawl.

"The number's right," Steve observed. "But it's not exactly what I expected, either."

She pulled the Honda in to the curb. The Mustang that had been on her tail for the past three blocks roared past in a cloud of bad language and half-combusted exhaust. *Rise above, Tory.* "This is the Riviera, isn't it?" she said. "I expected something a little more . . ."

"Posh?" suggested Neal.

"Well, less wedged-in," she said. But the houses that lined both sides of Alameda Padre Serra were not, by Santa Barbara standards, particularly impressive. The heart-stopping view of the city far below and the channel beyond must be what draws them, she thought. For sure it isn't the road. Clinging to every curve of the hillside, APS (as the natives called it) managed to be two lanes wide only by engineering sleight-of-hand. And the road's twisting narrowness seemed to bring out the frustrated racer in local drivers.

Jock's house was smaller than most, a white bungalow with a

dormer window, perched above its own cavelike garage, dug into the hillside. The garage door drooped on its hinges, and the concrete steps up to the house looked as if something had been chewing on them. "Car's in the garage: a red Triumph," Steve said.

"That sounds right," Neal observed absently. He was standing on the steps staring up at the house, shading his eyes with one hand. "I don't see any signs of life."

Tory's skirt was too tight for the high, steep risers, and she had to sidle awkwardly up the steps, with her two companions watching. The front door—badly in need of paint, she noted—had one of Jock's business cards wedged behind the dusty glass. Inside, the entry hall was dark, but she could make out paintings everywhere, hung frame to frame on the walls and stacked on the floor. She pressed the bell, which didn't work, and rapped the glass with her Academy ring.

From just behind her, Neal said, "Looks like nobody's home."

A part of her wanted to take his word for it, but she said, "Californians don't go out and leave their car behind. Anyway, what about Wilbur?"

Steve's shoes scraped on the concrete steps. His voice, a little out of breath, said, "I suppose the door's locked."

The brass knob was warm to her hand. And loose. "Not locked," she said, feeling her stomach tighten. She pushed the door open and leaned through it. Sharp smell of fresh acrylic paint, and under it the furry odor of dry rot. "Hello?" she called. "Anyone home?" The paintings, now that her eyes had adjusted to the gloom, were obviously Wilbur's, dozens of them.

Her eye caught, down the hall, a flash of movement from a beaded doorway curtain. "Jock, it's Tory Lennox. Come on out and sell me something."

There was a shuffling noise from behind the doorway. Beside her, Steve put his hand under the hem of his loose shirt. She took two deliberate steps forward, her high heels echoing on the uncarpeted wood. Now she could see Jock's feet below the beaded curtain—his tasseled loafers, made from the skin of some probably endangered reptile, were appallingly unforgettable.

"I wanted to show my friends the painting, Jock. I hope you put it aside the way you said you would." Steve and Neal, who had followed her silently into the hallway, were looking at her oddly.

"No, no—I've got it here, Tory." Jock's voice was shaky and higher than she remembered, almost an old man's. From Neal's expression he'd noticed the difference, too.

"Good," she said. "We'll just have a look." One quick forward step, on the ball of her foot, and she snatched the beaded curtain aside. Her first thought was that Jock, facing her and swaying slightly, looked nearly as dead as the man in Steve's photo. His face was the yellow of a faded legal pad, which made the circles under his glazed eyes appear nearly black. And although his tan slacks and striped shirt, with the top three buttons open, were immaculate, they somehow had the air of having been disarranged and then hastily straightened.

"You'll have to excuse me: I'm a little under the weather," he said, with a ghastly smile. "Let me get . . ." His reedy voice trailed into silence as his eyes lit on Neal. Jock's face turned a shade paler, and his smile went rigid. ". . . Get your painting," he said. "I put it right here." He turned, moving with clearly painful slowness, and began to fumble among the unframed canvases stacked on their edges along the wall.

"You look dreadful, Jock. What's wrong?" Tory asked.

"Fell down a flight of stairs," he replied, not turning. "Painful but not serious . . . Ah, here we are."

Even in the dimly lit hallway the painting—a lonely harbor edged with dark green beetling cliffs, and two urchin divers' boats, one a vivid Prussian blue, riding at anchor among bright red buoys—made Tory's breath catch in her throat. Jock suspended the canvas from an empty hook screwed into the wall and stepped back.

Neal leaned forward to peer at the date in the lower left-hand corner. "Painted two years ago, so the blue boat must be Matty Groves's *Cutthroat*," he said. "Wilbur sure got her right—trimmed down by the head. That was what sank her, in the end."

Jock caught Tory's eye. Even injured, he managed a faintly superior smile that annoyed her more than she would have expected. "I'm sure you recognize the place, too, Mr. . . . Donahoe: San Miguel Island," he said.

"Cuyler Harbor," Neal agreed, nodding. "I see you've still got Wilbur's big piece on the gallery wall."

"It's been sold," Jock said, his voice flat.

Steve, who had managed near-invisibility standing behind Neal, coughed meaningfully. "Oh, I'm sorry," she said. "Jock, this is Steve Merriam, of the Santa Barbara police."

She had to admire Jock's self-possession, as he murmured something appropriate and shook the cop's hand. Or perhaps he was just numb. In any case, Steve wasted no time: "I wanted to talk to you about Vernon Benjamin, Jock."

Jock's "Who?" sounded to Tory completely genuine, but a half-second later he blinked, then asked, "Is he a painter?" in a tone just this side of coy.

Steve put on his knowing cop smile and pulled the brown envelope from his pocket. "This is him. Ring a bell?"

"My goodness. He looks quite dead." *That photo was no surprise: Jock was ready for it.*

"Do you know him?" She could hear the frustration, tightly controlled, in Steve's voice and so, apparently, could Jock.

"I'm afraid not. Never seen him in my life—or his," Jock replied. His skin was parchment-colored, but he sounded entirely calm. And there was no shaking him. He'd never seen the dead Vernon Benjamin, nor either of the EMTs who'd carried Wilbur to the ambulance. Only when Steve mentioned the ophthalmologist, Dr. Merida, did Jock seem to waver.

"I did meet him," the gallery owner said. "At the TV show."

"For the first time," Steve said.

"Absolutely," Jock replied.

"Well, maybe we'll talk to Wilbur, then," said Steve.

"He's not here," Jock replied, too quickly.

"Oh? D'you know where he is?" Steve sounded bored, as if his question were number two hundred on a list he'd been handed. It was something Tory had noticed before in him: as he closed in on someone, his voice got slower and lazier, his normally alert expression seemed to blur with disinterest.

"Wilbur? I don't really know," said Jock. He probably meant to sound unconcerned, Tory thought, but the muscles along his jaw were bunched, and the whites of his eyes showed.

"You don't really *know?*" Steve demanded, coming suddenly, aggressively alive, as if he'd been plugged into a wall socket. "A blind man who's your meal ticket, and you just let him wander off to play in traffic? Give me a break, Jock."

Steve's first verbal assault didn't break Jock, nor his second, but at the third, his back against his own wall, he said, "He left early this morning. I think he was with his friend from the harbor. The kid."

"What kid, Jock?" Steve insisted.

Tory found herself feeling almost sorry for the gallery owner, who seemed near tears and completely flustered. "D'you mean Junior Halvorsen?" she said.

Steve's sidelong glance was venomous, and Jock nearly fell into her arms with relief. "Junior!" he cried. "That's it: that's the boy's name. A wiseass if there ever was one."

"Isn't that the boy who witnessed Wilbur's accident?" Steve's utterly neutral tone was an accusation in itself. An ugly tide of color flowed into Jock's face.

"Yes, that's the one. And no: I don't know where they went," he said defiantly.

Five minutes later, as they stood by the door, Jock said: "I suppose you're not really interested in the painting, Tory."

"On the contrary: I've brought a check. Certified," she said. Jock registered what looked like genuine surprise, while Neal simply nodded—but was it approval of her choice or confirmation of his worst suspicions? Steve, of course—once a cop, always a cop—tried to get a look at the amount, but Jock simply placed the check, still folded, in his pocket.

"If you'll wait a second, I'll wrap it," he said.

"That's okay. You can send it to my apartment—the address is on the check," she said.

His eyes met hers. "I think it'd be best if you took it."

Buckling her car seatbelt, Tory said: "Jock's got a certain amount of class. In spite of those awful shoes. Did you believe that about falling down the stairs?"

"In a one-story house? Sure," Steve said from the backseat, which he was sharing with the wrapped picture.

"My guess is that somebody worked him over," said Neal, beside her. "I wonder who."

"Perhaps a disappointed customer," Tory offered. "Someone who bought a blind painter's masterpiece and found it wasn't."

"So you don't think he's blind, either," Steve said. "Well, why don't we go see the man who really knows?"

"The eye doctor?" said Tory, unsurprised. "You've got it. But don't you want to have someone keep an eye on Jock?"

"You may be right. In fact, now that I think it over, I'm sure you are," Steve said. The clear respect on his face pleased her.

"You can use my cell phone to call in, if you like," she said. Without a word, Neal opened the glove compartment, took out the phone, and passed it over his shoulder. He was wearing what she thought of as his Inca look—blank and impenetrable—and she would have given a lot to know what he was thinking. Why do I care? she asked herself.

## MILPAS STREET; 1:15 P.M.: NEAL

"It should be right along here," Neal said, as Tory guided the Honda slowly down a stretch of Milpas a few blocks north of the 101 freeway. In the last couple of years, fast food places seemed to have spawned out of control on both sides of the street, outnumbering the remaining shops and offices.

"We could pull over for a quick bite," Tory offered. Her tone was noncommittal, but Neal remembered that the Coasties ate well before noon—and that Tory's conception of the basic food groups was largely restricted to grease, salt, and sugar. How she survived, much less bloomed, on such a diet still mystified him.

"There: 'Ramón Mérida, M.D.'" Steve said suddenly. Neal saw the lettering an instant later, on the front window of a one-story structure that had probably begun as a private home before being remodeled, more or less, into an office. "What's *cirujano oftálmico?*" he added and in the next breath half answered himself: "Ophthalmic something."

"Surgeon," said Neal. "Or surgery—I'm not sure which."

Tory deftly slipped the Honda into the only visible curbside

171

space. "Surgeon. It's on the sign by the door," she said, setting the parking brake. Her manner told Neal she'd gone into super-efficient mode, which meant she was feeling uncertain about something. It also meant she wasn't ready to talk about whatever it was.

He was reaching for the door handle when Steve said, "Hold on a second." And when they had turned to face him: "Look, I don't mind you guys coming along, but let's not get sidetracked here. It doesn't matter what kind of scam Jock and Wilbur are running. I'm looking for a killer, not a con man."

"What do you want us to do?" Tory asked. She sounded wary, Neal thought.

"My guess," he said, "is that the fraud is connected to the murder, and the good doctor's connected to the fraud. Whatever he can tell us about the murder's going to be incidental."

Tory was nodding impatiently even before Steve had finished. "Of course, the other EMT is the link. She's the one you want to find."

"But Merida's probably the one with the most to lose. If he knows about Benjamin's murder, he must feel real exposed. And if he doesn't"—a wolfish grin stretched Steve's unremarkable face— "if he doesn't, then I'm going to make sure he gets the full picture. Your mission, if you choose to accept it, is to play the nice guys— sympathetic, understanding, that kind of thing. Don't promise anything, but make him think if he cooperates, he could still come out clean. Okay?"

"I suppose so," Tory replied, without enthusiasm.

The waiting room, Neal guessed, had once been a screened porch. The badly fitted windows were clearly a later addition, and he could feel the uneven planking right through the thin carpet. Seated in an assortment of uncomfortable-looking chairs, eight or ten patients, most of them obviously Hispanic, regarded the new arrivals with resigned apprehension. Inside the original front door, behind a scarred desk, Merida's nurse, a solid, corseted blonde in her late fifties, sat like a watchdog, seeming to Neal suspicious and uneasy in about equal parts. Apparently she decided that Steve looked least unlike a patient. "Do you have an appointment?" she asked him.

"Not exactly," he replied. Stepping up to the desk he raised the edge of his shirt just high enough so she could see the bottom of his badge. "I need to talk to Dr. Merida. Would you tell him it's about Wilbur Andreas?"

A long moment of obvious reluctance, and then the nurse picked up the phone and punched a single digit. In the silence the interoffice ring was clearly audible through a closed door behind her. "Doctor, there's a . . ." Her voice dropped to near-inaudibility, ". . . police officer here. He says—" Interrupted in mid-sentence, she listened, a look of surprise on her face. "Why, yes," she said. "Two men and a woman." To Steve: "If you'll wait a couple of minutes, Doctor will see you."

"Steve?" said Tory, urgency in her voice.

"Let's go," said the police lieutenant, brushing past the desk. Tory was on his heels, moving fast in spite of her hobbling skirt; Neal, bringing up the rear, shook off the indignant nurse's grasping hand. The office door was locked, and Steve knocked hard, rattling the flimsy wood. "Dr. Merida? Police: open up!"

"What are you doing?" the nurse cried out.

Steve knocked again. Getting no answer he grasped the knob with both hands, lifting the door upward. "Hit it!" he gasped to Neal, who slammed into the wood with his shoulder. The door popped inward, and Neal, off balance, staggered into the office. It must originally have been the master bedroom, he saw at once—old-fashioned tongue-and-groove planking, with several coats of white paint slapped over the original stain. Across a big, cluttered desk lay a cellular phone on a doctor's white jacket, casually folded, and behind it the window to the street was half-open.

"Jesus!" snarled Steve, pushing past Neal. He thrust his head and shoulders out, just as Tory called from behind them, "In here! Quick!"

Still moving forward, Neal skidded on the waxed floor, bouncing painfully off the doctor's desk, before his Top-Siders gripped the highly polished wood. He knew from Tory's voice—anguished,

tightly controlled—that it was going to be bad, but nothing prepared him for what he saw. The bathroom off the office was small,
its open doorway narrow, and the blood was everywhere—gouts
like scarlet explosions on the flowered wallpaper, thick splashes
across the sink, the floor, and most of all the gray-faced man who
sat sprawled on the toilet, his head thrown back, arms clutched
across his chest.

Neal's instant impression was of a desperate body wound: heavy
red spurts gushed between the man's forearms, but Tory—on her
knees beside him, dragging at her belt—threw Neal a glance over
her shoulder, called out, "It's his wrists!"

*Tourniquet.* The thought galvanized him. As Tory wrapped two
turns of belt around the man's left forearm and drew them up
tight, Neal reached over her and seized the high, arching sink
spout. A single twisting wrench tore it free just above the faucet.
"Here's a lever," he said, working it between belt and skin.

"Other arm," was all she replied, twisting the spout to tighten
the tourniquet.

"Right." He yanked his own belt off, was half blinded by a spurt
of blood as he struggled to knot the leather around Merida's right
forearm. But what to tighten it? His eye lit on the plumber's helper
wedged behind the toilet. As he jammed the wooden handle beneath the belt, he heard Steve's voice from the office behind him,
rapping out instructions to the 911 operator.

"Not me—in there," said Tory for the third time, to the EMTs
with the litter. It was easy to understand their mistake, Neal
thought: though the drying blood gave her blue suit a curious rusty
sheen, it was still appallingly red against her pale skin—blotched
on both knees, splattered on her face and neck, and covering her
hands and wrists like gloves. She was leaning with her seat braced
against Merida's desk, but Neal no longer thought she might faint
or be sick.

Steve Merriam, who had managed to remain entirely unspotted,
put down the phone. "So Jock called Merida while we were en
route. I should've thought of that," he said, clearly annoyed.

The litter rolled out, two IV stands wobbling above the phalanx of attendants who didn't quite screen its occupant. As the wheels bumped over the office door's threshold, Merida groaned. Tory, already ashen, winced, and Neal moved unobtrusively to her side. His hands and forearms were as red as hers, but he had stripped off his shirt and tossed it in a wastebasket. He groped for something to say, came up only with "I think he'll make it."

"I wonder if we did him any favor," Tory said. Neal followed her gaze to a framed photograph lying on its back: a middle-aged woman with a heavy, brooding face towered over two young girls who looked as if they might grow up mirror images of her.

"What I wonder," said Neal, "is if he called our missing witness before he tried to kill himself." He was reasonably sure of the answer, wanted only to move Tory's mind off the track it was on.

"I'm betting he did, on the cell phone," said Steve. "Maybe he thought we couldn't trace it—lots of people think that, maybe because there aren't any wires to tap."

"I want to get this stuff off me," Tory said, speaking very precisely. "Neal, would you mind seeing me home?" Her face was expressionless, but he felt his heart surge.

"Of course," he said.

She could sense Neal willing himself not to ask if she'd like him to drive. At the curb she paused, feeling in her handbag for the car keys. Without meaning to she looked down; the sight of her own hand, rinsed of its sheath of blood but with reddish brown half-moons under the nails, made her stomach clench. She raised her face to Neal's. The concern in his eyes warmed her, even as it hardened her determination. "I'm all right," she said.

A matter-of-fact "Let's go," and he got into the passenger seat.

Her first attempt at putting the key into the ignition failed. She forced herself to take a long, deep breath and got it the second time. The engine caught and settled down, and she shifted into first. *Look, signal . . . go.* The Honda lurched twice getting away from the curb, to the accompaniment of blaring horns from behind them, and she saw from the corner of her eye that his hands, folded in his lap, were white-knuckled. "You can scream if you'd like," she said.

"Maybe later," he replied. She saw—or thought she did—a fleeting grin.

By the time she turned west onto Cabrillo, her nerves were under control. "You agree with Steve about the cell phone," she said.

"Yes. I assume Jock called Merida and Merida called Ms. X on it, to avoid the office line."

She nodded, glanced quickly off to the left, where Fools' Anchorage gleamed in the afternoon sun. The water was oily calm, but the *Prophet Jonah*, riding on her mooring, rolled slowly in the barely perceptible swell. Her purple-and-gold pennant drooped from the masthead. *What's happening out there?* "Here's what I think," she said, to dispel the possibilities. "I think Ms. X is more than just a link between the doctor and Jock. I bet there's a personal relationship."

"With Merida?" Neal asked. He didn't sound surprised.

"Probably with him, but maybe with Jock, too," she replied. "Do you remember what she looked like?"

"Not too bad—blonde, fortyish, on the stringy side," he replied immediately.

She found she didn't want to expose her theory to the light, but having gone this far, couldn't pull it back. "Would you believe her as Merida's lover?" Automatically she swung the Honda into the left-turn pocket for the harbor entrance, caught herself with a muttered "Damn!" and pulled back into the center lane.

He was silent until they'd passed the City College stadium and started up the hill to the Shoreline Park bluff, then said, "Tell me."

"We leave Jock, and he calls Merida to warn him we're coming," she said. "Merida calls Ms. X to warn her, but before he can get away himself, we've arrived. He panics and slashes his wrists. Make sense?" Her voice was under control, but her palms were damp on the steering wheel: shock, of course. She knew she'd be shaking in a minute—but in another minute she'd be home.

"Pretty much," said Neal. "But if you're right about Merida and Ms. X, that might make suicide look reasonable to him: career, reputation, family all blown—assuming Mrs. Merida's anything like her photo."

It took a man to think of suicide as reasonable, Tory thought, just as she started to shiver uncontrollably. She clamped down on the wheel, but it didn't help.

"Hundred more yards," Neal said.

*He could have patronized and said, "You can do it," and he could have put me down and said, "Pull over: I'll drive."* "Hundred and fifty," she said.

When she came out of the shower, wrapped in a towel, he was sitting naked on the end of her bed, scanning her annotated copy of *Federal Requirements for Commercial Fishing Industry Vessels* and stroking Atrocious with his free hand. The cat was lying on her back, all four legs outstretched, purring hoarsely. Tory's blood-stained clothes—and Neal's—were nowhere in sight. "Your underwear and my stuff are in the washer," he said, not looking up. "I put your dress in the trash."

"Thanks. The shower's all yours."

He got to his feet, tossing the booklet on the bed: "How anybody can make sense of those regs sure beats me."

"That's the way we like it," she replied, aware she wasn't quite matching his tone. Maybe that bare-bottomed insouciance was something men learned in locker rooms. Atrocious, conscious of being ignored, jumped off the bed and stalked out of the room, tail high.

"Toto Boyle called. Left a message—he sounded pretty uptight," Neal said.

"I'll call him back." *And get away from you before I make a fool of myself.*

She came up the stairs two at a time, and he must have heard her: his dripping head emerged from behind the bathroom door. "Toto?" he said.

"Erik, actually," she replied. "He wants to talk to you right away."

Neal looked surprised. "To me?"

"That's what he told Toto. He doesn't want me to come out to the *Jonah.*" *And in case you were wondering, the* Jonah's *the last place on earth I want to go.*

She had the strongest feeling that her unsuppressable thought, still wrapped in shame, had flown straight into his head. But all he said was, "Can I borrow a set of your sweats?"

"Of course. You know where they are." There was so much more she wanted to say, the words brimming up, but what came out was, "Atrocious won't do that for me: lie on her back while I scratch her belly."

She watched him run through and discard, in no more than a half-second, several probably suggestive responses—the kind that would have set them laughing, only a week before. "I guess she trusts me," he said mildly, and added, with a kind of smile, "Another instance of feline misjudgment, you were about to say."

"Was I? Why don't you put some pants on."


"I thought you said Erik didn't want you to come out to the *Jonah*," Neal said. He was standing at *Harbor 3*'s helm, and she found herself thinking how utterly right he looked behind the wheel.

"He did," she replied. *This could be a big mistake, but how can I not go?*

"You don't have to be on-scene commander all the time," Neal said, as if answering her unspoken question.

"I'm just a passenger."

"You could stay out of sight, in the cabin," he suggested.

"Maybe not *that* much of a passenger." And to cut him off: "Are you going to tie alongside?"

"No." For an instant she thought he was annoyed, then saw he was only preoccupied. Ahead of them, the *Prophet Jonah* was corkscrewing with sullen slowness in the building westerly chop. As Neal swung the patrol boat in an easy arc, Erik popped out of the after hatch, stood balancing on the deck. A moment later Erling's head and shoulders appeared in the hatchway. Neal stopped *Harbor 3* dead in the water no more than two yards off the trawler's quarter. "What's up, Erik?" he called.

The boy stood in a tensed crouch, his eyes fixed on *Harbor 3*'s padded gunwale. If he saw Tory, he gave no sign, but Erling had spotted her and was pulling himself laboriously out of the hatch.

His face was puffy and mottled, almost as if he'd been crying. Through the cabin porthole she saw another man's bulky shape. "What's wrong with Erik?" she asked.

Without answering, Neal reached out and twitched *Harbor 3*'s twin shift levers, one into forward, the other into reverse. In a sudden boil of wake, the patrol boat's stern kicked dangerously close to the trawler's side just as Erik coiled himself and sprang. He cleared the patrol boat's gunwale and landed in a heap on deck, just as Neal spun *Harbor 3* away. "Don't try this at home," he said.

"You've got to find my brother," Erik said, struggling to his feet.

"We'd love to," Tory said. "Is he still hiding in the brush with his friend?"

"No. Vern . . . went away. I don't know where he is," Erik mumbled, his eyes on the deck.

*Vern—Vernon. Of course.* Over the boy's bent head, Tory and Neal stared at each other. "Vern who?" Tory said gently. "What's his last name?"

"How should I know? I only met him once," Erik snapped.

*He's not angry; he's terrified. Why?*

It was as if Neal had read her thought and leapfrogged over it: "Was that when Junior and Vern had a fight?" He leaned forward slightly. "Down by the launch ramps?"

The boy's face was a mask of agony. "Junior didn't hit him!"

"Who, then?" Neal said. And as Erik hesitated, added, "Vern's dead."

Erik's face closed like a trap, and he shook his head. Neal's overdone it, Tory thought, but the boy said, all in a burst, "It was the other guy. He came in a Corvair, only it belonged to the woman."

"Blonde woman, thin, a little older than I," Tory put in.

Erik's eyes widened. "You already know, so why're you asking me?"

*Bingo.* "Did you hear their names—the guy's and the woman's?" she asked.

"Not his," Erik said. "Junior called her Lorraine."

"You'd recognize them again," Neal said.

"No!"

*He won't be pushed further, at least not now.* Neal seemed to read the message in Tory's eyes and shrugged almost imperceptibly. "So how'm I supposed to find Junior?" he asked.

Erik blinked several times before he said, "He went with Mr. Andreas."

"Mr. Wilbur Andreas, the blind artist," Tory said.

"Oh, he's not so blind," Erik said. Clearly Wilbur's sight didn't interest him much.

"Where'd they go?" Neal said.

The boy seemed to be having second thoughts, and Tory wondered if the uniform Neal was now wearing might have something to do with it. "Look, we don't want your brother or Mr. Andreas to get hurt. That's the most important thing."

"San Miguel," Erik muttered. And seeing Tory's bewilderment, repeated, "San Miguel, the island. That's where Junior and Mr. Andreas went."

## 4:30 P.M.: NEAL

Tory still didn't fully get it. Neal saw. "Whose boat did Junior . . . take?" he asked.

Erik shrugged, avoiding Neal's eye. "I don't know. A Trojan from Marina 2. Junior said the guy hides the keys under the dash."

Only one boat that could be, Neal thought. *"Alibi:* Single-screw, about twenty-five feet," he said to Tory. "Junior better hope the tank's full—she only carries fifty gallons."

She nodded. "When did they leave, Erik?"

"Before lunch," the boy replied.

"And why did they go?" Neal put in, as much to Tory as to Erik.

The teenager looked at Neal in disbelief. "I figured you knew."

Neal bit off the impatient retort half formed, and Tory said, "It's something to do with Wilbur not being blind, isn't it?"

Erik nodded slowly. After a long pause, he continued: "Some-body found out. They came to the house where Mr. Andreas was staying, beat up the guy who owns it"—Tory glanced quickly up at Neal—"because he wouldn't say where Mr. Andreas was."

"And where was he—Mr. Andreas?" Neal asked.

"He was there the whole time, hiding in this little attic," Erik said, with a shaky smile.

"So that was why he decided to run for it," Tory said. "He was afraid the same thing would happen to him."

"Oh, no," Erik replied. "The guy said he was going to make sure Mr. Andreas really was blind. They were going to put his eyes out—that's why he ran."

Can't say I blame him, Neal thought. "Look, Erik," he said, "Miss Lennox and I will find your brother. But I want you to tell this whole story to a friend of mine—"

"No," said Erik.

"—He'll make sure you're safe," Neal continued, as if the boy hadn't spoken. "And he'll find the man who wants to blind Mr. Andreas."

"I can't," Erik said. "I've got to stay here—on the *Prophet*."

"Look, Erik," Neal began, then saw Tory, behind the boy, shake her head. "Wait a second," he finished lamely. He took Tory by the arm—*Never thought of a woman's biceps as sexy before*—and with his back to Erik mouthed "What?"

She shook her head again. "Trust me," she whispered. Suddenly she looked past him, and her eyes widened.

Warned too late, Neal turned just as Erik leaped from *Harbor 3*'s padded gunwale back to the trawler. His timing was off, and the *Jonah*'s near side lifted as he jumped. He landed with a grunt of pain and lay for several seconds sprawled across the coaming before rolling into the cockpit. But what caught and held Neal's eye was Erling Halvorsen's face. The self-styled preacher was standing with one hand on the roof of the after cabin, glaring at Tory, his face disfigured by hunger and rage.

"I shouldn't have come," Tory said quietly. "Let's get out of here."

"First thing, we need a boat," said Neal, bringing *Harbor 3* up to its float.

"Can't use the one we're on?" said Tory, and in the same breath answered herself: "No, I guess not—not all the way to San Miguel."

"The boat could do it," Neal said, surprised at the automatic defensiveness in his voice. "But I can't take her more than a mile beyond the harbor unless it's a clear case of life-and-death—and the unsupported word of a fourteen-year-old," he added quickly, "isn't good enough."

"*Point Hampton*'s out on patrol," Tory observed. "I could call the CO down at Channel Islands, see if we can use his 41 . . ."

Not much hope there, and Tory knew it. Besides, Coast Guard Station Channel Islands was all the way down in Oxnard—an hour at least to get to Santa Barbara, and another hour and a half to San Miguel. "This is really ridiculous," Neal said. "We're surrounded by goddamned boats, and all we need is one."

"All we need," Tory corrected him, "is something fast and seaworthy and ready to go."

"Preferably with an owner who owes me a whole lot of money," Neal added. Stifling his frustration, he cleated the bow and stern lines before noticing that Tory hadn't moved. "What is it?" he asked, followed instantly by, "You've thought of something."

"I have indeed," she replied, stepping ashore. "Follow me."

Up the ramp, along the sidewalk past The Chandlery, and then down the next ramp, which led to the float where a dozen of Santa Barbara's urchin-diving fleet tied up. Something in the way Tory's behind switched from side to side (despite the coverall) conveyed both determination and confidence. She stopped alongside one of the smaller urchin boats, a locally built twenty-one-footer named simply *Boat*. Neal knew and cordially disliked the owner-skipper, Lloyd Desmond, who emerged squinting from the cuddy cabin when Tory rapped on it with her ring.

"How's my sweetheart?" he said, ignoring Neal. He was a powerfully built young man, a UCSB graduate student and part-time urchin diver, who had gone public in his long, convoluted feud with the city's Harbor Department, posting libelous handwritten notices on each of the marina bulletin boards and writing furious letters to the *News-Press* and the *Independent*. The mere mention of Lloyd's name could make Maria Acevedo grind her teeth audibly; she had forbidden any employee under her jurisdiction—including the Harbor Patrol—to have anything to do with him.

"Just fine, thank you," Tory said. "Lloyd, I've come to collect."

He seemed to know what she meant, though Neal didn't. "Name it, Tory," he replied, spreading his arms.

"I need to borrow *Boat*. Unofficially and right now. I'll have her back here tomorrow." She had—or at least conveyed—unassailable assurance, Neal thought. But borrow a man's boat? That was asking a hell of a lot.

Lloyd's full lips pursed in apparent thought. "You taking Donahoe with you?"

She didn't hesitate. "Yes."

"In that case . . ." Lloyd turned a wide smile on her. The pupils of his blue eyes looked to Neal a little more contracted than they should have been. "In that case—okay," he said. "Just bring yourself back in one piece."

"How's she feel?" Tory asked, as *Boat* eased up the harbor at fast idle.

"Not too bad," Neal replied grudgingly. "She'll do it, if she holds together." But he was being less than forthright: small as she was, *Boat* felt solid and quick under his fingertips, just caressing the steering wheel. She was overpowered, of course—the big 454, a V-8 truck engine, could barely be kept down to the harbor's five-knot speed limit. Running light, with half-full tanks and no cargo in the big midships hold, she should make close to forty knots in calm water. The forty nautical miles to San Miguel, however, were likely to be anything but calm.

"She'll hold together," Tory was saying. "I checked her out myself." Her quick, private smile was clearly intended to tease, and Neal decided to humor her.

185

"Some kind of special exam for Lloyd?"

"You could say— Neal, that J's going to tack across your bow."

"I see him, thanks." In fact, Neal had been watching the racing sloop for more than a minute as it short-tacked up the harbor toward him. The skipper was clearly so preoccupied in squeezing the last foot out of each leg that he simply failed to take anyone else into account. Neal dropped *Boat* into neutral, then had to jab her into reverse as the J-24 sailed into an obvious dead spot and sagged down on him. "I guess God protects people like that," he said, as the sailboat glided past with a yard to spare.

"Well, the Almighty's working overtime with that pinhead," Tory replied. "D'you want a course to San Miguel?"

"Let's see what the seas are like," he said. Just then, they rounded the high, square-cornered dredge, moored alongside the entrance channel. Out beyond the breakwater he could see the afternoon's first tentative whitecaps. "Hold on—here we go."

As he'd suspected, the wind had gone into the north a little: if he ran *Boat* close to shore, right along the kelp line, she'd be partly in the lee of the bluffs for the first seven miles. And since *Boat* had an essentially open helm station, with only a partial hardtop over the windshield, he wanted to stay in protected water as long as possible. He pushed the throttle all the way forward, felt the boat leap ahead, cutting the top neatly off a short, steep sea.

Beside him, he saw with approval, Tory was balancing on the balls of her feet, letting her bent legs absorb the shocks as the little boat seemed to bounce from wavetop to wavetop. But she had the thoughtful, almost abstracted look he associated with people in the first stages of seasickness—odd, because the jolting ride wasn't nearly as upsetting as swooping or rolling, and Tory had an iron stomach in any case.

She read his concern, and a mischievous grin lit her face. "Just trying to calculate courses," she yelled.

"Goleta Point to San Miguel," he yelled back.

She nodded. He could see she'd already worked out where they would have to leave the shelter of the land. "Two-fifteen, magnetic."

186

Memory and experience told him the course was correct; could he have plotted it on a mental chart while leaping around like this? Probably not. Losing her was the dumbest thing he'd ever done. "Two-fifteen magnetic," he called out.

## 1725 HOURS: TORY

A musician in mid-performance might, she thought, have the same look of total concentration Neal did, guiding *Boat* at twenty knots through seas that were now about six feet from trough to crest. The course brought most of the waves a little forward of the dive boat's beam and gave her a skidding, corkscrewing ride among the breaking tops and the inevitable cross seas. Neal held the old-fashioned wheel lightly, moving it barely a spoke in either direction, seeming to steer the little vessel with body English or maybe force of will. Tory considered herself a more than competent boat driver, but his helmsmanship transcended mere skill. *I could watch him do this forever*

The sky was if anything a deeper, clearer blue than when they'd started, but the wind and waves had both picked up dramatically. Back along the mainland shore, she knew, it would keep on blowing like this only until sunset. But out toward San Miguel the weather systems had a straight shot clear across the Pacific. Thirty-knot winds were ordinary out here, and seas of fifteen or even twenty feet—breaking seas, sometimes with two wave patterns running across each other. Only for a few hours before and after dawn was it likely to be calm, and even then the residual swell could roll you dizzy.

She'd been aboard the *Point Hampton* one day, riding as a guest on a search-and-rescue case that had taken them out to San Miguel in the teeth of a northwesterly gale. The eighty-two-foot cutter had been tossed about like a rubber ducky in a Jacuzzi, experienced Coasties holding on to anything solid and the less experienced bouncing off bulkheads, collecting bruises.

"There it is," Neal yelled. "Just on the starboard bow."

Sharp eyes, she thought: the haze was sneaky, not thick enough to perceive in itself, yet cutting visibility to about five miles. At first the island's outline was only a ghostly line across the lower sky, hardening by the moment as they approached. This early in the summer, much of San Miguel was still green, but it was the white swath of a windswept saddle that caught the eye. Off to port a few miles more distant lay Santa Rosa, with one peak twice the height of San Miguel's hills, yet it was entirely invisible, as was the even higher, much larger Santa Cruz, somewhere abaft their beam. The three islands, with little Anacapa, their easterly outrider, formed the barrier that created the Santa Barbara Channel and protected the mainland shore from storm seas. But sometimes, as now, the islands funneled the westerly winds and waves down the channel, increasing their strength and size.

"They'll head for Cuyler Harbor," Tory said, and then had to say it again, louder.

Neal nodded vigorously. "Not the best anchorage in a nor'wester, but the most obvious." He grinned. "And Wilbur knows what it looks like."

He throttled back well short of Cuyler's wide entrance, easing *Boat* off the wind until she was partly in the lee of Prince Island, the steeply menacing rock that marked—and partly blocked—the left side of the harbor mouth. As he did so, the apparent wind, and the accompanying noise, fell away dramatically, till it was possible to converse at nearly normal volume. But the wind was still out there: Tory saw that breakers had begun to curl around the high, grim outcropping called Harris Point, San Miguel's northern extremity. Whitecapped seas were reaching across the harbor entrance, toward Prince Island. "That passage looks pretty ugly already," she observed. "Another couple of hours, it could be impassable." But Neal, she realized, knew the harbor better than she—and he'd probably heard the nervousness that had put the words in her mouth.

"No place for a small, tubby, middle-aged Trojan," he said. "Which I don't see, by the way."

*A diplomatic way of saying pull yourself together, Tory.* "No boats at all—isn't that strange?" Even in the worst weather, she knew, the fishing boats already at San Miguel tended to hunker down and stick it out, rather than attempt the forty-mile run back to Santa Barbara.

"With this wind, they've probably moved around to Tyler Bight, on the south side," he said.

But she only half heard him: "Neal, d'you see that cluster of red floats, right in the westerly corner of the harbor? There's something in among them."

"Not a boat, I don't think," he said. "Does your buddy Lloyd have binocs in that cuddy cabin?"

"I think so. Wait one." He did, and good ones—rubber-armored 7x50s. Standing on tiptoe, she braced her elbows on the dashboard edge and brought the glasses to her eyes. A single stand of weirdly treelike plants on the shore leaped into view, and he panned downward. There were eight floats—spherical fenders that fishermen often used as markers—and next to them a rectangular, raftlike surface, nearly awash, studded with unmistakable fittings. "Neal, it's a cabin top, like a cruiser's wheelhouse." As she spoke, a sea swept the rectangle, and the trough that followed revealed for a moment the cabin sides that supported it. "Yes, that's what it is: a wheelhouse."

"The little son of a bitch sank her," Neal said, his voice iced with anger. "For five cents I'd leave him out here."

She recognized Neal's reaction as instinctive; he knew as well as she did that Junior had probably acted in panic: if the boat disappeared, there'd be no visible trace of him or Wilbur. But sinking even a fiberglass boat could be tricky—the little Trojan would go down eventually, but there was no telling how long air in her hull and cabin spaces would keep her partly afloat.

"Where do you want to anchor?" she said, as if he hadn't spoken.

"Inside the floats: right up under the big bluff," he replied. She started to swing herself out of the cockpit, onto the narrow side deck, and he said: "You might want to check the chain locker first, make sure it's free to run."

He was right, of course—stowed free, chain had a tendency to shake itself down into a solid clump after an hour or so of pounding through seas. *Boat's* cuddy cabin was brutally Spartan—a V-shaped berth with a bucket for a toilet; a galley that consisted of a gimballed propane burner with a pot on it and a Styrofoam ice chest too revolting to contemplate. Regulations required Lloyd to carry a dinghy, but a loophole in the regs allowed him to fudge with an inflatable plastic toy, which lived on the berth, wedged between the mattress and the overhead. At the berth's foot, an open locker held a couple of hundred feet of quarter-inch chain, badly rusted and smelling strongly of dead kelp.

Lying on her belly, Tory pried free what she estimated as a hundred feet of the chain, then got to her knees and unhooked the bungee cord ties that held the dinghy in place.

Neal had brought *Boat* into position a good deal closer to the sheer, unforgiving bluff than she would have done. The depth sounder was still reading twenty feet. "This'll do," he told her. "Let out ten fathoms for starters."

Tory dragged the plastic dinghy up into the cockpit, where it looked even more absurd than it had in the cabin. Neal regarded it in silence, his eyebrows arched eloquently, and Tory finally said, "I don't write the regulations. Do you want to see if you can find the oars?"

The silly little boat was rated to carry three, according to its label, but with just the two of them it seemed dangerously low in the water. Even so, the minute they cast off from *Boat*'s side, the wind threatened to blow them straight across Cuyler Harbor. Seated on the ribbed plastic floor, with Tory facing him and bracing his legs, Neal rowed like a madman. The oars were too short, the plastic oarlocks threatened to pull free from the sides with every stroke, yet somehow he managed to make headway across the wind, liberally splashing himself and Tory with icy spray.

At last the dinghy's bottom grated on the sandy shore, and Tory leaped out into knee-deep water, grasping the painter in one hand. Neal was still panting as he stepped gingerly over the side; with his weight removed, the dinghy took off, turned over in midair, and nearly yanked Tory off her feet. Together they wrestled it up the narrow beach, lashing it firmly to a heavy piece of driftwood. "Rowing back's going to be fun," Tory observed, raising her voice over the wind's intermittent howl.

"The Trojan had a dinghy, too—an Avon or a Zodiac. Junior and Wilbur didn't swim ashore," Neal said, brushing wet sand off himself. "When we find where they hid it, we should be able to find their tracks, too. Jesus, I hate sand."

A rough wooden staircase set into the sandy hill led upward, through a cleft, to the island's official campground, about a half-mile inland. "They won't have gone there," Neal said confidently. "The park ranger's station is up that way, and Wilbur must know it."

A hundred yards down the beach they found, in the grass above the highwater line, a scuffed track that might have marked where an inflatable had been dragged ashore—and the inflatable itself, deflated and half-covered with sand, a few yards farther up the slope. "You suppose they tried to bury it?" Tory asked, her head turned away from the stinging barrage of airborne particles.

"Could be. But nothing's going to stay buried while this wind's blowing," Neal replied. "I wonder if Junior remembered to bring the air pump," he added a moment later.

It was Tory who saw the marks, running up the hill just inside the edge of the grass line. The driving wind was quickly filling in the little hollows, which already had lost shape. In another hour or less they'd be gone completely, and even now—

"You're sure they're footprints?" Neal said.

Because she wanted them to be, her reply was a little quicker, a little more positive: "What else? Come on." The four words allowed what felt like a teaspoonful of sand into her mouth. She spat out what she could and led the way—staggering, slipping, eyes narrowed to slits. Up ahead what looked like a narrow gully cut into the hill. She paused to let Neal catch up and pointed toward it.

He nodded, his face screwed up against the flying sand. But when she turned away to resume the climb, he grabbed her arm. Setting his mouth almost against her ear, he said, "Not straight in—we'll come at 'em over the edge of the cut."

Makes sense, she was thinking, when she felt the pressure of his dry, gritty lips on her cheek. Before she could stop herself, she swung awkwardly toward him. In the shifting, slippery sand her feet went out from under her, and as she sat she knocked him over backward, to slip downward some ten feet in a miniature sandslide. He pulled himself to his feet, spitting and shaking his head—and laughing. She waited for him to struggle up the slope to her, extended her hand to grasp his. "Easy does it," she warned.

He was still grinning as he raised her easily, and she knew her expression was matching his. "Ready?" he said.

"Let's go."

The sand had filtered through the zipper on the front of her coverall, and as she lay on her belly at the edge of the gully she felt it working its abrasive way under the strap of her bra and the waistband of her tights. Still, she reflected, Neal must be even more uncomfortable than she was: a fine coating covered every visible inch of his skin, even his eyelashes, as he lay beside her.

Below them, at the bottom of the little ravine, Wilbur Andreas and Junior Halvorsen hunched miserably together, trying to create a human screen in whose lee they could start a fire. Their tent, pitched with its closed end into the wind, heaved and flexed as though it might take wing at any moment. Junior was spinning the wheel of a cheap plastic lighter, but the flame never lasted for more than a second. On the other hand, she thought, if he did manage to ignite the wretched collection of twigs and crumpled bits of paper that lay uneasily in a scooped-out hollow, the burning bits might easily blow away and torch the whole island.

She turned her head to Neal, saw he was watching her. She nodded, and he rose, his right hand on the butt of his automatic. Sand spilled from the holster: a good thing he wouldn't need a weapon against the two castaways below them, she thought.

## 6:55 P.M.: NEAL

The sound of crunching footsteps above and behind them, carried on the wind, brought Junior and Wilbur lurching to their feet—Wilbur off balance, so that he stepped into the hole filled with kindling and fell heavily to his knees. A pathetic pair, Neal thought: they had clearly soaked themselves to the skin getting ashore, and their drying clothes were streaked with salt where they weren't crusted with sand. Wilbur's round, red, unshaven face, topped by a windblown thatch of sun-bleached hair, made him look as if he'd been living on the street for months. His eyes, though bloodshot and dark-circled, still had the same unsettling intensity Neal remembered—as if they were seeing slightly beneath the surface of what he was looking at.

Junior, too, was damp, sandy, and bedraggled. His sly, calculating air had completely blown away, and he was only a ferret-faced sixteen-year-old boy—chilled to the bone, exhausted, frightened nearly out of his wits. Neal felt sympathy welling up, though he knew perfectly well that Junior would revert to his usual obnoxious self as soon as the danger was past.

"Game's over. Time to go home," said Tory. Neal glanced at her. Sun and wind had reddened her face, and her short hair, blown from behind, stood up like a blonde mane. Her coverall showed the effects of the row ashore followed by their scramble up the dune, but her calm authority was as complete as if she'd been wearing freshly pressed dress blues. Even if she quit the Coast Guard, Neal thought, its mark would be on her the rest of her life.

"You heard the lady," Neal said. "Let's go—we've got a long run ahead of us." *If we can get* Boat *out of Cuyler at all, in this wind.* He saw Tory watching him, saw she'd had the same thought. As Wilbur and Junior were packing up their gear, the teenager grumbling and whining, Neal said to her, "Maybe we ought to go up to the ranger's house, stay there tonight, and head back when the channel calms down."

She seemed uncertain, which was most unusual for her. "I just don't know," she replied, her voice low.

"What is it?" he said.

"I'm worried about Erling—and those kids," she said slowly. "Maybe it's foolish, but that look on his face . . ."

Maybe it isn't foolish at all, Neal thought, remembering Erling's expression of despairing rage. "We'll go down to the harbor. See how bad it looks," he said.

Twilight was approaching by the time they were on the beach, with the gear stacked beside *Boat's* absurd dinghy. (The air pump for the larger inflatable was, as Neal had suspected, still aboard the Trojan.) "No worse than before," Tory said.

He could tell she didn't really believe it, any more than he did. But *Boat* was still riding well in the westernmost corner of the harbor, jerking at her anchor chain like a nervous horse. The wind would almost certainly drop before dawn, but it would, he thought, pick up again with the sun. Better to get aboard now, be ready to take advantage of whatever window opened for them. The sun, already below the island's northerly ridge, would be gone soon. "Okay," he said. "Here's what we'll do."

They left Wilbur on the shore, sorting through his and Junior's food to assemble something for dinner. Neal and Junior, guided by Tory, carried the plastic dinghy upwind along the beach into the shelter of the overhanging bluffs. In the lee of the ridge the wind was gusting hard by now, and some of the gusts came right down the cliff. The run out to *Boat* was straight downwind, though, and all Neal had to do was guide the overloaded dinghy into a soft collision with the little urchin boat.

Even a couple of hundred feet out, however, the force of the westerly seemed doubled, whipping spray across the water. *Boat* was weathercocking from side to side, fetching up with a jerk of the anchor chain at the end of each swing. Tory leaned over the gunwale, looking worried: "Are you sure you can make it back to shore?"

Neal, holding the dinghy's doubled painter in one hand, tried to project a confidence he didn't feel. "That's a good long chunk of beach. I'll fetch up on it someplace." If he missed—if the dinghy, carried by the wind, blew through the shallow, rock-strewn gap between Prince Island and the San Miguel shore . . . well, that didn't bear thinking about. The next land to leeward was Ventura, seventy miles away.

He released the bitter end of the dinghy's painter, pulled the braided line into the boat, and braced himself as well as he could for the first stroke. "Hey!" called Tory. He looked up into her face. "Good luck." She'd been on the point of saying something more, he was almost sure of it.

Two yards out of the urchin boat's lee, the westerly seized the dinghy. For a moment, Neal thought the toy boat might take flight, and then it was all he could do to keep from being spilled into the harbor. When at last he had the dinghy's quarter precariously into the choppy waves, he was appalled to see how far it had already been pushed. Digging his heels into the flexing plastic sides, he pulled with all his strength.

Once, as the little boat bobbed over a wave top, he missed a stroke. Only by flinging himself across the windward gunwale did he keep from capsizing. When he could see the sandy bottom, he jumped over the side with the painter between his teeth. The water was chest deep and not much over fifty degrees. The driving spray felt like hail. Ashore, Wilbur had settled in the shelter of a boulder, a heavy plastic bag beside him. He was staring out toward Prince Island, seemingly oblivious until Neal was only a few feet away, striding through calf-deep water with the dinghy behind him.

"Makes a hell of a composition," Wilbur said. "Be better if that little boat of yours was red, though."

You couldn't be angry at someone like that, Neal decided. But you could—indeed, had to—be firm with him: "Just pick up the goddamned groceries and follow me," he said.

With two people aboard, he knew, the dingy would be considerably jumpier than with three. As soon as he'd shoved off and climbed aboard, Neal spun it so its stern was facing *Boat.* He quickly discovered that his own back, catching the wind, made a surprisingly effective squaresail, leaving the oars free for steering. Wilbur, squatting on the inflated floor as he'd been told, watched him with interest. Tory was leaning out over *Boat*'s gunwale; she'd taken the long-handled gaff from its rack in the cockpit and taped something that could have been a sock to cover the needle-pointed hook.

Even so, Neal was glad she wouldn't need to use it to snag the inflatable as it went by. Dragging both oar blades to slow the boat, he was calculating the final approach that would lay him neatly alongside, when from behind Prince Island a long, low hull appeared. She was dark blue, sixty feet or a little more—a blown-up version of the cigarette boats Neal had seen so often back in his Caribbean days. Tarted-up versions of offshore racing powerboats, the cigarettes could race across even the turbulent Gulf Stream at forty knots. In Neal's former world, they had a limited market as symbols of virility for wealthy, mostly older men, and a much wider application as high-speed carriers of drugs, especially cocaine.

Along Southern California's bare, exposed coast, a cigarette was at once too obvious and too slow to make a good drug smuggler. Just the same, Neal felt his heartbeat race: there was something predatory about the blue boat as she hovered just outside the line of breakers that now stretched clear across the harbor entrance.

"Neal!" Tory called, snapping him back to his task. She'd never taken her eyes off the dinghy, which was about to blow right past *Boat*. She extended the gaff and Neal, stretching, managed to grab it at the last instant. For a long moment he was sure the load was too much—she'd have to let go of the gaff or go overboard with it. One look at her set jaw and he knew which it would be, and he prepared himself to release the hook the instant he saw her over-balance. Slowly, slowly, she dragged the dinghy and its load in closer to *Boat*, until finally Neal could reach out with his free hand and clamp on to the gunwale with a death grip. The gaff's hook, despite its wrapping, had scored the knuckles of his right hand painfully. Ignoring it, he pulled the oar from its plastic lock to keep it from scraping *Boat*'s hull.

"Pass up the food, Wilbur," Neal said. The artist obeyed with helpful eagerness, nearly capsizing the dinghy as he did so. "Now yourself. No—don't stand up; easy does it: grab my shoulder . . . now the gunwale—the edge of the boat . . . now stand up, but slowly."

Tory, who had dropped the gaff, held out her hand and Wilbur took it. He pulled himself up, legs scissoring wildly. One sandy foot caught Neal in the forehead, nearly spilling him backward; the other neatly hooked the free oar and spun it into the water. As Wilbur rolled into the cockpit, Neal grabbed desperately for the aluminum oar, watched it sink inches beyond his fingertips. *Screw it—I'll buy Lloyd a half-dozen when we get home.* He passed Tory the dinghy painter and swung himself aboard. "Did you see our visitor?" he said, nodding toward the stern.

"I don't like it," she replied. "Boats like that remind me of the Seventh District: plastic-wrapped bundles hidden below and square grouper floating in the wake." She reached into the cuddy cabin, where Junior was huddling under an oil-stained beach towel, and passed Neal the binoculars. "What do you make of them?"

Bracing his back against the cabin, he focused the glasses on the other boat's cockpit, aware as he did so that it was now nearly dark.

Below the lazily spinning radar antenna three human heads were visible above the windscreen. One of them had an oddly shaped pair of binoculars pressed to his eyes—electronic night glasses, Neal thought bitterly: another tool the patrol's budget was too lean to buy. "I know one of those guys," he said. "But I bet you know him better . . ." As he spoke he turned to Wilbur, to discover he had climbed over the coaming and was standing on the narrow side deck, looking vaguely back at the newcomer. "Jesus, Wilbur! Get back in here!" Neal snapped.

Startled, Wilbur lost his balance. One flailing hand knocked the binoculars out of Neal's grasp, the other clutched at the vertical radio antenna, snapping it off its mount. Neal leaped for the binoculars, and Tory, lunging for Wilbur, tripped over him. Wilbur, still holding the antenna, toppled overboard. He came up a second later without it, gasping and yelling. Tory grasped his outstretched hand and Neal, recovering, grabbed the other. Tory, he saw, was already braced with her knees against the cockpit coaming. "One, two, three—heave!" he said, and Wilbur was back aboard, spraying water in all directions.

"God, that's cold!" he gasped, sprawling on the deck.

Tory was already leaning over the side. Neal called to her, "What about the antenna?"

She straightened without a word, holding up the coaxial cable; it ended in a moplike tassel of braided wire.

"Shit," said Neal with feeling.

He was groping for words to expand on the theme, when Wilbur, who had picked up the binoculars, cried out, "That's them! What's-his-face Celeste and the guy who beat up Jock!" For the first time, fear twisted his face.

## 2015 HOURS: TORY

She took the glasses from Wilbur's unresisting hands. The image was dark, but she could just recognize two of the men on the distant bridge. "They were in the gallery when I bought my painting," she told Neal: "The older one seemed to be in charge, and the one with the ponytail was just hanging around."

"The main guy is Mr. Celeste; the ponytail works for him—name's Felix. He's the one who's supposed to . . ." Wilbur's words seemed to dry up. He shook his head. "Supposed to make sure I really can't see," he said, spitting the words out fast.

She turned the center focus knob. Felix's profile was clear, but his features were completely in shadow now. "You heard him say that?" she asked.

She caught Wilbur's nod as she lowered the binoculars. "In Jock's house: he stashed me up in the attic. I heard them . . . what they did to him." He shivered uncontrollably for a few seconds and went on: "It was Mr. Celeste. He told Jock he had a choice: me really blind—or dead. Then they beat the shit out of him. It was, like, a sample, they said."

Neal draped a mildewed sleeping bag over Wilbur's shoulders. "And after that they left?" he asked.

Wilbur nodded again, pulling the sleeping bag tightly around him. "They said they'd be back. Jock told me to run for it while I could."

"You told him where you were going?" Tory asked. But even Wilbur wouldn't have been that foolish.

"I didn't know where I was going," Wilbur said plaintively. "Except to find Junior—he was the one decided to come out here."

"Then how—" Tory began, her eyes going to the other boat. In the last gleam of sunset, the radar antenna's white arm flashed as they turned. "Oh," she said.

"We have met the enemy, and he is us." She could hear Neal's wry smile in his voice. "They must have been outside Jock's house when we were there, and just hung on our tail."

"So we led them out here." If she stopped to let it sink in, she would only lose her temper. That she was sure of—but practically nothing else. "What do you think they'll do now?" she said to Neal.

From just the silhouette of his cocked head, her memory's eye supplied the complete picture of him: eyes narrowed, lips drawn slightly back, concentrating with his whole body. He didn't answer for a minute, and she was on the point of repeating her question when he spoke, his voice detached: "That's a professional skipper out there—I'd bet money on it—and you can tell he doesn't want to run those breakers." Perhaps he sensed her question, because he added, "Just look at the way he's handling her, easing up to the breaker line and then falling back. As if somebody's pushing him, but they can't quite make him jump."

Neal could be right, she thought: now that he pointed it out, the big boat had been moving in and dropping back, though she'd seen no pattern to it. "They must know we don't have a transmitter," she said, thinking out loud.

His laugh was humorless: "Even if they missed our little slapstick number, they can see the antenna's gone. And they can see we've got no chance of rowing ashore while the wind holds."

"We could put up a flare, see if that brings the ranger out. Or even drive *Boat* up on the beach and run for it," she said.

As Tory had expected, the mere suggestion of beaching—probably wrecking—*Boat* snapped Neal's head around. But he didn't reject it out of hand, which told her how seriously he took the situation. "Beach the boat," he said slowly, as if the words were sour. "In the dark, with two landlubbers aboard . . ."

He didn't need to say more. Out on the hovering cigarette boat a light flashed and died. "What do you think they'll do?" she asked.

"Wait till the wind drops and then make their move," he replied, so promptly she knew he'd thought it through. "Moon's in the last quarter, but with radar they don't need light till they're right on us. And as long as the wind stays in the west, we won't hear them coming till it's too late."

"Like the Coast Guard boarding a drug boat, only in reverse," she said. "But do you seriously think this Mr. Celeste would kill a cop and a Coast Guard officer, just to keep his scam intact."

"You bet your tail he would," said Wilbur unexpectedly. "If you're in his way—*squish.* Felix, the ponytail . . . he was all set to push me out a window."

"Obviously, I don't know," Neal said, as if Wilbur hadn't spoken. *But you've made up your mind.* She waited.

"I met this Mr. Celeste, for just a couple of minutes," he said at last. "I got the feeling he's a major heavy, a serious bad guy. Certainly, the way he had Jock worked over . . . that's not exactly Chamber of Commerce tactics."

"If you were that kind of person," she said, thinking aloud, "it'd be so easy, once you had our boat." The reality of it was beginning to sink in. For the first time she felt the chill in the driving wind.

"If it was me in charge," Neal said, "I'd leave *Boat* where she is. Take the four of us offshore a couple of miles and push us overboard."

*It would work. Even if they found a body or two.* "How about applying that imagination of yours to our side of the problem," she said.

"Why don't we run for it?" demanded Junior from the cabin.

"What have we got to lose?" He sounded angry and desperate, at the end of his rope.

"In this weather, a boat the size of theirs has all the advantages," she replied. "Did you say something, Neal?"

"I was just thinking: weather's not the only card in the deck."

She waited until it was clear he wasn't ready to explain. Whatever was taking shape in his head, he had to work it out, and she had to give him the space to do it. She could feel Wilbur and Junior watching her expectantly. With more spirit than she realized she had, she said, "Okay, everybody—at least let's get something warm in our stomachs. Wilbur, what did you bring us to eat?"

Junior barely touched his half of the canned beef stew, and he fell asleep sitting, wedged between the cabin bulkhead and the side of the boat. Wilbur devoured both portions greedily, then crept below and curled himself up under the blanket. "Alone at last," said Tory, emptying a second can of stew into the pot.

Neal, his back propped against the helm, had been staring through the binoculars at the passage between Prince Island and San Miguel's beach. He grunted, swiveled the glasses around to focus them on the cigarette boat, a black patch against the dark, spray-flecked seas. "It's not so great," he said at last, sliding down on his haunches, out of the wind: "They've got us in a box. Even if we could get *Boat* through that breaker line, we'd never get past them." He paused, and Tory nodded. "I could run the passage inside Prince Island—"

"What about the rocks? And the kelp?" The chart was clear in her mind, maybe too clear—charted dangers often looked larger, more perilous than they turned out to be.

"—But they could just dodge around behind Prince and catch us coming out," he continued.

He was really talking to himself, not her, she saw. And she also sensed he was laying out the impossible courses of action just to clear them from his head—which meant there was some viable plan down at the bottom. At least, that was what she hoped. He had paused again, and despite the dark she could see his head was angled toward her. "So what do we do?"

He was silent. *There isn't any plan.*

"We wait till they make their move," he said suddenly. "Wait till they cross the break—we'll see that, even without a moon—then slip the hook and run like hell out the east pass."

*In the dark, with them right behind us?* The objection was in her mouth when he went on.

"*Boat* draws maybe two and a half feet—less, when she's planing. They must need more like five, and they don't know the passage. Even if their skipper has the nerve to follow me, he won't try to catch up."

"But even so, once we're in open water—"

"We should have enough of a lead so we can duck around Cardwell Point, at the east end of the island, and up into Tyler Bight. There'll be other boats there—he won't try anything in front of witnesses."

One faint hope piled on another, she thought. The pass between Prince Island and the beach looked wide and clear in daylight, but the harbor between *Boat* and the channel was pocked with reefs, festooned with the slippery, ropelike strands of kelp that could wind themselves so effectively around a propeller and shaft. Unmarked Cardwell Point was a long, low spit of land that trailed off into an even longer sandbar. More than one knowledgeable skipper had come to grief on it. And even if *Boat* survived that hurdle, who was to say there'd be anyone else in the anchorage at Tyler?

All her fears flashed past in the fraction of a second. Neal was waiting for her reaction. "We'll have to leave Lloyd's anchor and all that chain. I'll set it up," she said.

CUYLER HARBOR: 11:45 P.M.: NEAL

*I'll set it up.* By God, you couldn't ask more than that, he thought—especially since he knew she saw the holes in his plan as clearly as he did. Maybe even clearer: He'd noticed before that Tory tended to think of every boat as an eighty-two-footer, with an eighty-two's assets and liabilities. *Boat* was tiny by comparison, but she had a tiny boat's advantages, and he planned to make the most of them.

From the bow, nearly within arm's reach of where Neal stood, came the subdued clatter of chain. Tory was draped over the cabin top, her knee insecurely hooked over the grabrail, so she presented just an amorphous shape even to a pair of night glasses. She was pulling the rest of *Boat's* chain anchor rode, foot by foot, out the deck pipe and lowering it over the side. When she was done, only a single figure-8 of chain around the deck cleat would remain to be cast off.

The wind had dropped a good deal in the last hour, but it was still blowing about twenty knots in the anchorage itself—harder outside—and there was still a visible line of breaking sea across the harbor mouth. But it was no longer a serious barrier, Neal thought. Certainly not to something as big and powerful as the cigarette boat. In that captain's place, Neal knew he would already have made his move—would've made it when he first arrived, with *Boat's* crew falling over each other and her cockpit in chaos. Failing that, he would have brought the cigarette through the eastern pass when the wind-driven seas were at their height, closing off any escape through Cuyler's primary channel. With a spotlight and a good depth sounder, it wouldn't have been that risky. But the cigarette's captain hadn't. Not a macho daredevil, then: primarily a yacht skipper. But if he worked for Mr. Celeste, when push came to a gun in the ear, he would do what his boss ordered.

From the foredeck, Tory's low voice, harsh with strain and fatigue: "Pass me the buoy."

The buoy was, in fact, one of *Boat's* life jackets, with a short length of very light line carefully tied through the armholes. Neal extended the bitter end of the line around the windshield. Tory's fingers, wet, cold, and slippery, touched his hand and gave it a quick squeeze. As the line ran out, he stood lost in thought.

She clambered around the windshield and back into the cockpit, stood there for a moment, sucking her knuckle and staring forward with the numbness of exhaustion. It was more than he could resist, and he took her in his arms. He felt her cheek slide along his, but suddenly she stiffened and pulled back.

"What—"

"Behind you!"

The cigarette boat was moving—it must have been underway for a couple of minutes. "Cast off!" he said, but she was already climbing back out onto the narrow side deck. His hand groped for the key, found it. *Boat's* engine block was still warm, and the big 454 caught instantly. From the cabin he heard cries of alarm as Wilbur and Junior struggled up from unconsciousness. A head thrust out, and Neal pushed it back. "Stay below!" he roared. The last thing he needed was Wilbur crashing around on deck, screwing things up.

The cigarette boat was through the breakers, coming toward them fast. "Tory!" he yelled.

"Chain's jammed on the cleat!"

In the dark, working by touch alone, it wasn't surprising. But why now? The cigarette was nearly on them, and suddenly two powerful spotlights on her bridge wings picked out Tory, kneeling on the foredeck. "Get clear!" he called. And when she hesitated—she must, he knew, be blinded—he bellowed, "Get clear and hold on!"

A loud *crack!* off to starboard, and sparks flew simultaneously from *Boat*'s stemhead fitting. Tory, still on her knees, recoiled, and Neal pulled the throttle lever all the way back. The gears connected with a *thunk* that threw Tory forward, but as the urchin boat reversed, picking up speed, she managed an ungainly, flailing lurch back into the windshield, where Neal, reaching awkwardly around the side, pinned her in place with his free arm.

The overstressed engine's scream was drowned for a second by a burbling thud, as a wave slammed into and over the transom. The windshield pane next to Tory exploded in splinters, followed an instant later by the flat crack of a second shot, and a rending crash from forward as the bow cleat pulled free, taking its backing plate and several square inches of deck with it.

The spotlights were still tracking them, focused a little ahead of *Boat* but swinging fast. The cigarette herself was fully up on plane turning toward then, and Tory yelled, "He's going to ram us!"

*Fuck that.* Neal pushed the throttle–shift lever forward to neutral, heard the engine drop in response, then rammed it all the way ahead. How to destroy a transmission, he thought. But the urchin boat seemed to gather herself under him and then leaped ahead, just as the cigarette shot past her stern, missing the outdrive by a couple of feet. Two more shots rang out from overhead, but Neal barely heard them.

He yanked *Boat*'s wheel hard over, throwing her into a turn that buried her gunwale and nearly pulled Tory from his grasp. In the cabin, soft, heavy weights slammed downward into the hull, accompanied by yells of pained surprise. Behind them, the noise of the cigarette's engines abruptly dropped off. As he straightened *Boat* on her course for the eastern gap, Neal risked a look astern.

The cigarette was dead in the water, spotlights aimed close aboard, their beams weaving back and forth. "What's happened?" Tory called.

"He's either hit the Trojan or fouled in those red floats," Neal yelled. He pulled the throttle back and *Boat* dropped off plane. "You want to join the rest of us?"

She slid feetfirst through the broken windshield and half jumped, half fell into the cockpit, landing with a gasp and a crunch of broken glass.

"Are you all right?" Neal said.

"A little winded," she said. Her teeth gleamed pale green in the glow from the instruments. "That was my breast you had a death grip on. Should be some interesting bruises tomorrow."

"Oh," he said.

"But thanks." She leaned forward, lips pursed.

"I'll take a rain check," he said. "Here they come again."

She was looking at him oddly, and he realized that the adrenaline had completely taken over. He felt supremely confident, ready for anything. As he pushed the throttle forward, he heard a double crack from astern. "Two guns," Tory said. "Sound like rifles."

He nodded. The wind through the smashed windshield tore at his face, driving the smells of kelp and gull shit up his nostrils. Without the glass he could see much better, but the green lights from *Boat*'s instrument panel were far too bright. And then they were gone, muffled by a folded cloth Tory held over them. "Thanks," he said.

"*De nada.*" And then, a few seconds later, "Aren't you awfully close to the beach?"

"Yes." Another look behind. The cigarette was back up on plane, picking up speed, her spotlights groping through the dark. *Fine: blind yourself, you son of a bitch.* He twitched the wheel back and forth, dodging the beams.

"He's closing," Tory called. "No, he's holding position, about two hundred yards back and maybe ten yards farther off the beach."

"Gives him time to pull up if I hit a rock," said Neal. The wind was snatching the words from his lips. "Figures he'll catch me in open water."

Tory didn't answer. He felt her free hand around his waist, groping: the automatic—she was taking it from his holster. *Fine. She's better with the damn thing than I am, and it'll give her something to do.*

"Jammed with sand," she said. "I was afraid of that."

The spotlights caught them for a second. Before he jogged out of their beam, he saw a long streamer of kelp under the bow to port.

"That wouldn't stop them anyway," he said.

She heard the—what? expectation, maybe—in his tone and fed him the line: "What will, then?"

It came from astern, a full, heart-stopping second late: the unmistakable ringing crash of metal hitting rock. Tory's jaw dropped, and Neal glanced back to see the cigarette, already dropped off plane, slewing to port. "Unmarked rock," he said. "The divers all know about it, though."

"They're coming back on course—must still have one prop left," Tory said.

"They'll never catch us on one engine," Neal replied. "Let's go home."

"I haven't seen the cigarette boat for the last hour and a half," she said, lowering the binoculars. "Tell you the truth, they could be right alongside and I might not know it. I'm pretty tired."

The first few miles out of San Miguel had been genuinely terrifying: roller-coaster rides down unseen waves that roared up behind them with the sound of express trains, and the screaming voices of the wind all around. But Neal's intuitive reactions, coupled perfectly to *Boat*'s responsiveness, had given her perspective: this was what commercial fishermen lived—and died—with every day. And with each mile they put between them and San Miguel the seas dropped, the wind slackened; *Boat* was now planing easily at fifteen knots or so down gentle four-foot swells, well clear of the shipping lanes. Even though the world outside was restricted to a few feet of spray-splattered darkness, her apprehensions had faded to nothing.

Neal was slumped against the cockpit side, steering with one finger. His face, tinted green from below by the dashboard lights, looked a million years old but not unhappy. "My guess is the cigarette's limping back to wherever she came from." His wide mouth curled in a wry grin. "I'll bet you whatever you like that six hours from now Mr. Celeste is going to have an ironclad alibi for last night."

She knew Neal was probably right, knew she'd probably feel angry and frustrated about it—later. Right now, emotion was too much trouble. All she wanted was to lie down and let unconsciousness sweep over her.

She ducked and peered into *Boat*'s cuddy cabin: a green glow from the back of the instrument panel gave the triangular space a faint fluorescence, so she could sense more than actually see Junior and Wilbur, wrapped in whatever they'd managed to find, huddled on the V-berths like bundled rags. "You really think Wilbur's safe now?" she asked.

"From Celeste? Pretty much," Neal replied. "It's just like I told him: once everybody knows he isn't blind, there's no more secret to keep. I mean, he may have to deal with some fraud complaints, but those'll land mostly on Jock's head."

"I certainly hope so," Tory said, and yawned.

"What I wonder is who killed that guy Benjamin."

"Benjamin who?" said Tory automatically. "Oh, my God—that's dreadful. The homeless guy: I'd forgotten about him completely."

"Yes," said Neal. "And so will everyone—unless Steve Merriam can get somebody to rat on somebody else. That's how this kind of case gets broken."

"I suppose," she said vaguely. *I just don't want to think about it. Not now.*

"And your friend Lloyd'll get his boat back," Neal went on. "Most of her, anyway." *He's leading up to something.* "You never told me what made him so willing to loan her to you."

That she could handle: "He thinks I saved his life."

"Did you?"

She shrugged. "Who knows for sure? I was doing the regular checkout on *Boat*, and I found a leak around the fuel intake hose. Just a slow drip, but it was right next to where the wires to the stern light were chafing through on some raw fiberglass."

He was silent for several seconds; she could almost feel him reconstructing the scene in his head. Finally, "He's right. You did save his life."

Funny: the emotionless certainty in Neal's voice was twice as convincing as Lloyd's passionate gratitude. And twice as satisfying, too. *Well, consider the sources, Tory.*

He lapsed back into silence, but she had a feeling he was nerving himself up to talk about the two of them, and she wasn't ready. Up ahead to port the lights of the breakwater began to slide from behind the bluff that had concealed them. Looking for something neutral to talk about, she focused the binoculars on the harbor entrance, now a couple of miles ahead. She felt her gut tighten. "Neal, there's something going on—look at those blue strobes."

Each blue strobe light meant one law enforcement boat, and she counted six. She exchanged startled looks with Neal, who pushed the throttle forward hard. A few minutes later, as *Boat* sliced in toward the harbor entrance, she saw that one of the flashing blue lights was on the forty-one-footer from Station Channel Islands, idling just off the breakwater. In the entrance channel itself, silhouetted by the light of Stearns Wharf, hovered the Harbor Patrol's rigid-hull inflatable, with the unmistakably military outline of Officer Lance Dalleson at the wheel and a solid-looking female figure at his side.

"Could that be your boss?" she said.

"Could be and is," Neal answered. His fatigue seemed to have evaporated.

"I don't think I've ever seen Maria in a boat," Tory said.

"She hates them," Neal replied absently. His voice hardened: "Sweet Jesus, even the county sheriff's navy is out. Must be the end of the world."

"Uncle Tom Cobley and all," Tory agreed. "Look at the black-and-whites on Stearns Wharf. What do you suppose is going on?" But some part of her brain knew the answer, while another part wouldn't let it surface.

"Here comes Taffy in *Harbor 2*. She'll have the true word," Neal said, cutting the throttle.

Officer Taffy Hegemann had grown up on small boats, and she

handled them like extensions of herself. She swung *Harbor 2* so close alongside that Tory could easily have stepped across, but her excited shout must have been audible on upper State: "Neal—is that you? Thank God you're back!"

"Major trouble," said Neal, not quite under his breath.

Taffy's head cocked forward as she identified the other occupant of *Boat*'s cockpit: "Tory, everybody's looking for you, too! They need you—now!"

"What is it?" Tory called out. But she could almost put a name to her fear.

"Follow me!" Taffy called. Triggering *Harbor 2*'s siren, she gunned the engine, leaving *Boat* rolling hard in her wake as she headed into the harbor.

As Neal swung *Boat* past the east breakwater, and the launch area opened in front of them, it was like a curtain going up. Over *Boat*'s engine the sound of chugging generators, pierced by insistent, electronicized questions and commands, floated across the dark water. The stage was the black asphalt parking lot, its usual complement of boats and trailers pushed away to form a disorderly barrier that shut out Cabrillo Boulevard behind. In the foreground, within a perimeter of uniforms, an unmistakable field headquarters centered around the Santa Barbara Police Department's emergency response van. Under the piercing glare of improvised lighting, a knot of suits and uniforms—was one of them a Coast Guard admiral?—moved toward the launch ramp's finger piers.

All at once, the dreadful, amorphous suspicion crystallized into certainty. "Erling's killed the children," she said. *Naming calls. Erase that thought. If only I could.*

Tory knew that near-exhaustion was the screen between her and the anxious faces clustering around. The effect was a little like being underwater, except for the difficulty of connecting one thought to the next. She might have surrendered to the sense of detachment, had it extended to her physical body—raw with chafe, crusted with salt, and bruised in surprising places.

"Miss Lennox, I want to be sure you realize this has nothing to do with your duty as a Coast Guard officer," the admiral was saying. "It's your decision to make, but I'm personally not in favor."

"Understood, sir," she replied. Rear Admiral Terrell, a short, wiry, energetic man with a bristle of gray hair, was known behind his back as the Terrier and sometimes, because of his size and snappishness, Yorkie. Right now he was unusually diffident—maybe he was genuinely concerned for her safety or maybe this was the way he always behaved at zero-dark-thirty in the morning. The question somehow didn't seem important to her—Lieutenant Victoria A. Lennox USCG was another person, a distant acquaintance.

Fatigue aside, what made concentration nearly impossible was the mob of *eminenti* swirling around her. Besides the admiral and Tory's own immediate boss, a commander, Long Beach had disgorged the district chief of staff, a captain, the lieutenant commander in charge of Public Affairs, and a miscellaneous gaggle of junior officers. Distracting enough, and that was only the Coast Guard: the Santa Barbara PD was on hand in full force, from the chief on down, plus delegations from the county sheriff's department and the CHP, and a half-dozen suited "observers," presumably from the FBI. The mayor of Santa Barbara, a reformed realtor, hovered around the fringes of the law enforcers, assuring anyone who would listen (at the moment, one Coast Guard JG) that this kind of thing had never happened before in Santa Barbara—was, in fact, inconceivable—probably wasn't really happening at all.

Beyond the police perimeter, the media had set up shop in their customary style—vans with satellite dishes on the roof, sweatered heavies hefting their Steadicams and still photographers with gyroscopic lenses the size of baseball bats, all standing around in clusters, drinking coffee and arguing about whether the fog would roll in with the dawn to spoil their shots. It reminded Tory of a bad morning back in Seventh District—the wreck of a Haitian sloop in the Miami Beach surf; ragged, half-naked black bodies on the beach in front of the towering hotels.

What made this scene different were the fishermen—silent knots of unshaven figures standing just outside the lights. They had, Tory realized for the first time, an early-morning uniform of

215

their own: faded plaid shirt with the sleeves rolled up, stained jeans or khakis tucked into knee-high black rubber boots, a Styrofoam coffee cup in one hand. She could feel their eyes on her, the one person they knew among all the officials. The one they'd blame, whatever happened.

Where was Neal, anyway? He'd gone off in search of Steve Merriam, dragging Wilbur and Junior in his wake. Without his supporting presence, she felt exposed, angry. And afraid.

At the same time, the analytical part of her mind was working overtime, appraising yesterday's events aboard the *Prophet Jonah*— one version, anyway, in the form of a taped interview with Pete Burns, the fisherman-babysitter-guard Toto Boyle had placed aboard.

After a tense afternoon on the trawler—the children huddled at one end of the main cabin, apparently too frightened to speak; their father at the other, deep in agonized conversation with himself—along about dusk Erling had gone forward to his own tiny quarters, to pray, he said. Burns had begun talking to Martha, who was washing up the lunch dishes in the galley dishpan, with the nominal assistance of the three younger children. Up in the bow of the boat they could hear Erling. "He was, like, groaning," Burns told the police later, his bewilderment coming through clearly on the tape. "Every once in a while you could hear him yell out something," he added.

"Yell what, Pete?" said a second voice.

"I don't know, man. Just, like, stuff," Burns said. "All I know, he was really hurting."

(Burns's face suddenly took shape in Tory's memory: shifty eyes set close, an extra chin usually blurred by beard. But that was misleading; he was a solid citizen, longtime skipper of a successful crab boat. A man to be believed.)

"Give us an example, Pete."

"Well, a couple times he yelled out, 'Why hast thou forsaken me?'" A pause. "That's in the Bible."

"Okay. You remember anything else, Pete?"

"Yeah. Just before Erling, like, blew his stack, he said—let me make sure I got this straight . . . He said, 'Reign in hell or serve in heaven?' Like he was asking somebody a question. A minute after that, he came bursting out of that cabin—I knew he was going to kill me."

"How'd you know that, Pete?"

An unsteady laugh. "Well, he was waving this bread knife. That was my first clue. I didn't hang around: my skiff was tied up alongside, and I got the hell out of there."

Burns had fled ashore and hunted up Toto, who was at home watching TV. The two of them were dithering loudly when Toto's wife woke up, absorbed the situation in one quick take, and called the police. Two SBPD officers in a Harbor Patrol boat had gone out to the *Prophet Jonah,* only to be warned off by Erling, shouting at them from inside the cabin.

The Harbor Patrol officer at the helm had been Gaspar Ortega, who was then produced to add his own account of what had happened next. Red-eyed and rumpled, the young officer was clearly intimidated by his audience, who now included Maria Acevedo, his boss's boss. Still, his story was clear and detailed—and, to Tory's ear, a little stale. No telling how many people he's told it to, she thought. Or how much it's been improved along the way.

Erling had been out of control, Ortega said. Bellowing threats and explanations, all mixed together.

"What's that supposed to mean?" Maria snapped.

"He kept yelling about sin," Ortega replied apologetically, as if sin—as opposed to felony or misdemeanor—was not his department. "He said three of his own children were already damned to hell, and part of it was his fault." The young officer turned to Tory, met her eye, looked away. She knew what was coming an instant before the words emerged: "He said it was your fault, too, Miss Lennox. For tempting him more than he could stand."

From somewhere deep inside she found the strength to ignore the suddenly embarrassed faces, the quick, appraising glances. "Go on, Gaspar," she said.

"But he knew how to save his bad kids, he said. The same way he was going to save the other two, who were still innocent."

217

"How?" Like a whipcrack, Maria Acevedo's voice derailed Gaspar. "How was he going to save them?" she demanded.

"I don't know," Ortega confessed. "Something about sacrifice. Some guy was going to show Halvorsen what to do."

"What guy?" said a hard, official voice behind Tory.

"Not a name I'm familiar with," Ortega replied, sounding defensive. "Abraham: said like it's a last name." His dark eyes were still locked on Tory's. "Do you know anybody around here named Abraham, Miss Lennox?"

The chief of police was standing just across from Tory, his eyes in shadow. He must have read her expression, because he said, "You know this Abraham, Miss Lennox?"

She stifled the giggle that might so easily run away with her. "In a manner of speaking, sir. The Old Testament: Abraham and Isaac."

"Oh, my God," said somebody.

*No, not your God: Erling Halvorsen's.*

"The thing is," Gaspar continued, "Erling wants you there, Miss Lennox. Nobody else. 'If she doesn't come, I'll start without her.' That's what he said, and I think he meant it."

"Oh, he means it, all right," Tory said. In that moment, everything came clear. She turned to the admiral, saw they were on the same wavelength, if only momentarily: "Sir, you remember what the old-time Coasties say?"

He nodded. "'You've got to go out; you don't have to come back.' For the record, I'm still not in favor."

"Thank you, sir."

She had changed into a fresh set of coveralls, he saw, and done something to her hair, but in the first gray light of dawn she still looked desperately tired. And determined: when Tory's jaw set like that, there was no way she was going to be deflected. He slipped between a couple of sheriff's deputies, came up behind her. She was talking to someone in SWAT gear, an older man Neal vaguely recognized.

"I'm sorry, but that's how it has to be," Tory said, her voice flat.

"I still think you should leave it to us," the man replied—his name was Nordlinger, Neal suddenly recalled. "Once you're on that boat, you're just another hostage." But he had already lost the argument, and he knew it.

"What's happening?" Neal asked.

She turned. "Oh, there you are." Of her several voices, it was the one he liked least: coolly superior, the lady of the house to a clumsy servant.

And the worst part was that he automatically reacted in character, explaining himself: "I had to dispose of Wilbur and Junior.

219

Took longer than I thought it would." *Whoa, tiger. I won't be manipulated like that.* "They said you're going out to the *Jonah.*"

Nordlinger, clearly scenting an ally, said, "You're the chief of patrol, aren't you? Maybe you can reason with her."

From Nordlinger's point of view, Neal knew, there was nothing to discuss. Tory had no training in hostage situations. Even worse, she was part of Erling's obsession: her mere appearance on the *Prophet Jonah* could send him over the edge. She was, he saw, perfectly aware of all the risks—had written them off at a cost he couldn't begin to appreciate. That wasn't cool superiority in her voice, it was iron self-control. What she required from him, he knew, was exactly the same thing. "Sorry I can't help you, Captain," he said. "Miss Lennox knows what she's doing."

They walked in silence across the asphalt, toward the finger pier, with every eye on them. Neal could feel the tension crackling all around, but they were apart, in the eye of the storm. It was a moment for confidences, and she broke the silence first: "Thanks for back there. Even if you didn't mean it."

*Thirty yards to go: a dozen steps. Cut to the chase, Donahoe.* "I love you."
"I know."

"What I did—" he began, and she rode down his halting words. "If I took your hand, I wouldn't be able to let go."

It was so much more than he'd expected that he let two precious steps go by before he spoke: "Which boat are we using?"

"The inflatable, so Erling can see there's no one else aboard." Her tone was businesslike, but he heard—or thought he did—the slightest quaver behind it. "Lance Dalleson's going to drive me out, though: you're too close to the bone."

Every fiber in him protested, but he knew she was right. An ex-Marine without fear or imagination, Dalleson was the ideal choice. "There must be something I can do," he said.

They were at the foot of the pier. Dalleson was standing by his boat. He was in uniform, though without his equipment belt. Tory stopped, faced Neal. "I know it's not your MO," she said, "but a prayer wouldn't hurt."

"Do my best."

"For all of us," she said, her tired eyes suddenly intent. "You, me, the kids . . ."

"Even Erling," he said.

"Especially Erling." She smiled, and he knew he would never forget it. "See you in a bit."

He knew what had to be done: "Take it slow," he said, and walked away.

"Four hours," said Chief Washington. "What's that bastard up to, anyway?" The chief's voice had an edge you could shave with, Neal thought, even if his face bore no more expression than a mahogany piling.

"Don't ask me," Neal said. "You're the one with the binocs."

Washington looked down at the rubber-armored 10x50s he was holding as if he hadn't noticed them before. Without a word he handed them over. Neal adjusted the focus for his own eyes and forced himself to pan slowly across the scene before him. He and the chief were standing at the very end of Stearns Wharf, partly sheltered by the shedlike structure that held the radio beacon transmitter. From their vantage point he could see several dozen other figures, uniformed cops mostly, hidden from the anchorage by the aquarium, the Nature Conservancy office, and the shops. Three black-and-whites, spaced evenly along the wharf, were the only sign of an official presence—or the only sign visible from the *Prophet Jonah.* The whole idea, Neal had been told, was to let Erling know he was surrounded, without making him feel like the center of the universe.

Except for a few more black-and-whites, Cabrillo Boulevard was empty—blocked off from the foot of State Street all the way east to the Milpas intersection. And East Beach was totally bare. If you listened closely, you could probably hear the beachfront hotel owners' teeth grinding in unison.

Fools' Anchorage looked normal, too, if you ignored the three Harbor Patrol boats and the Coast Guard forty-one-footer idling around its perimeter. Only a trained eye could see that the fleet of moored semiderelicts were riding a little more sluggishly than usual, a little lower in the water, thanks to the sharpshooters hidden aboard them. You had to give it to those guys, he reflected: they were absolutely invisible. Even the brown pelicans and a few of the braver seals had returned to their regular places. The smell aboard those boats must be incredible, and as the sun heated up the layers of birdshit that encased them, it would only get worse.

Finally, almost reluctantly, he fixed the binoculars on the *Prophet Jonah*. She looked no different from the other boats, no sign of life except for the purple-and-gold pennant already beginning to lift in the westerly breeze. If the weather guessers were right, it would be blowing hard by early afternoon, from a little south of west. Short, steep seas that would make the moored boats pitch badly—a refinement of hell for the hidden marksmen, though it wouldn't bother Tory and the Halvorsens much.

Tory. *Did I do the right thing? Should I have stopped her?* He shook his head angrily: that kind of thinking was stupid. And pointless. If you couldn't handle the idea of Tory Lennox being herself, you didn't qualify as her lover. Maybe prayer was the answer, though his fumbling attempts had just made him feel foolish.

*What's she doing now?*

ABOARD THE *PROPHET JONAH*, FOOLS' ANCHORAGE; 1330 HOURS:
TORY

She came awake with a start, from a dream of Neal: he was beside her in a place she didn't recognize, and he looked worried.
"We can't do this anymore," he said, and then she woke.

The boat was pitching heavily, digging its bow into the seas and
then fetching up with a perceptible tug on its mooring line. From
the light coming through the ports, she judged it must be early afternoon. Nothing in the *Prophet Jonah*'s main cabin seemed different, though. She was sitting on Erik's bunk, with her arm
protectively around his shoulders; from the tenseness of his body
she knew he was awake. Wrapped in a blanket, Martha sat stiffly
on her other side—wide eyes focused on nothing, the tracks of
dried tears still clear on her face. From above and behind Tory,
quick, hoarse breathing told her that Anneke and Leif were still
huddled together in Martha's berth.

And Erling was still there, too, slouched on the top wheelhouse
step at the forward end of the cabin. From where he sat, he could
see out small ports on either side or the larger window at the end

223

of the deckhouse, but he seemed uninterested in what might be happening outside the boat; his fixed stare devoured her. Which Erling was he now? That, she realized, was the life-or-death question for all of them. Without meeting his red-rimmed eyes—just feeling them on her was unsettling enough—she reran what had happened since Lance Dalleson had brought the Harbor Patrol's inflatable alongside the seemingly deserted *Jonah,* just as the sun was clearing the mountains to the east.

"Come on board. You're late." Erling's muffled, disembodied voice had made her jump, and then she saw something move behind the small, opened port at the forward end of the cabin.

"You sure you want to do this, Miss L?" Lance's whisper was just audible over the outboard's liquid muttering.

*Of course I don't. And you're not making it easier.* She tried to stiffen her resolution with a mental picture of the Halvorsen children, but what memory kicked up was the disapproving face of Nordlinger, the SWAT team captain. "Here goes," she said: up onto the inflatable's gunwale, using its slight elasticity underfoot to help make the longer step to the trawler's side deck.

"Now go away, officer," said Erling's voice, at the level of Tory's knee.

She saw that Lance hadn't heard over the sound of the outboard. "Sheer off," she called. "I'll be fine."

"That's better," Erling said, as the inflatable pulled away. "Now . . . Tory: you'll have to come in by the pilothouse. The main hatch is, shall we say, unavailable." *He sounds as if he's enjoying this: I don't like that at all.*

He'd been waiting for her in the shadows at the foot of the steps into the cabin. Something cold and sharp touched her neck just above her collar. "Please hold still." His free hand patted her down—clumsily and, she could have sworn, maliciously. "Just a precaution, you understand."

Nothing crazy about him, she remembered thinking. He might be your textbook stickup artist: a little tense, but completely in control.

And then the knifepoint was gone, and he'd gasped out, "Thank

God you've come!" She'd turned to face him, moving slowly and carefully. The face before her was that of a man on the rack, a soul in torment. Her defenses collapsed before the desperation in his eyes, and suddenly his arms were around her, imprisoning her. "You feel it, too," he breathed in her ear. "I knew you did."

"No! Erling, stop!" He was far stronger than she'd expected, and the knifepoint was pressing the base of her skull, forcing her face into his shoulder.

"Father! Let her go!" The voice was Martha's, harshly desperate, but Tory couldn't see her—couldn't see anything, could barely breathe, her nose crushed hard into rough flannel, smelling of mildew and sweat; rasp of his beard against her ear.

"Don't you understand, child? She's been sent," Erling panted. "She'll save you—and me. She can save all of us, if she wants to."

Through the heavy canvas of the coverall Tory could feel him rising against her. For the first time she had to fight down a wave of sheer panic. *A knee in the groin isn't the answer. Not while that knife's where it is.*

Erling again, breathing hard: "It's true, isn't it? You're the messenger I've begged Him to send . . . the lamb of God." His knife arm pressed her to him, the other hand groped for openings.

"I won't be saved like that!" Martha cried out.

"Don't blaspheme, child," Erling said. And in Tory's ear, "Turn around. Slowly." With one hand he grasped her by the hair, with the other held the knife to her throat. "Please," he implored, and Tory knew he was speaking as much to his other self as to her.

She shuffled around until her back was to him. Four pairs of eyes were fixed on her—three wide and glazed with terror, one showing nothing but despair. Across the main cabin hatchway at the cabin's aft end, Erling had nailed two heavy planks, effectively sealing it off. Now he was pressing against her from behind, holding the knifepoint under her chin. He released her hair—she saw from the corner of her eye his hand move down—and was groping for the zipper on the front of her coverall. "Erling, this is wrong," Tory heard herself croak.

225

"Of all God's . . . creatures, you should understand," he replied. His fingertips had found the zipper pull.

In a single motion Martha was on her feet. "She doesn't know what you need, Father. Only I do." Her big, red-knuckled hands were behind her, and a second later her shapeless dress fell to the deck. Her slip had been cut to fit a shorter, heavier woman, and it hung on her strong body like a tent.

But Erling, of course, knew what it hid. Tory heard his breath hiss, felt a stab of pain as the knife jerked involuntarily upward. She cried out, and Martha's eyes widened: "Father, *no!*" she moaned. Her eyes rolled up, and she collapsed to the deck.

"You're bleeding," Erling said, amazement clear in his voice.

The knife had pulled away as reflexively as it had stabbed. Tory's hand darted to the wound: warm stickiness ran down her fingers, but no pulsing gush. Relief rushed through her, and for a moment she thought she might faint, too. She turned within the circle of Erling's arm; his face, shocked and horrified, loomed inches from hers. The knife—rust-caked blade with oozing redness clinging to the point—was touching her coverall. She was shaking almost un-controllably, and the weakness made her furious: "Of course I'm bleeding, you son of a bitch. Give me that thing before you really hurt somebody."

It had very nearly worked. He looked down at the knife as if he'd never seen it before. "Give me the knife, Erling," she'd said, slowly and distinctly. *That was my mistake: I should've just grabbed for it.*

His eyes went from the blade to her face. "You're not my angel," he said slowly. "You're not from God at all." Horrified rage twisted his face. "I know you—get away from me!" He pushed awkwardly at her, and she stumbled backward, away from the knife—tripped over Martha's half-naked body and fell against the berth.

Her head had struck the wooden frame—the lump felt as if it were still rising—and for several minutes she'd been too dazed to move, her blue-clad legs sprawled over Martha's pasty white ones. The girl had recovered first, dragged herself free. "Are you all right, Miss Lennox?" she'd asked anxiously.

The instinctive response—"Please: call me Tory"—was halfway

to her lips, followed closely by helpless laughter, when her gaze lit on Erling. His face was a battleground of raw emotion—lust, hatred, shame, fear—so undisguised that watching him was like peeking through a keyhole. And his lips never stopped moving, forming soundless words of agony. He was clutching the knife so hard his knuckles were white, his hand trembling as if he were struggling to keep it from doing—what?

"I'm all right, Martha. Thank you," Tory said quietly. She pulled herself up. "You must be freezing. Here: put this blanket around you."

Martha allowed herself to be wrapped in the grubby blanket— Erik's, by its unmistakable smell of teenage boy—and seated on the berth. Only then did she begin to cry.

The vibrating silence had endured for an hour—an hour that felt like years—when Erling broke it abruptly. "Why not in the form of a woman? Lucifer to Lucy—that is within your power, surely."

He was, Tory realized, talking both to her and to himself. *Patience, Tory. Just take an even strain.* "Erling, it's only me," she said. "You've seen me around for months: Lieutenant Victoria Alexandra Lennox, United States Coast Guard. The fishermen's sometimes nagging conscience." She paused. "And your friend."

It won her the sweet, unaffected, innocent smile she remembered. She felt her confidence begin to revive; but as she watched the smile became knowing, derisive. "That's what you would say, of course."

"It's who I *am*, Erling," she said. "Not Astarte, not Cleopatra. Just me. I can get you out of this nightmare, if you'll let me."

"Show me your feet," he said.

"What?"

"You heard me." He pointed the knife. It was, she saw, no longer shaking. "Take off your shoes."

*Who's speaking—the lecher or the maniac?*

"Do it. Please," whispered Martha, without turning her head.

Slowly she unlaced her deck shoes and kicked them away, tugged off her heavy wool socks. "See? Plain old ten and a half mediums. No cloven hoof."

His quick, startled glance told her she had guessed too well. And then his face changed again. *Not just his expression. It's like his flesh shifts under the skin. And I don't think I'm going to like this Erling at all.* He started to say something, pulled it back at the last moment. He smiled, and Tory shivered uncontrollably. But he was looking past her shoulder. "Anneke, come here," he said.

"No." Tory's exclamation was echoed by Martha.

"Anneke, come to me," Erling repeated. Calmly paternal, but Tory could sense the uncontrolled darkness beneath it. "I am your father, Anneke. A good little girl obeys her father."

At the rustle of cloth above and behind them, Tory and Martha both half turned. With amazing speed, Erling darted forward, grabbed Erik's arm, and dragged him out of reach. "Father!" Erik cried. But the breath was crushed out of him as Erling wrapped one great arm around the boy's chest and squeezed. Behind Tory, Anneke and Leif wailed in terror.

"Quiet!" Erling's deep roar rattled the cabin fittings. Martha flinched away, and the two smallest children subsided into stifled whimpering. Erik's wide-eyed stillness reminded Tory of a shot deer. *He's in shock; maybe that's best.* Erling surveyed the scene with satisfaction. "That's better." To Tory: "You see, I am captain of this ship—and this family."

"If you say so," she replied. Agree with anything, she told herself—if it buys you time. But she knew there were some demands she could never give in to.

"It's the Bible that says so," he corrected her. "And the Bible is the word of God."

*I recognize that look: he's edging up to something.*

"The captain," he repeated, nodding. He seemed to be talking to himself, but his eyes kept darting to Tory. "It is a question of rank, *Lieutenant* Lennox—and rank, as you military people say, has its privileges."

*So: there it is.* "True enough," she said, surprised at her own calm.

"But if you were a military person, you'd know the privileges come after the responsibilities—a long way after."

"But I am responsible to only one," he replied mildly, his eyebrows rising. "'Captain under God'—isn't that the nautical phrase?"

*If only I weren't so tired, I might be able to beat him at this game.* "What they teach us," she said slowly, "is that responsibility goes up *and* down. You have to answer to God, but you're answering on your crew's behalf."

He didn't like that version, she saw. His face closed, and for several minutes he sat lost in thought—but not so lost he wasn't clearly aware of every movement around him.

"In the end, however, I am the one God speaks to," he said suddenly. "I am the one charged with carrying out His instructions." He was looking right past Tory, at a spot on the bulkhead just over her left shoulder. "I must pray for guidance."

*Oh, God, let him close his eyes. Just for a minute.*

She might have spoken aloud: smiling indulgently, Erling said, "I think I must preserve you from temptation, Miss Lennox. Please lie down on the floor—the deck. On your stomach." The rusty knife moved up toward Erik's neck. He blinked and shivered.

Tory waited until she saw the point indent the boy's skin. "Oh, please," Martha whispered.

"All right," Tory said. Stiffly—*a good thing I didn't try to jump him*—she edged off the bunk, dropped to her knees, and lay down in the narrow space.

"Turn your head away from me. Put your hands behind your back, please. Good." Something small and light landed on Tory's back. "Martha, please tie Miss Lennox's wrists with that cord."

Even if Martha had known how to fake a knot, Erling gave her no opportunity. At his instruction, she lashed Tory's wrists together with a dozen turns, then wound a dozen more turns at right angles to the first, between the wrists. "I think you call it a seizing," Erling remarked. "Quite effective."

*You got that right. It'd take me five minutes just to unwrap this lot.*

Silence, except for the noises of the old boat flexing in the choppy sea, the muted slap of waves against the hull. The minutes fled past, and Tory's mind, like a fly in a bottle, dashed itself against one desperate plan after another. And then she heard a movement, followed by Erling's voice, sorrowful yet determined, say, "So be it, Lord. Thy judgments are just and righteous altogether." A different tone, now—the sorrow still there, behind a screen of paternal kindliness: "Erik, go sit beside your sister. Try not to step on Miss Lennox."

Erik's sneakered foot came down next to Tory's face, distracting her for a second. *What was that other sound? Scrape of something hard on wood.* And then, entirely without warning, cold liquid splashed across her back. A piercing, pungent, all-too-familiar smell seared her nostrils: gasoline.

FOOLS' ANCHORAGE; 2:00 P.M.: NEAL

The water running down the side of *Harbor 2* tugged at him, trying to spin his body as he clung to the short length of line. Every time he twisted, the air tank on his back thumped the patrol boat's chine. He looked up and saw Officer Taffy Hegemann's round, concerned face staring down at him. *Will you for Christ's sake stop looking over the side? If Erling's watching you he's bound to guess something's going on.*

But with the mouthpiece clamped between his jaws and both hands wound in the towline, there was no signal he could give. He wondered for a moment if Taffy was deliberately trying to shake him loose: she'd been against the plan from the start, an hour and a half ago, when the Navy technician looked up at the watching faces surrounding him and said, "I don't like what I'm hearing, folks."

The tech, an angular first-class petty officer with an electronics patch on his sleeve and a submariner badge on his chest, had arrived with the improvised hydrophones, a loan arranged by Admiral Terrell through Navy friends at Long Beach. According

231

to the young lieutenant who'd also accompanied the equipment, the underwater receiver allowed a listener to hear absolutely every subsurface sound between Ventura and Coal Oil Point, "from a depth charge down to a seal fart—sorry, ma'am."

Maria Acevedo, the only woman present, had brushed off the apology with an annoyed wave. "Can we hear what this Halvorsen is saying—inside his boat?" she demanded.

"No question, ma'am. The only problems are distortion and too many noises at once—it's like picking one voice out of a . . . a crowded restaurant. That's why we need Petty Officer Durham, here. He's our interpreter."

From Petty Officer Durham's condescending smile, Neal guessed he had a saltier simile in mind, but in minutes after setting up his gear on one of the launch ramp floats, he was able to isolate the noises coming from the *Prophet Jonah.* Isolate but not translate, it soon appeared. "I'm pretty sure about the people," Durham said, after half an hour. "One adult male, two adult females—"

"Two?" said Maria to Neal. "Who's the other one?"

"Martha, the older Halvorsen daughter," Neal said. And to Durham: "Who else?"

"One teenager, probably male . . ."

"That's Erik."

". . . And one, maybe two small children." He looked up at Admiral Terrell. "That tally with your count, sir?"

The admiral's hard stare passed the question on to Neal, who said, "Sounds right. The small children are a boy, Leif, and a girl, Anneke."

"What are they doing—can you tell?" said Nordlinger, the SWAT captain.

"Well, not exactly, sir," Durham replied. "They're talking, mostly—at least, the male adult is. Fine speaking voice, but a very hostile man." He made a minor adjustment to two dials on the console before him, shook his head. In the morning sunlight, his forehead was gleaming with sweat. "I can get a word here and there . . . It's kind of disconnected," he said slowly. "But I have to say I don't like what I'm hearing, folks."

"That I believe," said Nordlinger unhappily. He turned: "Mr. Mayor, we've given that Coast Guard gal long enough. We're going to have to take a hand."

The mayor's mouth opened and closed, but it was Maria who said: "'Take a hand'—what does that mean, Leo?"

"Apply some pressure," the captain said quickly. "Loudspeakers, spotlights, more visible patrol boats. Get a conflict resolution team out there. No rough stuff, though."

*Not yet* hung unspoken between them. "I'm not going to have a Ruby Ridge in my harbor, Leo," Maria said.

"It's not exactly your harbor, Ms. Acevedo," the Coast Guard captain put in. "That's joint federal-state waters outside your breakwater."

"As I understand it," the county sheriff's representative put in, "it's kind of a jurisdictional free-for-all out there. And the county's got a very good dive team—"

Suddenly everybody seemed to be talking at once, until Maria pitched her voice to cut through the clamor: "Screw jurisdiction," she snapped. Into the stunned silence that followed this blasphemy, she said, "Neal, you're the only one here who really knows this situation. What do you think?"

The faces turned to him as one. From their expressions he guessed that half those present would be happy to see someone else pick up the ball, while the other half looked ready to fight any plan not their own. Neal knew exactly what he had to do, knew there wasn't a hope in hell of getting agreement from such a diverse collection of experts. There was, in fact, only one way to pull it off, and for that to have a chance, he needed help from the last person he could expect to give it. "I think we should wait another two hours," he said. "See how things look then."

Maria, clearly startled, threw him a quick, questioning glance. Before the others could do more than clear their throats, she said, "That's settled, then. We'll get out of Mr. Durham's hair, talk to our own people, and meet back here at . . . one-thirty.

Neal, come with me." Barely out of earshot, striding across the warm asphalt, she said from the corner of her mouth, "Okay, what's really on your mind?"

Halfway through his explanation, she was shaking her head, but she waited till he'd run down before she said, "Out of the question. Neal, you're as crazy as Nordlinger."

But he saw her mental door wasn't completely closed. "Look, Erling Halvorsen's a ticking bomb. From what his buddies have told me, he'd welcome the chance to go up in smoke, if he could make it public enough. Tory was the only person with a chance of getting through to him, and it sounds like she couldn't do it. So now we have to take him out, quick and neat."

"That's what the SWAT team's for," she said.

His "no" was pure instinct; she waited while he assembled the reasons beneath it: "Too big, too noisy, too slow. Nordlinger's boys might sneak up within, oh, two hundred yards before they had to rush the *Jonah*. But that's two hundred yards of open water: Erling can hear propellers through his hull damn near as clearly as that Navy guy can—he could kill everybody aboard before a team could reach him."

"And you think you can stop him alone?" she asked.

"I have to."

*But that was then. This is now: Maria was right—it's crazy to think I can pull this off. All I'll do is get Tory killed—if she isn't dead already.* As if in response to his thought, *Harbor 2* slowed to idle. Above him, he heard Taffy's clear voice call out, "You're relieved, Bill. You and Joanie go refuel."

It was the signal that Taffy had *Harbor 2* lined up so the *Jonah* was precisely due east of the patrol boat. Now or never, Neal told himself. He rapped twice on the hull and let go of the trailing line. He'd deliberately overweighted his belt by four pounds, so he went down like a stone, twenty-five feet to the bottom. As usual, the water off the harbor was like cold soup—thick with suspended particles that didn't bear thinking about, visibility about ten feet. Over the years, everything that could possibly be thrown off a boat had wound up somewhere on the floor of Fools' Anchorage. Some of it had sunk out of sight in the odorous muddy sand, much of it had corroded into mysterious, skeletal shapes that would loom up suddenly out of the brownish fog. But he'd dived this stretch of harbor bottom dozens of times, and some of the larger chunks of debris had become old friends. Besides, it was the only approach to the *Prophet Jonah* that had a chance of being unseen as well as unheard—and only an experienced diver would be able to pick out his bubbles from the wind-whipped surface turbulence. That was the theory, anyway—though, come to think of it, he had no idea if Erling had ever dived in his life.

Two hundred yards, swimming through next-to-nothing visibility in currents that no one had ever bothered to chart. The target at the far end was composed of three old engine blocks chained together, a heap now almost entirely invisible under several years' gathered silt. But this time, if he got off track, he couldn't surface to check his position. His navigation had to be spot-on the first time. To give himself an edge, he'd divided the run into three parts: from his kickoff point about fifty yards west-southwest, to the hundred-and-fifty-pound mushroom anchor that was currently holding a dismasted sailboat, awash to the gunwales; change course there, about ten degrees more to the south, and kick another seventy yards to a forty-foot section of abandoned dredge pipe, nearly buried but showing an unmistakable curve just above the surface. The last leg, a little north of west-northwest, to the *Jonah*'s mooring, was ninety yards—longer than he liked, but there was no really memorable marker in between.

Even as he was mentally reviewing the courses, the dismasted sailboat's mushroom anchor loomed into view off to his right, lying on its side with about a third of its circumference showing above the mud. He glanced down at the wrist compass he'd borrowed from Officer Joanie Westphal. His course was correct, which meant he'd have to allow slight offset on the next leg—a calculation that would be easy enough on paper, with nothing but potential embarrassment hanging on the result.

*Stop second-guessing.* He finned to a spot right over the old anchor, aimed himself as precisely as he could, and kicked off into the gray-brown murk. The dredge pipe appeared right on schedule, a quarter-round running almost at right angles to his course, and he felt a gush of relief. Now for the final leg, the longest one. Once more he corrected his course for the current and finned off, hugging the bottom and staring ahead for the vague lump that was his mark.

The thought struck him halfway, more or less: had he added or subtracted the current correction? He couldn't remember. There was nothing to do but press on. Seconds passed with no sign of the *Jonah's* mooring. Surely he must be within a few yards of the trawler, but where the hell was the hillock of mud-covered metal? Slowly he kicked upward until he could see the mirrored surface moving uneasily above him.

And there it was, no more than a dozen feet away, the deep, chunky hull festooned with ribbons of weed, the bronze propeller half-eaten by corrosion. But emotion was making him breathe far too frequently. A steady stream of bubbles erupted from his mouthpiece. If Erling was looking over the side, he couldn't help but see them. He grabbed at the *Jonah's* rusted chain mooring rode, felt the sting as a barnacle slashed his finger. But cut fingers, he'd decided, were preferable to the clumsiness of gloves.

Holding the chain in one hand, he pulled off his fins and watched them slide away toward the bottom, then unhooked his buoyancy control vest and air tank and slipped clear of them, still holding the mouthpiece clamped between his teeth. Next his weight belt, which he reconnected through one armhole of the vest. Now he allowed thirty seconds of rest to get his breathing back to something like normal. As he hung from the chain, holding the tank and weight belt in his free hand, he ran once more through what he had to do.

The *Jonah's* high, plumb bow was the trawler's only blind spot

and her mooring chain the only ladder. But speed was the key.
Speed and nimbleness. And luck.

*In five minutes I could be dead.*

*Go.*

ABOARD THE *PROPHET JONAH;* TORY


She'd managed to fight her way to her knees, expecting every second to hear the scrape of a match, feel the searing heat engulf her. Gasping from the gasoline fumes, she straightened and met Erling's mild, concerned stare. "Why?" she demanded. "Why, for God's sake?"

He was holding the gasoline container—the one she herself had bought for the dinghy—in one big hand, the box of wooden matches in the other. He nodded: "Exactly: it is for God's sake I'm doing this."

The sharp stink of gasoline filled the cabin, stabbing at her eyes. She was too desperate to hide the rage that swept over her. "That's revolting. What God would burn children alive?" As he cocked his head, considering, she measured the distance between them. *If I were on my feet, with my hands free, I'd stand a chance.* With desperate strength she pulled her wrists apart until she could feel the thin cord cutting her skin, but the tiny amount of slack was nowhere near enough.

"For my children—my darlings—this will be their purgatory," Erling replied seriously. "A few minutes' pain, and then eternal bliss. For myself . . ." His mouth twisted in bitter self-reproach. "Perhaps a small foretaste of eternity. But that is for my master to decide."

"And me?" Tory said. "Where do I fit in?" *Fight for every second* clashed head-on with *It's over.* Never give up, she ordered herself. *Never give up.*

"It took me some time to realize," Erling replied. "You were my temptation, a thing that almost replaced my faith. So it is fitting that you should be my sacrifice."

Behind Erling—had she really seen it?—an instant's glimpse of something black, spiky, gleaming wet. *Neal's hair.* It was too much to hope for—but hope was all that remained. *How can I help him?*

Erling raised the gas can. "This will make it faster," he said, and swung it, sluicing her with the contents from breast to knees.

Stunned, she watched frozen as he dropped the container, extracted a match, and held it poised to strike. "Wait!" she cried.

He paused. "Please, Tory: don't prolong it," he said, voice tinged with sorrow.

*Have to distract him.* "At least let me stand," she said. "I don't want to die on my knees."

"All right. But don't do anything foolish."

With exaggerated awkwardness, she raised herself to one knee, watched with horror as the match rose and scraped and lit. Impossibly, she pushed off from her half-kneeling position, wobbled, caught her balance, and hurled herself head-first into his belly as the lighted match sailed past her and landed on the damp floorboards, igniting them with a *whoosh.*

Erling's gasp was followed an instant later by a grunt of pain as his back struck the *Jonah's* steering wheel. At the same moment, a wiry figure in dripping black neoprene slammed through the wheelhouse door shoulder-first, scattering broken glass and rotted wood in all directions.

"Tory! Are you—"

"Get the kids!" she cried, staggering into the binnacle as Erling pulled himself up and brushed her aside.

Neal's black-clad arm swung up in a spray of blood. Something metal caught the sun and descended, struck Erling's skull with the sound of a melon dropping on concrete. Soundlessly he collapsed, and Neal's dive knife clattered off the wooden deck beside him.

Tory dropped clumsily to a sitting position, her hands scrabbling for the knife. Inches from her nose she saw the scarlet fire extinguisher mounted on the binnacle. Neal had paused at the foot of the wheelhouse steps; a foot in front of him the cabin was a wall of fire and smoke. And then, from behind the flames, a high-pitched scream of terror. "Neal: on the binnacle!" Tory called, sawing furiously at the cords around her wrists.

But he didn't hear her. Lowering his head, he plunged into the fire. A second later, Martha, coughing and choking, reeled into view, the blanket around her shoulders crackling. From behind the smoke, Tory heard a solid thumping—Neal trying to force the cabin door. At that moment, the cords binding her wrists finally parted. She reached for the extinguisher and yanked it free, only dimly aware of the blood sheeting down her forearm.

The extinguisher, she knew, was good for only a few seconds. She aimed it at the base of the flames, squeezed the handle, panned it across. Miraculously, the fire died under the fog of white powder, revealing Neal and the two littlest Halvorsens. But already tendrils of flame were inching back across the floorboards. "Neal, this way!"

He turned, tucked one petrified child under each arm, and leaped across the smoldering deck. But where was Erik? Then, as the fire crackled fully back to life, Tory saw the huddled lump beneath the upper berth blanket. Without thinking, she jumped down the steps, onto the cabin floorboards. "Tory, no!" screamed Martha. Clad only in the ragged, scorched slip, she crawled up onto the lower berth, reached out, and dragged her brother's limp figure to safety.

"Outside, everybody!" Neal called from the side deck. "Outside now!" His voice galvanized Tory. She looked down and saw the flames had crept toward her bare feet till they were only inches away. Suddenly his powerful, long-fingered hands—she didn't have to see them to recognize their touch—took her gently by the biceps. "Come on, love. Time to go."

COTTAGE HOSPITAL, SANTA BARBARA; 5:00 P.M.: TORY

Everyone had insisted she spend at least the night in Cottage
Hospital, and she finally gave in. It was a mistake, as she discovered
almost immediately: her room was jammed to the door; among the
faces she recognized were her boss from Long Beach, the district
chief of staff, the mayor, Maria Acevedo, and the chief of police—
all singing her praises a cappella. They were so grossly flattering she
found herself at a loss to respond, and they appeared ready to camp
out forever. Admiral Terrell arrived soon after, accompanied by a
fourragèred aide bearing a sizable bouquet of roses. Relief had
made the admiral testy: his prepared remarks, in which he compared
her to Joan of Arc (and who, she wondered, had supplied *that* refer-
ence), were delivered in quick, barking bursts.

To make it worse, Tory caught a quick glimpse of her reflection
in a stainless steel pitcher. She could, with an effort, discount the
distorting effect of the curved surface, the windburned cheeks and
sun-swollen lips—but not the double chin caused by the tight bandage under her jaw or the scorched, frizzy bangs and the shaved
patch on the top of her skull. And the dire hospital gown had

clearly been designed as revenge on the female sex generally. *I look like an ancient madwoman who's just fallen down a flight of barbecues.*

Just when she was coming to the conclusion that nothing short of screaming hysteria would clear the room, a formidable nurse appeared and ordered everyone out. "We need our rest," she said, making it sound like a death sentence. But no sooner had the crowd ebbed, with the nurse nipping at their heels, than the door opened again, tentatively.

"Oh, *Christ,*" Tory heard herself say.

"Afraid not," said a familiar voice, and Steve Merriam's homely, grinning face peered around the corner.

"Come on in," she said, forcing a smile.

"I brought a friend," Steve said, his expression so arch that she knew who it had to be. *My God: it's like a first date—my face on fire and my heart in my throat.*

For several seconds all she could take in were his dark eyes, which seemed to be lit from within. Then she became aware of the blisters, smeared with glistening ointment, on his face and neck, the heavy bandage wrapping his right hand. "How's it going, tiger?" he asked, shifting awkwardly from one foot to the other.

"Kiss her and find out," muttered Steve, not quite under his breath.

Several minutes later, she released Neal reluctantly and he straightened up. "I think you'll live," he said.

Behind him, Steve, who had been staring out the window, said, "I thought you might like a quick look at the scorecard."

"Oh, my God, yes!" she exclaimed. "The children—what about them?"

"In better shape than either of us. At least physically," Neal put in. "They're right upstairs, while the city tries to figure out what to do about them."

*Some awful foster home. Split up, probably.* "Isn't there anything—" she began, but Neal interrupted.

"Don't hold your breath, but there's an uncle—their dead mother's brother—up in Oregon. Seems he's been trying to trace them for months. Might come to something, might not."

"Junior, however, may be otherwise occupied," said Steve. "Grand larceny aside, we're holding him as a material witness—he saw what happened to Vern the homeless."

Tired as she was, Tory could see Steve was itching to tell her, so she fed him the line: "And that was?"

"They were arguing about money, and Jock popped him. Says Junior. Jock says it was self-defense: Vern went for him with a knife. We could go after Jock for manslaughter—maybe. But this is not the kind of case that prosecutors salivate over."

"Meaning Jock gets away with killing someone?" she said, thinking: I ought to feel outrage, but mild irritation's the best I can do.

"Not necessarily. The City Attorney's already talking about going after Jock's profits from the paintings."

"The paintings—Wilbur," she said. "What happens to him?"

"Wilbur's in the clear, unless somebody files a complaint for fraud," he said.

"And why should they?" Neal broke in. "Wilbur's been on all three networks today, and the prices of his stuff are still going up. The new restaurant in the old Naval Reserve building just offered some incredible amount for that huge *Fools' Anchorage* painting."

"Well, good for Wilbur," she said. "I just hope he spends it foolishly, before some new Jock gets hold of him and picks him clean."

"Yes. Well, that's all I've got to contribute," Steve said, with a sideways glance at Neal. Without warning he darted forward a step and, like a great clumsy bird, planted a dry peck on Tory's cheek. "Get better soon."

"About us," Neal began, when the door had closed behind the cop. He seemed to be having trouble finding the words he wanted, and Tory let him grope. "I figure you'll get that half-stripe now." He paused again. "I just wanted to say, I wouldn't mind Alameda at all . . ." A grimace of frustration twisted his lean face. "This isn't coming out quite right."

"I certainly hope not," she said, deadpan. "But I don't want you in Alameda . . ." His face fell so completely she didn't have the heart to continue. "I'm staying here. I got a year extension in the Marine Safety office."

244

*Most men really are little boys, at some level.* The glow in his eyes seemed to have extended to his entire face.

"I won't ask you about getting married—yet."

"Don't," she said firmly. And then her emotions burst through, and she was smiling so hard her face hurt, and crying at the same time. "Not yet," she said.